The Book Hunters of KATPADI

When it opened its doors in January 2016, Biblio became India's first full-fledged antiquarian bookshop, dealing in rare books, fine editions and the book arts.

The Book Hunters of KATPADI

A Bibliomystery

PRADEEP SEBASTIAN

hachette INDIA

First published in 2017 by Hachette India
(Registered name: Hachette Book Publishing India Pvt. Ltd)
An Hachette UK company
www.hachetteindia.com

2

Illustrations by Sonali Zohra
Art direction by Bhavi Mehta

ISBN 978-93-5009-223-1

Hachette Book Publishing India Pvt. Ltd
4th & 5th Floors, Corporate Centre,
Sector 44, Gurugram 122003, India

Typeset in Mrs Eaves OT 12.5/15
by InoSoft Systems, Noida

Printed and bound in India
by Manipal Technologies Limited, Manipal

MIX
Paper from responsible sources
FSC™ C043100

For Lovy

Book collecting, I would have you know, is a full-time occupation, and one wouldn't get far if one took time off for frivolities like reading.

A.N.L. MUNBY

I remember John Sparrow's definition of the book collector as having two pleasures, of which the first was to remark, 'Now I have the complete set,' and the second, 'But I don't think you do, do you?'

COLIN FRANKLIN, Book Collecting as One of the Fine Arts and Other Essays

It's not bad, bibliophily.

S. BARKWORTH, The Nijmegen Proof

Contents

Epilogue

Part One

I

The Priest in the Bookshop

On a Tuesday in February that felt like it would be the last cool evening in Chennai before the sweltering heat engulfed the city, a priest in a black cassock and white clerical collar hurried into an antiquarian bookshop, strode up to the young woman at the desk and demanded to know why the shop was trafficking in stolen books.

Startled, Kayal looked up from the book catalogue she was working on.

He was possibly in his early sixties, Kayal noted, short but fit, with gelled silver-black hair severely combed back. The white clerical collar band made his black cassock look more like a tux.

'I'm Reverend James Satya, a chaplain at MCC... Madras Christian College, you know,' he announced in a rather plummy voice, and looked expectantly at her, as if the introduction was explanation enough.

'You mentioned something, Reverend, about, uh, stolen books?'

'I'll come to that later. First, tell me...you deal in old books, correct?'

'Antiquarian, yes.'

'Which section is that in the bookshop?'

'That depends on what you're looking for. Nearly everything we stock is antiquarian in some sense.'

'I'm looking for antiquarian theological editions.'

Kayal pointed the priest to a complex of glass bookcases across from her desk and returned to the catalogue.

Months later, the two bookwomen of Biblio – Neela, the owner, in her early forties, and Kayal, her young associate – would recall that it was after the priest's visit that a series of highly charged bibliophilic events came to grip their lives. On this pleasant February evening, however, the only thing on Kayal's mind was finishing up work on Biblio's first catalogue of rare, fine and first editions. For several months now, she and her boss Neela had been working on this catalogue with great relish, and Kayal wanted the bookshop to herself for the rest of the evening to work out the tricky business of identifying modern Indian first editions.

Take Upamanyu Chatterjee's *English, August*, for instance. She had before her the 1988 Faber UK hardcover edition and the ₹40 Rupa paperback. Both were first editions, but if you followed the flag – as you had to in determining these things – it would have to be the Rupa edition, scruffy as it was, that counted as the real thing. The Faber edition in hardcover and handsome binding looked more like how modern first editions were supposed to, but it was in Rupa's paperback edition that the book had been read first by most in India, the author's country of origin. So Biblio had decided that both editions would be included in the catalogue and offered as firsts.

Not surprisingly, the Rupa paperback was the scarcer edition. All through the eighties and nineties, copies of it had been commonplace – you could have them for as little as ₹50 from pavement hawkers – tattered, well-thumbed, flying from hand to hand as the book's popularity spread by word of mouth to create, arguably, the first cult novel in modern Indian English fiction. (For those who felt that Sasthi Brata's *Confessions of an Indian Woman Eater* was more deserving of the title of 'first cult novel', Biblio had that too in the 1973 Sterling paperback, Delhi, and the 1971 Hutchinson hardcover, London, along with his autobiography, *My God Died Young*, 1968, Harper, New York.) Today, you would be lucky to find copies of the first Rupa printing (they would most probably be circulating-library copies, coming apart at the seams), while you could still source copies of the Faber edition in good condition from online antiquarian bookshops.

But the catalogue would have to wait, Kayal realized; the priest had materialized at her desk once again, looking terribly impatient, even upset.

'The sign says to ask for assistance with the books in the bookcases,' he began. 'The cabinets are all locked...'

'Just ignore the sign, Reverend. We have those up simply to discourage people who handle books far too, um, informally. It helps to hint that the books in the glass bookcases are rare and valuable and need careful handling. You'll notice that the key for each bookcase is left in the lock itself. Please feel free to take the books out and have a look at them.'

The Reverend hurried back to the cases without another word.

'Some of those books haven't been priced yet, though...' Kayal called after him. But she had lost him; he was too preoccupied with opening and closing the cabinets' glass doors, one after the other, in a somewhat frenzied manner. A collector-priest, and such a keen one too! Curiouser and curiouser, thought Kayal.

Biblio was located in the leafy neighbourhood of

Adyar, just beside the Theosophical Society, whose vast wooded grounds, thick with banyan groves, keep the streets in the area a little cooler even through Chennai's humid afternoons. When it opened its doors in January 2016, Biblio became India's first full-fledged antiquarian bookshop, dealing in rare books, fine editions and the book arts. In setting it up, Neelambari Adigal had avoided the typical commercial retail spaces occupied by most Indian bookshops and housed it in a place befitting a cosy antiquarian business: her Adyar home, a traditional Karaikudi cottage built in the 1930s. For years she had run her antiquarian bookshop from a Besant Nagar flat as a by-appointment-only business, but she had been yearning to make it an open, brick-and-mortar bookshop. And her Adyar cottage, it struck her one day, had just the space and atmosphere such a rare bookshop needed. In remodelling the cottage to fit Biblio's image, she had retained everything that was traditional and charming about it: The red-tiled roof, the red-oxide flooring, the famed Karaikudi teak doors and pillars (that had come all the way from Burma), the little courtyard garden with jasmine and champak trees and the brick path that led from the gate to the entrance through the garden.

It was not just the location that made Biblio stand apart. When Neela had planned its interiors, she had paid special attention to the way books would be stocked and arranged in her shop. Absent was the atmosphere of purposeful clutter you usually saw in second-hand bookshops, with volumes overflowing from shelves, piled up on the floor and along the aisles. A friend who ran a second-hand bookshop had once remarked to Neela, 'The moment I shelve everything and bring order to the bookshop, customers stop coming. Now I leave everything lying around and they're happy.' As charming and welcoming as that might seem to casual browsers, Neela knew that an antiquarian bookshop that served the serious book collector couldn't afford to have books lying around in joyful chaos. Biblio's stock of rare, fine and first editions, displayed in glass-enclosed bookcases, were meticulously stocked and beautifully arranged.

Upon entering Biblio, the first thing you saw was a riot of pulpy, lurid colours – the bright yellows and reds and greens and oranges of vintage paperbacks, displayed face-up because they were collected for their cover art. Past this cosy veranda-room of genre titles, the bookshop opened out into the spaciousness of its glinting heart – the room with the glass cabinets housing the shop's most valued stock. Kayal worked out of a large desk placed in a corner from where all the bookcases were in full view. Turning a house into a bookshop had certain advantages, such as more rooms, tucked-away spaces – like the one leading off from the heart of the bookshop, which Neela had turned into a compact office for herself, and a third room that doubled as stockroom and kitchen, which could be reached from the garden.

Kayal's favourite section in the bookshop were the shelves dedicated to the book arts – the art and history of manuscripts and the printed book. Here, you could find an entire range of books and ephemera dealing with typography, bookbinding, papermaking, calligraphy, memoirs of antiquarian booksellers and collectors, bibliographies of presses and biographies of bookshops. Kayal had persuaded her boss that Biblio should, yet again, score a first by being the first Indian bookstore to devote not just a shelf or two but an entire section to these subjects, making theirs a deep and comprehensive collection of books on books gathered in one place. After all, this was what Biblio was all about – curators and evangelizers of the art and craft of the printed book.

The bookshop had fallen silent; except for the priest, all the other browsers had left. Kayal looked at the time: 8.20 p.m. – ten minutes to closing time, and if the priest wasn't gone by then, she would have to shoo him out. She turned her attention again to the catalogue. Pricing modern Indian first editions was a challenge, but she and Neela had been looking forward to the task. The whole point of putting out the first-ever book catalogue of modern Indian firsts was to not only inspire Indian bibliophiles to collect

Neela knew that an antiquarian bookshop that served the serious book collector couldn't afford to have books lying around in joyful chaos.

books from their own country but also to set up some debate and discussion on what could be viewed as a true modern first edition in India and how much it would be worth in the antiquarian book market.

Against the Faber *English, August* edition she lightly pencilled in ₹5,000 and against the Rupa paperback, in its near-fine condition (the spine wasn't cracked and the cover was bright, with no edgewear or creases), ₹3,000. She smiled to herself, remembering its original list price. 'If you happen to own a decent 1988 copy,' Neela was fond of telling fans of the book, 'and you aren't too attached to it, bring it in and Biblio will be happy to give you ₹1,500 for it.' Neela herself owned a very interesting association copy of the book – inscribed to Dev Benegal (in part, it said, 'Thanks for getting it right...') and signed by Upamanyu Chatterjee – and she had been itching to include it in the catalogue. But Kayal had talked her out of it; it was the kind of thing you regretted parting with the moment you sold it and Kayal was aware that no one knew this better than her boss, the best – and perhaps the only – Indian bookwoman in the rare-book trade.

'But think of what an exciting first-catalogue item it would make!' Neela would remind her every now and then.

'That it would,' Kayal would reply wistfully, looking longingly at the very desirable inscription, and then gently pry the book out of her boss's hands and slide it back into one of Neela's many personal bookcases (housed in her swanky Besant Nagar beach-front apartment) that held, among other bibliophilic rarities, her exquisite private collection of association copies and signed firsts, including a presentation copy of *Sir Vidia's Shadow* from Theroux to Naipaul, with a manuscript inscription on the front flyleaf that read, 'To Vidia: A small tit for a large tat'.

'Ah-ha!' the priest suddenly exclaimed.

A discovery, perhaps, Kayal wondered, looking his way; one of those tiny eureka moments that every collector experiences with a find.

Smiling, she looked up from her catalogue...to see him glowering at her. He had an armload of books and his expression suggested that he could, at any moment, do something uncanonical with them. He brought the books over and carefully piled them on the desk. They were mostly late seventeeth-century and early eighteenth-century hymnals, liturgical prayer books and church manuals whose pages had foxed and binding loosened, giving off that musty whiff bibliophiles got high on – what Orwell had once referred to as 'the sweet smell of decaying books'. Except for one volume in the lot, they were not valuable so much as out of print.

Kayal could see why these books would interest a clergyman, but now she had the task of having to tell him they were not for sale – at least, not just yet.

'Reverend, I'm sorry,' she began, 'but these books haven't been priced and catalogued yet.'

'And why not?' he asked with a mystifying smirk.

'They need to be restored and, in some cases, even rebacked.'

'Which is…?'

'When the binding shows signs of becoming detached, we reback the book by having the spine remade. And when that doesn't help we remove the original binding and replace it with a contemporary binding. It's a lot of work, but we know a skilful bookbinder right here in Chennai who does a fine job of restoring books.'

'I'm not here to buy these books, but to claim them back, Ms…?'

'Kayalveli – Kayal. *Claim* them back?'

'The books in question, Ms Kayal, are stolen property,' declared the priest. 'I'd like them returned to where they belong.'

'And where's that, Reverend Satya?' asked Kayal, in a slightly sharper voice now.

'The library at Heber Chapel in Madras Christian College. Look.'

He opened the books to their paste-down endpapers and pointed to the chapel seal which was clearly decipherable. 'The gift of Bishop Heber, Heber Hall, MCC, Tambaram,' it said.

'I came here today because more than one faculty member has informed me that they've seen books belonging to the chapel library in your stock. Now I come here and discover that you have a shelf – a *whole shelf* – of all our very old library books here. I don't understand what your interest in these books could be and how you came to possess them.'

'Did you not deaccession these books some three months ago because they were taking up much-needed shelf space?'

He looked uncertain for a moment, then replied, 'Our very devoted chapel librarian, Robert Arulpragasam – soon to retire after thirty years of faithful and dedicated librarianship – persuaded us that it might be the best course of action to make room for newer, more updated holdings and to clear our shelves of clutter. But the collection wasn't thrown away. He asked if he could have the books – he was terribly attached to them, you see, having been their custodian for over three decades – and we gladly made a gift of them to him. And, might I add, that in deep appreciation of our gesture, our dear, venerable Arulpragasam gifted the library a bookcase full of beautiful leather-bound books from his personal collection. Each of them, no doubt, of considerable value.'

'And in return you let him have these shabby old books?'

'It's the least we could do after he had replaced them with all those sumptuous-looking ones. He was deeply sentimental about these old books and offered to take them off our hands and look after them.'

'So they are really his books, then. Wouldn't that be correct, Reverend Satya?'

'Indeed! And it now looks like someone has taken or stolen these books from him somehow, and sold them here!'

'Not just someone, Reverend. The librarian himself.'

Momentarily stumped, Reverend Satya opened and shut his mouth a couple of times. Then, recovering, he said brightly, 'Ah, I see now. Arulpragasam donated the lot to the bookshop, no doubt.'

'No, not donated, Reverend. Sold. For quite a pretty sum too.'

'But...but these are not valuable books! Th-they're just very old.'

'You're right in assuming that most old books are not really valuable, as people often tend to believe. Their value is more sentimental than anything else. But once in a while some of these books do turn out to be that rare thing: Truly valuable and scarce editions of important books; books that continue to matter now. To a collector interested in antiquarian books, especially someone who collects hymnals and prayer books from this period, they would be invaluable.

And, yes, in this lot that Arulpragasam sold us there are one or two fairly interesting editions.'

'Then all I can say is that it seems to me our Arulpragasam was doubly generous! The leather-bound books that replaced these out-of-print editions must surely be worth more, perhaps even be valuable in the extreme.'

'Can I come and see the leather-bounds myself?' Kayal asked, her curiosity surfacing in spite of herself.

'They are not for sale,' the priest replied icily.

'Biblio has no interest, I can assure you, in buying them. Reverend, will you sit down for a moment, please? There's something I want to show you that may interest you. And then, perhaps, some things about this whole affair will become a little clearer to you.'

He nodded and took the chair by her desk.

'Leather-bound books,' said Kayal gently, 'are pretty but most of the time their only value is decorative. With a few exceptions, they are not collected; I doubt the books Mr Arulpragasam donated so generously are worth anything in the antiquarian market. What is valued, plain though it may be, is a book in its original cloth binding, not one bound in decorative leather. And these books that he took away from the chapel library are all in their original binding and boards, not rebound in contemporary binding. Look at this one.'

She picked out the one item in the lot that was carefully wrapped and handed it to him.

He opened the book and exclaimed, '*The Book of Common Prayer*! But we have several more of these! It's been the Anglican liturgical prayer book for centuries now.'

'But I bet you don't have very many copies as old as this one; my guess is, probably none whatsoever.' She showed him the title page, pointing to the year of printing: 1662. 'This is a fairly scarce, sought-after edition. It's not often that you can turn up something printed in the seventeenth century here in India – and in this condition too. Your librarian must have known it would fetch something, because he sold it to us for a considerable sum.'

At first, the clergyman seemed silenced by this revelation, but then he spoke up again. 'You did mention there were some exceptions to leather bindings that are the valuable sort…'

'Those are bindings by bespoke designer binders such as Sangorski and Sutcliffe, Zaensdorf, Zahn, Middleton – custom-made for collectors, with gold tooling, gilt edges, marbled paper and raised bands in all kinds of sumptuous leather. I doubt if the bindings Arulpragasam donated are fine bindings, though I can't be certain until I've seen them. In fact, it's possible that they could be prize bindings.'

'Prize bindings?'

'It was quite common for well-endowed European and English schools to award their star pupil, say someone who had stood first in Latin, a well-known classic rebound in leather. Such custom binding was usually carried out by a local binder, and though many were quite attractively designed and bound, they are nevertheless, craftsmanship-wise, fairly standard, and nothing close to the work of the designer binders I've just mentioned.'

This time, the priest remained quiet and Kayal held her tongue, allowing him to work it out for himself.

When he finally spoke, he looked troubled, sad. 'What you aren't saying, Ms Kayal, is that apart from how valuable and rare these books are, they were the college chapel's most prized treasure; something we ought to have carefully preserved instead of discarding.'

'Yes, you should hold on to them. Recover them if you can.'

'How do I do that now? We can't ask for the books to be returned.'

'I have an idea about how you can get them back,' Kayal told him. 'It involves paying a surprise visit to your dear Robert Arulpragasam and playing a little antiquarian trade trick on him. Give me a few weeks, Reverend Satya, and I'll have something worked out.'

'We have a month. Robert is on leave; on a trip, I believe, to his native place near Madurai. But please keep in mind that the librarian we are both referring to is not the librarian of the main college library, which has always been separate. Arulpragasam is the librarian for the small library at Heber Chapel. Here's my phone number and address. I live on campus, of course.'

'And Arulpragasam – is he on campus too?'

'Yes, at least until the end of the next month. He's retiring, as I mentioned, and has, apparently, already found a nice house in East Tambaram.'

Kayal saw Reverend Satya to the door, locked up for the night and stepped out of the bookshop.

Outside, it was hotter now, with only a mild trace of sea breeze in the wind. She hailed an auto and jumped in, yelling, 'Alwarpet!' She simply wasn't in the mood tonight to haggle with the driver over the outrageous fare he would inevitably demand. She usually took the bus home, but it had been a long evening and her grandmother would be waiting up for her to begin dinner, no matter how late it got.

Amudha Paati was still puzzling over her granddaughter's choice of career. She had imagined her granddaughter as a college professor with a cushy UGC salary and pension, so when Kayal had announced she was quitting academics for Biblio, Paati hadn't known what to make of it.

'But, *kanna*,' Paati had argued, 'there are so many shops around Moore Market hawking old books. Why must you do the same?'

'Paati, those books are just second-hand, not antiquarian.'

'You know, *kanna*, that's exactly what they say about that famous roadside bookstall in Luz Corner. They say you can find all kinds of treasures there; once a lucky passer-by found a copy of Vairamuthu's poems, signed and inscribed to Ilayaraja.'

This had given Kayal pause. 'Well, that *is* a find. Hmm, wish I'd snapped that up... Makes you wonder, though, doesn't it, how it got there?'

2

The Young Antiquarian

The next morning, Kayal caught the 23C bus to Besant Nagar. Neela wanted to see her about going on a little book-scouting trip for Biblio. Since Neela knew how much her associate enjoyed sitting on the balcony of her sixth-floor apartment that overlooked the beach, a pot of fresh-ground organic coffee by her side, she had asked Kayal to drop by for a leisurely chat. Pokisha, Neela's neice, who clerked part-time at Biblio, had the morning desk at the bookshop, so Kayal wouldn't have to be back until later.

Getting off at the stop before the bus terminus, Kayal made an important detour to the Murugan Idli Shop which served the best chutneys (five of them!) in Chennai on a plantain leaf, so you could wipe off every bit of them with soft, steaming idlis and crisp dosas. They served ghee pongal too and decent filter coffee, but those weren't for a vegan like Kayal. Still, a satisfying breakfast at Murugan Idli needed to be followed up with some strong coffee and Neela's hundred-per-cent single-origin Arabica dark roast, drunk black, was just the thing. A million times better than the milky, overly sweet degree coffee served in most Chennai restaurants.

It was only 9 a.m. and already the day was sticky with humidity. It seemed unseasonably hot for February. Neela's apartment was at least half-a-kilometre away, but Kayal decided against taking an auto. She would take the path along the beach to make her walk a little more pleasant. For most of Kayal's adolescent life, Chennai had simply been the city she had grown up in and she had chugged along like every other Chennaite, trying not to mind the blistering heat, the exasperating philistinism of her college mates and the comical worldliness of her relatives. The things that connected many a Chennaite to their city – food, music, Tamil cinema and festivals – had left her mostly unmoved. But in her last year of college at Stella Maris, the city had suddenly changed for her. Kayal had stumbled upon colonial Madras while on an impromptu heritage walk through the city, and had fallen swiftly under the spell of its English and Indian antiquaries.

Kayal liked reminding people that the origins of the East India Company had not been in Calcutta, nor in Bombay, nor Delhi, but right here in her city. The other Raj cities had been more deliberate enterprises, and could boast of the best examples of colonial architecture. But Madras was the first Indian city to establish and nourish the institutions the British would later became famous for: The first hospitals, the first schools and colleges, the first government, the first railways, the first churches, the first libraries – and the first bookshops. It was fascinating to think that Robert Clive had been here when he was just a teenager, a still unknown soldier trying to find his footing at Fort St George, then a small garrison town.

What captivated the blooming antiquarian in Kayal was not life in the city as the British knew it, but life in Madras, the first 'modern' city in India, as its original inhabitants must have experienced it. While there seemed to be, if not very much, at least sufficient sources that could tell her how the British had fared in her city, she found very little about how her own people must have felt about life in a burgeoning metropolis. To dig up more telling sources about the average Madrasian became Kayal's new-found mission, focusing on the role Indians had played in the early establishment of libraries and bookshops in the country. Higginbotham's, the oldest bookshop in

India, was one of the starting points she'd considered. But just as Kayal was digging her teeth into the beginnings of Madras's antiquarian book culture, her parents, both of whom worked in the railways as administrators, got transfer orders to Salem. It was only when it looked like she would have to leave the city that Kayal realized how attached she had become to it. Luckily for her, Amudha Paati was stubborn about not leaving Chennai with the rest of the family and to have her granddaughter stay on with her seemed the best solution under the circumstances.

Years later, Kayal would again face a career decision that might have taken her out of Chennai, but life would steer her in another direction instead. With every indication that she would be awarded a scholarship to do her doctoral research at Jadavpur University's School of Cultural Texts and Records in Kolkata, Kayal had been ready to leave the city, and that was when, with such sweet timing, Neela had appeared, asking her if she would help her set up an antiquarian bookshop. She had sensed in Kayal that bibliophilic intimacy with the physical and bibliographical make-up of a printed book that was so important to antiquarian bookselling and collecting. To show that she was serious about taking Kayal on as an associate at the bookshop and investing in her, Neela had straightaway sponsored Kayal's trip to the Colorado Antiquarian Book Seminar, a one-week course that introduces young booksellers to the rare-book market. After that course, Kayal didn't have to think too much any more about what she wanted to do with her life, and where she wanted to be: She knew Biblio was the place for her.

Neela, a tall woman with a heart-shaped face and dark, sardonic eyes, was on the balcony, with a pot of steaming black coffee already waiting beside her. She waved, asking Kayal to let herself in.

'Come join me out here,' Neela called out as Kayal stepped into the apartment, appreciatively breathing in the heady smell of brewing coffee.

Kayal was rather surprised to see Neela dressed in a ravishing dark green Bengal cotton sari, already dressed to go out. Neela had only just returned from an antiquarian book fair in Europe; she usually came back jet-lagged and a little out of sorts from these far-flung, book-buying trips.

'Hey, I thought you were staying in today,' Kayal remarked, pouring herself a large cup of coffee and slurping greedily.

'Change of plan. We're meeting Nallathambi Whitehead later at Amethyst. He may have an assignment for you.'

'For *me*? That should be interesting,' Kayal remarked, still looking a little surprised.

Whitehead was a book collector of particular importance, one among a small band of wealthy, significant collectors in India. He was also India's pre-eminent collector of the books, manuscripts and letters of the polymath and explorer Richard Francis Burton.

'Have you breakfasted at Murugan's or will you have a bite here?' Neela asked.

Kayal rubbed her tummy, grinning contentedly, before filling her boss in quickly on the news from the bookshop. Neela was particularly curious about the priest's visit. 'Did you say the books were all stamped as belonging to Bishop Heber or to Heber Hall?'

Kayal thought for a few seconds, conjuring up the endpapers in her head. 'No, I'm sure they all said: "The gift of Bishop Heber."'

'My God, could it be?' Neela muttered softly to herself.

'*What*?' Kayal had never seen her boss look so surprised at anything she had said to her.

'I can't be sure just now, Kayal. I'll tell you more when I know. But when you go to see Reverend Satya at MCC, I want you to call me – I have some questions for him.'

'Okay. Look, this should interest you.' Kayal dug out a book from her bag. 'Found this at Luz Corner for you.'

'Ardizzone's *Indian Diary*! Kayal, this is wonderful! Look at all these lovely pencil-and-ink sketches made in the fifties. Bazaars, quaint little railway stations, old restaurants…' She turned the pages. 'Did you know he had visited India?'

'I had read something about it, but don't know much more.'

Edward Ardizzone, a favourite with both of them, had been one of England's most brilliant and best-loved illustrators of children's books. He had written and illustrated the Little Tim series, the delightful *Johnny the Clockmaker* and the lesser-known bibliophilic treasure *Sarah and Simon and No Red Paint*, with its fetching sketches of children browsing in a Dickensian antiquarian bookshop.

In 1952, he had been invited by UNESCO, along with four other artists, to be part of a workshop-seminar for the production of audio-visual aids in India. He had spent a total of three months in Delhi, Bombay and Mysore, briefly stopping in Bangalore. Every day, Ardizzone would send back to *Punch* the sketches he was making of scenes and objects and people that caught his eye in these cities and the magazine then published them. On his return, he did several watercolours of the scenes he had witnessed in India, which would become part of a celebrated exhibition.

'My turn,' said Neela. 'You just *have* to see my loot from the fair this year… I found a couple of gems.' She delicately placed a boxed set and two clamshell boxes between them on the coffee table. She unboxed a Kipling set, every copy signed by the author; 1930, bound in tan morocco, all edges gilt, raised bands, marbled endpapers – the works. 'These other two, though – I'm more pleased about these,' she continued, removing a folio-sized book from its slipcase.

Kayal leaned forward. Her boss had a personal interest in looking for fine editions with an Indian or even South Asian connection at these antiquarian book fairs abroad. The previous year, she had returned with books by Ananda Kentish Coomaraswamy published by the Essex House Press. What had caught her eye this time?

'*India Love Poems.* Translated by Tambimuttu, with colour lithographs by John Piper, impeccably printed by the Rampant Lions Press in 1967 on Velin Arches paper,' Neela announced, her voice triumphant.

It was, indeed, a handsome production, thought Kayal, taking it from Neela's hands. Meary James Thurairajah Tambimuttu, though little known in India, had been a legend in London's literary circles during the fifties and sixties. A Tamil poet from Sri Lanka, who had emigrated to England, he had quickly established himself as the editor of an important poetry journal called *Poetry London* that published the early works of Auden, Eliot, Corso and Ginsberg.

'I'm guessing you were equally excited about what you paid for it?' Kayal said, teasing, as she handed it back.

This limited edition of two hundred copies was never listed in the market for less than £2,000.

'Seven hundred pounds,' said her boss, grinning. 'And I have no idea why the dealer had it priced so low, but I wasn't going to educate him, was I?'

Biblio would price it at either £1,200 or £1,500, making it the most competitively priced copy on the market.

While Kayal pored over the items from the antiquarian book fair, Neela got up to brew more fresh coffee. Kayal found herself drawn particularly to an artist's book by Susan Allix, *The Golden Temple Mail to Bharatpur: Indian Encounters,* letterpress with six colour etchings in a special binding that used doublures of Indian yellow handmade paper from Jaipur. Noting the price her boss had paid for it, she gave a low whistle: £2,700.

Returning with a fresh pot, Neela rested her gaze on Kayal reading in the sun. The light had caught her face in profile and seemed to deepen the glow of her dark complexion, emphasizing her angular features, the sharp nose and the delicate, swooping curve of her neck.

Neela sat back down next to Kayal and asked, 'Interested in making a book-scouting trip to Ooty?'

'Totally. What's up?'

'Beardsley School in Lovedale will be deaccessioning some of their library material later this month and I thought there might be something there in the way of out-of-print children's books for Biblio.'

Kayal gave her boss a sceptical look. From past experiences of rummaging through library discard sales, they knew these were a hit or miss. Most of the time, they had been a miss – just tattered reading copies of hardcover classics and popular paperbacks. Very rarely, they had got lucky and come up with some very early reprint editions of famous children's books; ex-libris and therefore bearing the mark of the usual library treatment – heavily adorned with library stamps on every other page, card pockets stuck on to the paste-down and ex-libris labels – all of which brought down the value of the edition. Still, if they were out-of-print, and hard-to-come-by, they deserved a place on Biblio's shelves.

'Well, if nothing, it'll get me out of this sauna.'

'Exactly,' Neela chuckled. 'But there's something else too – which is why we're meeting Whitehead in a bit. While you're in Ooty, he wants you to check something for him.'

'Really? Is there some fabulous bibliographical treasure we don't know about hidden there?'

'He's being very mysterious, I have to say. Wouldn't actually disclose what it was. He sort of mentioned in passing that there might be something interesting, bibliophily-wise, in Ooty, but he didn't fancy making a trip all the way there to discover it was nothing. And that's when I mentioned that you might be going up there to do some book-scouting. He became pretty excited at that; said you could help him when you were there and then asked if he could see us both this afternoon.'

'Okay. Let's see what he has to say. Meanwhile, I'll get cracking on booking my train tickets to Ooty and finding a decent hotel.'

'Here's the name and number of the librarian at Beardsley. You need to give them a rough idea of when they should expect you.'

3

Sir Richard and the Collector

Half-an-hour later, they left in Neela's black Honda Brio for their meeting with the Burton collector, Nallathambi Whitehead, taking the long, pretty stretch along the Marina Beach Road. As they sped along, Kayal turned up the air conditioning. The traffic snarled once they moved inland, preventing them from making their way easily to Royapettah where the café and boutique, Amethyst, was located.

Both women dearly missed Amethyst's first location in Gopalapuram, where a fully restored colonial mansion in a tangled, overgrown garden in the heart of the city had been magically transformed into a café with an unmissable old-world charm, especially if you took a table in the colonnaded veranda. The present location, with its cobbled paths, luxuriant garden and period furniture, tried its best to remind you of the old Amethyst. In fact, many of its patrons continued to be the old regulars: Artists, expats and Tamil movie-industry folk, perennially sipping on tall, cool glasses of freshly made fruit juices or a variety of Italian coffees. Characterized by its solid colonial hangover, Amethyst was the closest thing to a Peninsula or a Raffles that Chennai had, a place where it felt as if you could spot Greene or Maugham in the corner at any moment, nursing a drink and scribbling on sheets of paper.

Afternoons were a particularly good time to grab the best tables, and the two women picked one on the veranda with a large ceiling fan lazily rotating above it. They ordered a generous pitcher of pulpy jamun juice, which promptly arrived, looking cool and alluring. As Kayal reached out for the jug, Neela excused herself to say a quick hello to someone she knew at another table. As she rose, she leaned over and cautioned her associate. 'If Whitehead turns up, remember not to bring up Arcot's name.'

Sipping on her juice, Kayal tried to recall what she knew about Nallathambi Whitehead and 'Arcot' Manovalan Templar, Whitehead's rival and owner of Heritage Auctions, the only book-auction house in India. The two men had been brought up in Katpadi, a township of Vellore, a small, teeming city in the North Arcot district of Tamil Nadu. They were proud of their origins, often reminding people that it was in Vellore, one of southern India's oldest cities, that the first Indian revolt against the British had actually broken out, predating by over half-a-century the more famous Sepoy Mutiny of 1857 that was sparked off in Meerut. The two men were not only contemporaries but had been childhood friends, though, over the years, they had turned rivals, competing and fighting over many bibliographical treasures. Rumour had it that rare books weren't the only thing they had fought over. There had apparently been a woman – a mighty and ravishing bibliophile-huntress, as Neela liked to call her – who had, in the end, spurned both suitors. Naturally, they blamed each other for her swift departure. Rumour also had it that the Ziegenbalg Bibliophiles, a society of book collectors in Chennai, knew why she had fled, and though none of them would say it outright, they suspected that the Katpadi rivals had each hoped to secure a place in her heart with the intention of laying his hand on her enviable rare-book collection.

Kayal looked around for Nallathambi Whitehead. No sign of him yet. She spotted the Tamil singer-actress Andrea Jeremiah at the next table, and in the garden, director Gautham Vasudev Menon and his crew animatedly discussing what could only be a new script. When Neela returned to the table, Kayal asked, 'What's the deal with Templar and Whitehead – are they still rivals in collecting?'

'Well, no, not exactly in collecting, though they are still rivals. See, once upon a time, they were busy trying to outdo each other in their conquest of rare and fine books. But once Templar went into the auction business, it turned competitive. If something interesting turned up in the antiquarian market here, Arcot Templar would try and see that it was placed with him at Heritage to be auctioned. At an auction, a rarity can go either way; it may realize a price that falls well below what it should have gone for or – as is frequently the case – considerably more than anyone had estimated. And once too often, Templar would get wind of items that Whitehead was hoping to acquire and convince the seller to auction it rather than sell privately. Nothing wrong at all, normally, in what Arcot Templar was doing, but things being the way they were with the two of them, it got personal. Each suspected the other of trying to snatch what should rightfully have been his. But if Whitehead has a rival in collecting now, it's the Englishman Viscount Ricky Pilkington.'

'Pilkington?'

'The English collector in London. I'll fill you in later – I think Whitehead's car just pulled up.'

Kayal spotted the collector's vintage Morris Minor gliding into the garden. They watched him slide out with some effort (which he tried hard to conceal), even though his driver held the door wide open for him. The man was clearly under strict orders from his employer to not assist him while stepping out of the car in public.

A tall, portly man in his early sixties, with a full head of white hair, Whitehead never left his stately bungalow in anything but a custom-made suit, suspender pants and bowler hat, with small, perfectly round Da Vinci eyeglasses and an ornate walking cane to complete the ensemble. The suspenders and walking stick were a necessity, but the hat was clearly an affectation.

'Ladies,' he grunted, acknowledging them as he slowly sank into a cane chair.

A waiter rushed to him, brandishing menus. Whitehead dismissed him with a wave of his cane and turned to Kayal.

'What do you know about Richard Francis Burton, Ms Anbuchelvan?'

Kayal wasn't expecting to be addressed, much less queried. 'Well...' she responded, 'I guess what everyone knows: Translator, explorer, *Arabian Nights*, first white man to take the Hajj to Mecca, his troubled quest for the true source of the Nile – that sort of thing. Oh, and also that he spent some time in India.'

'The most crucial years, Ms Anbuchelvan, the most *crucial* years!' bellowed Whitehead, growing visibly excited. 'Arabia, Africa and England feature strongly in any discussion on Burton, but little is said about his India experience except as a footnote. The seven years he spent in India, from 1842 to 1849, in his early twenties *formed* Burton. This country made him the Burton the world knows and admires. This is where he discovered his gift for languages, his abilities as a translator, his love for libraries, his passion for and curiosity about other cultures, his interest in Arabic and Islam. This is where he entertained the idea of trying out disguises in order to "go native", received his first exposure to a variety of sexual practices and developed his lifelong anthropological interest in this area.'

There was a brief silence as Whitehead paused to take a sip of water. And then, shifting his piercing gaze back to Kayal, he asked, 'And what do you know about me and my connection with Burton?'

'That you collect him fiercely,' answered Kayal, refusing to be intimidated.

'But I'm not just another Burton collector, Ms Anbuchelvan! I'm the second biggest collector of Burton material in the world – something your employer should have told you about me before our meeting.'

'Come now, Nallathambi, you were being so coy about this meeting to begin with!' Neela protested feigning indignation, but suppressing a grin. 'You didn't say it had to do with Burton, did you?'

Whitehead ignored her and resumed. 'You see, Ms Anbuchelvan, among private collectors, only the collection of Viscount Pilkington truly rivals mine. I might also add that with his collection and mine put together, we've long surpassed the achievements of the great Burton collectors of the past, such as Quentin Keynes, Edward Metcalfe and Burke Casari. Of course, the Burton holdings with institutional collectors like the British Library and the Huntington Library beat us all. But that is as it should be; institutions and museums have resources and funds that private collectors lack. In any case, a great part of the Keynes and Metcalfe collections are now at the British and Huntington libraries, while among private collectors, I own the scarcest Burton material in Asia. Now, I hear you are making a little trip to Ooty and this is where I'd like you to assist me with something.'

'I'm looking forward to it, Mr Whitehead.'

'Good. There's a fellow up there who says he has some Burton material from the Indian years, something he thinks no other collector could possibly have. He isn't willing to tell me what it is. He wants to show it to me, instead.'

'What Burton material could he possibly possess that you don't already have?' Neela wondered aloud.

'It could be a number of things. Surely you didn't think I'd finished with Burton entirely, did you, my dear Neelambari? I may have all his books in their first and variant printings, but I don't have several of his manuscripts.'

'Yes, but how is he so sure *you* don't already own a copy of whatever it is he has?'

'Because he – the chap's name is Kenton Selvaganesan – claims that no one in the world could possibly have another copy. It's a Burton manuscript, apparently.'

'And he didn't even hint at what it might be?' Neela asked.

'This is how it all began. Two weeks ago, I received a phone call from a man who identified himself as Kenton Francis Selvaganesan – the Francis was a nice touch, I thought – a history teacher at the Beardsley School in Ooty. He said he had some Burton material on him that he was in a terrible quandary about. He didn't know what to do with it and wanted my counsel. My interest was immediately aroused and I asked him to tell me more – and, before that, to also tell me how he knew of my interest in Burton. He said he had chanced on newspaper references to my last great Burton acquisition – well, you'll remember the news stories – talking about how an Indian collector had paid the highest price ever offered for that fairly scarce Burton pamphlet – '

'The 1853 *Bayonet Exercise*,' Neela volunteered, nodding.

'Yes, *A Complete System of Bayonet Exercise*. Satisfied that the man wasn't wasting my time, I asked him to tell me about the Burton material he had and how he came to own it. Apparently, a family Burton had known while he was recuperating in Ooty has had it in their possession all these years – that means, for more than a century. He listed two of the three items: two books that had belonged to Burton, with his ownership signature and annotations in the page margins – a very common feature with Burton – and a letter Burton had written from Karachi, after he returned there, to a woman he had known in Ooty. Nothing unusual in that; Burton was always writing letters, except that it's the first I have heard of one addressed to someone he knew during his stay in Ooty. All this was very well, as I'm always interested in adding books to my collection that contain Burton's scribbles, as well as his letters. But what was the third thing, I asked. He had mentioned three.'

Whitehead paused to wipe his brow.

'There was silence over the phone, even some hesitation,' he went on. 'Then the voice on the other end said, "It's a Burton manuscript." I was, as you can imagine, riveted by this piece of information. But he regretted that he was not at liberty to reveal what the manuscript was at that moment. Was he a crank, after all, I asked myself. Someone out to make quick money from me? With Francis as a middle name? When I asked him about it, he said his mother had apparently been some kind of devotee of Burton's and had stuck her son with that name. He was really quite tired of people asking him about it. After I had gathered my wits, I said a manuscript *would* be special, but why did he think it was so unique? "From the time this came into my possession," he answered, "I have been researching Burton enough to be convinced of its singularity." And then he suggested I come down to Ooty and look at it myself; he would rather not describe it or reveal more.'

'And you told him, of course, that you could not travel and that he should bring the Burton material here to you,' prompted Kayal. Whitehead suffered from severe gout and the only travelling he was capable of was confined within Chennai. It had been years since he had travelled anywhere out of the city.

'Hmm,' Whitehead grunted, annoyed at being interrupted, 'but the schoolteacher said he was unable to make a trip to Chennai any time soon – his mother was recovering from a stroke and he could not leave her unattended. To bait him, to draw him out, I said that if the material was, indeed, as unique as he claimed, and if it could be authenticated and its provenance verified, I would pay more for it than any Burton collector he could think of offering it to. But he remained firm. It would have to wait. And now you see, Neelambari, why I jumped at the chance of Ms Anbuchelvan checking on him when she's in Ooty. I've rung him since and told him that someone from Biblio might look in, adding that the bookshop was the nearest thing I could think of that would serve his best interests and mine; a knowledgeable third party, with expertise in these matters that could also remain objective and perhaps even serve the best interests of Sir Richard Francis Burton himself!'

'Hmm...certainly intriguing,' remarked Neela, 'and worth looking into. Come on, Nallathambi, what's your guess about the Burton he has? He's from Ooty, remember?'

Neela was grinning now, because she knew what Whitehead must be thinking.

'I admit I would be overjoyed if it were the Pilpay manuscript,' he replied, leaning back in his chair and closing his eyes, as if making a wish.

'Yes, of course, *Pilpay's Fables*,' said Neela softly. 'The first thing Burton ever translated.'

When he opened them, Whitehead's eyes were twinkling.

'But how do you think he – this Kenton – came upon it? How would it come to be in Ooty?' asked Kayal, watching them both closely.

'Because, young lady, Burton was in Ooty. Admittedly, not for very long, but he was there.'

'*Ooty*? I thought he was stationed in Bombay.'

'Not at all!' snorted Whitehead. 'He was never stationed in Bombay – though he did land there and often went there later to write his language exams. He was posted to Baroda and then to Sindh – Karachi, specifically. In 1846, Burton was asked to take a vacation to convalesce from sickness and fatigue. He went to Goa, Calicut and then, finally, to the Niligiri hills, to a sanitorium in Ootacamund. He quickly grew bored and restless in the hills and set down to learning more new languages. By now, he already knew Hindustani, Sanskrit, Gujarati and Marathi. On his return to Sindh, he would learn Punjabi and Sindhi. But now in Ooty, using a local tutor, he began learning Telugu and Toda. Oddly enough, there is no record of him learning or even attempting to learn Tamil.'

Whitehead paused as the waiter began laying out their food: Lemon linguine (without the garlic) for Neela, aglio olio peperoncino (without the cheese) for Kayal and a large piece of tiramisu for Whitehead (even though he had begged off ordering lunch, murmuring something about a diet).

Spooning out a creamy layer of the pastry, the collector continued. 'But something else Burton did in Ooty, while recovering from a bad eye infection, is of particular importance: He made his first foray into translation – a Sanskrit text of the *Hitopadesha*, retranslated in Hindi as the popular fables of Pilpay, something like an Indian Aesop. Burton discovered that he liked translating; enjoyed it so much, in fact, that he knew that's how he wanted to use his genius for language. However, he didn't complete the entire translation there. He returned to it later and finished it in 1847. The Pilpay manuscript is in the Huntington Library now. And, rather strangely, this first Burton translation was the very last of his works to come out in print – it would be published for the first time in book form only in 2003.'

He now looked imploringly at the two women. 'But I hope both of you can also see why part of that early translated manuscript – or a version of it – may have been left behind in Ooty? As to how this man, Kenton Selvaganesan, came to acquire it – if, indeed, that is what it really is – I do not know and cannot say. And this is where you come in, Ms Anbuchelvan. If you can coax him into at least telling you what the manuscript is, even if he won't show it, it will give me sufficient incentive to pursue it. If it is a holograph copy of the Pilpay fables, I cannot wait; I must have it.'

'Well, I think none of us can wait to find out!' declared Neela.

Kayal felt a sudden rush of adrenaline at the thought of the impending trip. She would soon be there, in the presence of a mysterious Burton manuscript; she would also be the first one to describe it to Neela and Whitehead – a rare and unexpected privilege.

Whitehead spoke again. 'Hopefully, we've beaten Arcot Templar to this. If he gets wind of it, I can handle it, but not a whiff of this should reach Pilkington. With his large Burton holdings, he's the only collector standing between me and the title of the world's greatest Burton collector. And stumbling upon something like an early version of the Pilpay manuscript – or any Burton papers – is what will bring me closer to becoming the foremost Burton collector in the world. Ms Anbuchelvan, I can't stress enough the importance of keeping mum on this.'

Kayal shot Neela a please-fill-me-in-on-this-now look.

Her boss elaborated quickly. 'Viscount Ricky Pilkington, from the house of Tresham, is a bit of a nasty business. A rich, titled revisionist scholar who plans to build a museum showcasing, in his words, "the glory of the British Raj". He has been obsessively collecting all kinds of antique Raj material for a decade now, with a particular focus on Burton. He's both reviled and admired in Britain...' She paused and added after a moment, 'It's sad to see such revisionist leanings in a young, moneyed scholar-collector. '

'Well,' Whitehead said, 'we've seen that before – the droves of wealthy German collectors, scholars and journalists pursuing Third Reich material and nearly salivating over it.'

'In my meeting with this schoolteacher in Ooty, should I bring up the subject of what he might want for this Burton item?' Kayal asked, addressing the collector.

'Not necessary at all,' Whitehead replied at once. 'I think I can afford whatever price he names. My dear Ms Anbuchelvan, you look quite chastened! Let me hasten to assure you that I may be able to pay what Kenton asks for not because my funds are unlimited but because Burton material, even the scarcer ones, are not very expensive. Well, at least not as forbiddingly so as some of the other things I collect.'

'Usually, a Burton first edition, even one in good condition, can be had for $500,' Neela chipped in. 'Some of the scarcer titles are available for a few thousand and his autograph letters start at $5,000 or so and go up a little more, but not much. The rarest of Burtoniana, such as the ones from the Quentin Keynes collection that sold at Christie's in 2004, did not meet the auction estimates. If I remember, two of the scarcer Burton pamphlets that Christie's thought would sell for between £15,000 and £20,000 realized only £11,500.'

'But why hasn't it risen over the years – the value, I mean?' Kayal asked.

'Sadly, interest in Burton today isn't very high,' replied Whitehead. 'Except for the occasional scholarly paper or monograph, I would say he's almost on the verge of being forgotten. Ms Anbuchelvan, I think it might be useful if you came along with me now to see some, if not all, the Burton material I have. I think it's important you do this before you make the trip. Also, it would be a good idea for you to begin reading up on Burton. And I have just the books for you. Several good biographies to pick through – Farwell, Brodie, Lovell, Godsall, and two bibliographies – Penzer and Casada. James Casada is the key book here for existing Burton material. Neelambari, my dear, I hope you can spare her for a little longer?'

Neela noticed Kayal's hesitant expression and reassured them both that she had no objections. 'That's fine,' she said. 'Kayal, I can take over the bookshop for as long as you need to be out. I'll give Pokisha the day off as well. I haven't been to Biblio in a while and I'm rather looking forward to chatting to the customers. It'll also give me time to catch up on the catalogue.'

Whitehead reached for the bill, but Neela swooped it up, saying it was Biblio's pleasure.

4

The Patron Saint of the Baker Street Irregulars

Whitehead's driver, Inba, took an illegal U-turn at Thousand Lights Mosque to squeeze on to Mount Road. At Spencer's, traffic was clogged, but the Morris was luxurious and cool, and Kayal relaxed a little. She wondered why the collector had chosen Burton, of all people, as his special interest and what made him pursue the Orientalist so obsessively. Perhaps, she thought, the answer lay in the biographies of Burton he had pointed her to. Whitehead had fallen silent, and when she turned to him with her questions she saw he had dozed off.

Turning back to watch the city crawl by outside the window, Kayal tried to remember what else she had heard from Neela about Whitehead and Templar. In the way some Indian Catholics name their children after saints, Protestants in India tended to name their offspring after famous white missionaries who, sometimes, also doubled as headmasters and headmistresses at mission schools. Both men, it seemed, had been named after an English missionary called Templar Whitehead, who had acquired the image, throughout North Arcot, of a formidable school headmaster, founding one prestigious missionary school after another – including the one in which the two men studied. The parents of Arcot and Nallathambi,close family friends who had venerated Templar Whitehead and his growing empire of mission schools, had named their children after the man, splitting his name between their sons: one became Templar and the other, Whitehead.

Kayal could never get over the oddness of hybrid Christian names; at college she had known fellow students and teachers with names like Janice Jananayagam, A.B.C. David, Carlyle Velu, Copernicus Manoharan, Sigmund Saravanan and Archibald Arokiaswamy. In the cultural heartlands of Tamil Nadu and the deep south, from Madurai to Thanjavur, Nagercoil to Tirunelveli, it wasn't uncommon to find neighbours called Stalin, Khrushchev, Kennedy, Socrates, Bernardshaw (pronounced and written as one name) or Faraday; and once, there had even been an English literature student from Madras University named Shakespeare Selvakumar, who – when his name was called out by the professor marking attendance – would answer loudly, 'Present, saar!' (Shakespeare Selvakumar was also known for once famously answering this way when asked 'Who is Keats?': 'Keats is the plural of Keat.') Kayal could quite easily picture an English missionary called Templar Whitehead in Katpadi, preaching and teaching and gathering acolytes.

Was that what explained Whitehead's attraction to Burton, she wondered, the shared colonial past? She recalled other details Neela had filled her in on regarding the origins of the two collectors.

The English headmaster after whom the two had been named had a passion, one he was very shy about. But he had shared it with his two favourite pupils; he was, he had confessed to the boys, a bibliomaniac of the first water. This love of rare books had been passed on to him by his father, who had been an antiquarian bookseller in the university town of Cambridge. Templar Whitehead's father would stand with a wheelbarrow of books outside Kings College every day, waiting for undergraduates to finish their tutorials. The young bibliophiles would come in droves, snatching up the lovely editions he offered at attractive bargain prices. They didn't have to go up to London to those expensive, finely appointed bookshops. It was right here, outside their university doors – a mobile antiquarian bookstall.

Antiquarian editions were not the only thing the headmaster seemed to have had a zeal for: Real estate – acquiring prime missionary property – was the other thing he lusted after. The missionary remained a bachelor, amassing both rare books and real estate at a giddy speed. At his deathbed, he bequeathed all his holdings in India, along with his superb and valuable antiquarian library, to his star pupils and namesakes in whom he had recognized the spark of bibliomania. He made them his legal heirs, urging them to share his legacy equally. Always itching to flee Katpadi and now armed with the resources to do so, Templar and Whitehead relocated to Madras. Templar quickly invested a part of his fortune in building Heritage, while Nallathambi turned to real estate and played the market. Collecting books had by now become their grand passion and their recent prosperity enabled them to fully pursue it. Both Templar and Whitehead went on to build their libraries on the foundation of their mentor's towering private collection.

Beside her, the collector stirred. Kayal sensed Whitehead had awakened from his nap and asked the question which had been on the tip of her tongue for some time. 'How did you come by your Burton collection?'

Whitehead nodded approvingly. 'Good question, Ms Anbuchelvan. A great deal of my best Burton material comes from the collection of Quentin Keynes, whose library came up for sale in 2004 at Christie's. In my own quest for Burton, Quentin Keynes has been my bibliophile hero. I had the opportunity to meet him once, when he invited me to tea and to have a look at his collection. This was quite unusual, since he was known for keeping his collection very private. Only in his last years did he allow scholars access to his Burton material, particularly the correspondence – and it was the biographer Mary S. Lovell who was fortunate enough to see some of this material and let it inform her work.

'Keynes was the great-grandson of Charles Darwin, but perhaps, more pertinently – at least, where bibliophiles are concerned – the son of the great scholar-collector Geoffrey Keynes, who inspired so many young bibliophiles in England to see collecting as a form of scholarship. When the Keynes collection came up for auction, I made every effort to secure the best and most high-end material. But I lacked experience and so I lost out to the bigger players, who ranged from wealthy private collectors to institutional libraries with deep pockets. But I did manage to bid on several smaller lots and got significant wins. When we reach home, I hope to be able to show you some Burton rarities that I managed to snag from other sources as well. And, of course, I am indebted to your boss for putting much of it together for me... Ah, here we are now.'

The car turned into a quiet cul-de-sac. They had reached Whitehead's bungalow in Egmore twenty minutes later than a ride through Chennai's afternoon traffic should have normally taken. Whitehead said they needn't bother going through the main house and guided Kayal through a door leading into what he called 'the east wing'. She had been inside the house once before, very briefly, while on an errand for Neela, but had only caught a glimpse of the large library downstairs that ran into several rooms. When she had mentioned it to her boss, Neela had dismissed it as a large collection of mere reading copies to distract visitors and keep them away from the real thing upstairs. Now, Kayal noted with mounting excitement, that they were headed up.

A little elevator took them to the second floor where it opened into a finely appointed private library. She wasn't surprised to see that all the furniture and furnishings here were made of glass, leather or wood. It was a large, circular room, with a glass wall on the side that overlooked the vast green garden below. Panelled walnut bookshelves, filled to the deep with attractive editions, lined the rest of the walls. Sofas and armchairs, plushly upholstered in real leather, were scattered around, with anglepoise lamps placed next to them. In various corners of the room stood illuminated museum-quality glass-counter display cases that probably held some of the rarer material from Whitehead's collection.

This must be one of the most beautiful book rooms in all of India, thought Kayal, as Whitehead led her further in.

'I have a few calls to make,' he said. 'So look around, make yourself comfortable. I'll be with you soon. If you need me, I'm in there – the adjoining room inside.' He pointed to an ornate wooden door and ambled over to it, walking cane in hand.

Kayal had the library to herself now. Not a library full of reading copies, but a room full of sparkling editions. A great book collector's private collection, authentic and accomplished. There was so much to see, where was she to start? The books on the shelves would have to wait, she decided, quickly walking over to the display counters to take a peek. The material – a mix of ephemera, broadsides and books – was carefully displayed, spread open to key pages so that visitors could focus right away on what was important about them. The glass cabinet counters had mirror-base panels, lockable castors and chrome side lights. The glass all around meant that you could look but not touch. One display held Gandhi's own copy of *Hind Swaraj* and a second pair of eyeglasses that had belonged to him (not the one that was nearly auctioned at Sotheby's was Kayal's guess). Interestingly enough, juxtaposed to Gandhi's things was what looked like a typed, draft copy of the Indian Constitution, with annotations and corrections in Ambedkar's manuscript hand. In another part of the room, a larger display counter held scientific first editions; one, Kayal could see, was by Darwin. So, she thought, puzzling it over, the display counters held interesting items but hardly the prized highlights of Whitehead's collection. From her year at Biblio and Neela's accounts of purchases made for all the collectors over the years, Kayal was somewhat familiar with each collector's high spots, all of it obsessively pursued and bid for or bought at fabled prices. Whitehead was not strictly an antiquarian man. His primary interest, contrasting peculiarly with everything else that hinted at the old-fashioned in him, was the modern.

Intrigued, Kayal moved to the shelves, scanning them quickly and saw that they held hypermodern firsts and fine bindings. Beautiful books in beautiful editions. But these too were far from scarce or rare. Whitehead's bibliophilic treasures must be somewhere else – in the room he had disappeared into, perhaps, a room full of locked bookcases? And where was all the Burton material?

'You won't find them there,' the collector called out, re-entering the room, as if reading her mind.

'Pardon?'

'The Burtons. We'll get to them soon, but it's your first time up here and you should have a quick tour.'

'Now you're coming perilously close to reading my mind, Mr Whitehead! Lead on.'

'Let's move to the display at the other end of the room.'

That was the glass counter she hadn't had a chance to view yet.

Just a glance told her that it was full of Sherlockiana. At first, it looked like a random assortment of interesting Sherlock Holmes material. Then it became apparent that the display was devoted to Vincent Starrett.

'The patron saint of the Baker Street Irregulars!' Kayal exclaimed in delight.

'Ah, I see you are a Sherlockian.' Whitehead sounded so pleased he was almost purring.

'Not really, sir. Just a buff. You must tell me more about Starrett.'

'I was going to whisk you through this quickly, because the material here is not difficult to find, but since you've turned out to be – perhaps a Holmesian? Well, never mind, I'm going to open the display and let you see the books up close. They are all association copies.'

With a practised hand, he swiftly unbolted the castors, smoothly sliding the glass sideways. He took out two books and showed her the titles.

'*The Private Life of Sherlock Holmes*. 1933. You know, don't you, that Starrett's first book was so influential that it got Christopher Morley to introduce the Baker Street Irregulars? This copy is inscribed to Morley. The next one, *221B: Studies in Sherlock Holmes*, edited by Starrett, was the first ever book of Holmes scholarship to be published, setting off a trend. This one is inscribed to the *Baker Street Journal*'s finest editor, Edgar Smith.' Placing the books carefully back inside, he picked up two more. '*The Adventures of the Unique Hamlet*, the first – and still the finest – Sherlock Holmes pastiche to date, inspiring scores of others to try their hand at something similar. This one is inscribed to Arthur Machen. But to appreciate Starrett, to see why I have a display devoted to association copies of *his* work – which are, by no means, expensive or difficult to find – you have to look at Starrett, the Holmes collector, not the scholar.

'Starrett was a struggling bookman in Chicago in the twenties. He put together not once, but thrice, the handsomest rare Sherlock Holmes material anyone had ever gathered until then. When he found a first printing of *The Hound of the Baskervilles* for $1.50, he noted it was "a trifle high". He even managed to find that extreme rarity – the first ever appearance of Sherlock Holmes in print, *A Study in Scarlet*, from the very scarce 1887 *Beeton's Christmas Annual*.'

Whitehead removed another slim little volume authored by Starrett, encased in an acetate wrapper. 'You must know the widely quoted sonnet Starrett penned here – "221B".' And though the collector had it open to the page, he recited the last lines from memory, murmuring most of it so that Kayal only got a whiff of swirling yellow fog, the ghostly shapes of gas lamps and a lonely hansom cab splashing its way through the rain.

Whitehead paused. 'I did say he had to do the collection three times over, didn't I?'

Kayal nodded, even though it wasn't really a question.

'Well,' Whitehead continued, picking up another book from the case, 'financial difficulties forced him to sell his precious collection thrice. The last time he was forced to sell the Holmes collection, he felt he would never collect again. The collection was to be sold by Scribner's, who had prepared a catalogue, and Starrett's loss and the difficult circumstances surrounding the sale had become public knowledge.

'And then something remarkable happened, something wonderful that you wouldn't expect to happen today. He received a letter out of the blue from a fellow collector called Clendening. But let me read a few lines of that letter from Starrett's own book, *Born in a Bookshop: Chapters from the Chicago Renascence*. And this copy, by the way, is Starrett's personal copy, with his iconic Sherlockian bookplate, designed and printed for him by Fridolf Johnson of the Mermaid Press.'

Whitehead slipped on his eyeglasses and read in a voice thick with emotion:

'My dear boy, I find that I am not getting as much fun out of my Holmes collection as I had anticipated... I hear that you have just parted with your own collection, and I think you ought to start another. Why not start with mine? It is small, but goodish – it contains a number of the better pieces that you might have difficulty duplicating – and I am boxing it up this afternoon and getting it off to you tomorrow morning. You will really take a load off my mind if you will accept it.

'The letter ends here. And then Starrett adds that the box contained some twenty of the most desirable items in the field, including "the desperately rare first printing" of *A Study in Scarlet*, and ends by saying, "I suppose no finer thing ever was done for one collector by another."'

Whitehead replaced the book reverently, slid the glass back into place and gestured to Kayal. 'Now, if you'll come with me, I will introduce you to *The Hound of the Baskervilles* from 1902 and that rarest piece of Sherlockiana: The actual printed pages on which Sherlock Holmes first made his appearance. After which, we shall look at the Burtons.'

5

In the Rare-Book Room

The adjoining room into which Whitehead had first disappeared turned out to be fairly small, but not without its own little surprises. No wooden shelves, no glass cabinets; just chrome. Instead of shelves there were alcoves, niches and compartments of varying sizes and shapes around the room. The room itself had been made even more blindingly white by the glare of tiny gallery lights around the ceiling, and Kayal sensed at once that the room was temperature-controlled.

'This room holds my essential collection,' Whitehead said, his hand gesturing towards the chrome alcoves.

At the centre of the room stood a small, simple rectangular table with a pair of chairs – all chrome again – facing each other across it. To place one or more of these incandescent printed treasures on it, Kayal imagined, and then sit down to caress them, study them, lose oneself in them...

'All my rare Sherlockiana are here,' said Whitehead, standing before a long, vertical alcove in the far corner of the room. 'Here it is, in publisher's red cloth without a dust jacket, just as it was issued in 1902.'

He handed her a short, squat, reddish book with a gilt spine: The first printing of *The Hound of the Baskervilles*. A perfect, unblemished copy, the text and illustrations sharp and bright throughout.

'And here is that elusive item.' Whitehead removed a small steel box and opened it, indicating that Kayal should look inside.

Sheathed in archival Mylar was a slightly wrinkled magazine. He gently coaxed the brittle thing out of its protective covering. '*Beeton's Christmas Annual* from 1887.'

It wasn't an immaculate copy, Kayal could see, but no other collector in India owned one. On the market, it was valued at $200,000. Whitehead's fellow collectors and rivals would have loved to have got their hands on it – if only they could unearth one. It seldom surfaced anywhere but at auctions and, when it did, was snapped up by wealthier American, European and Japanese collectors who enjoyed long associations with these famed auction houses or had important connections there. But this had been Neela's find, her book-hunting coup, and Nallathambi Whitehead had been the beneficiary because she had wanted to honour her oldest and most loyal customer by offering it to him first. Except for his old rival Arcot Templar, who hissed and spat in frustration, the other collectors, good sports all, had congratulated the collector and the book dealer.

'Few know that the first version of *A Study in Scarlet* that appeared in book form the following year, 1888, has now become just as rare. It was illustrated by Conan Doyle's father and not so hotly sought because those illustrations don't measure up today. I must also confess that there's just one other great piece of Sherlockiana that I wish I had – the original holograph of the Holmes story, "The Adventure of the Greek Interpreter", sent to the *Strand* magazine in 1893 and the only Conan Doyle holograph hitherto offered for public sale. But, alas, it continues to elude me…

'And, now to the Burtons,' said the collector after a pause, stowing away all the rare Sherlockiana in an instant and reaching for his beloved Burtons.

'I want you to at least see the material relating to his Indian years. Just so you have a sense of what the original editions look like, the kind of paper used in his manuscripts and letters, his handwriting in these documents. Why don't we sit down? If you can take a seat, I'll assemble them on the table. I have wonderful editions of *The Book of the Thousand Nights and a Night*, with entire sets, and all the variant *Kama Sutra*s – though Burton declared that it was published by the Kama Shastra Society in Calcutta, it was actually he and his friends who printed it privately in London – but these volumes won't serve to make a point now. You are welcome, of course, to see them at another time. I just get rather tired of people showing interest only in the *Nights* and the *Sutra*s and little else of Burton's.'

Whitehead spent the next few minutes looking for the material he wanted to pull together, nimbly using his cane to navigate around the alcoves. As she sat down now on the stylish, ergonomically designed chrome chair, Kayal found herself facing, just across the room, another large alcove, with three long-running compartments containing a series of colourful hardcover spines. Most were dust-jacketed; a few were cloth boards with gilt-edged titles on the spine. Kayal realized, with a little gasp, that she was looking at Whitehead's famed collection of Victorian detective and mystery titles, along with modern first editions of the highest of the high spots in mystery fiction. In the few minutes she got to herself before the collector joined her, she squinted, with a little shiver of excitement, to read the titles from where she was sitting: *The Moonstone*, *The Big Sleep*, *The Maltese Falcon*, *The Mysterious Affair at Styles*, *The Big Clock*, *Kiss Me Deadly*, *The Daughter of Time*, *The Nine Tailors*... The rows stretched on and on.

Her boss, who had once again played a vital part in assembling this collection, had told Kayal that the copies were all immaculate first editions, with tight binding, unfaded spines, sharp and fine-looking pages inside and dust jackets that glowed so intensely, they could have been airbrushed. One of those copies sitting unassumingly on the shelf, Neela had told her, was among the holy grails of inscribed first editions: *The Maltese Falcon*, inscribed to Raymond Chandler by Dashiell Hammett. You couldn't put a price on something like that, Neela had said, sighing.

Kayal turned her attention back to the table. The collector had assembled the material, placing all of it closer to where she sat. He took a seat across the table from her.

'This one is *Goa, and the Blue Mountains*, the first book of Burton's own fledgling attempts at writing, an interesting enough account of his stay in Goa, Calicut and the Nilgiris. It won't be a bad idea for you to dip into this monograph, since it deals with Burton's days in Ooty. This second item is a fun book, *Vikram and the Vampire*, which he translated with his wife Isabel. Also issued from the non-existent Kama Shastra Society in Calcutta.'

Kayal liked all the black-and-white illustrations representing Vikram and the ghost. So far, from what she could see, all the editions were plain. The boards were a dull yellow, the pages ordinary and the printing standard.

'This one is a little scarce: *Falconry in the Valley of the Indus*, 1852,' said Whitehead. 'And now, to the really scarce Burton book: *A Complete System of Bayonet Exercise*. Only ten copies of it have survived,' he said, placing it in her hand. 'You are now holding one of them.'

It was more a pamphlet than a book. And quite plain-looking too, thought Kayal, except for a typographically pleasing title page. Kayal handed it back to him.

'However,' the collector went on, producing two other pamphlets, 'the *Bayonet Exercise* is not really the rarest of Burton material, though it is scarce. That honour goes to two other publications. One is *The Guide Book: A Pictorial Pilgrimage to Mecca and Medina*, London, 1865; the other, perhaps rarer still, is *Stone Talk: Being Some of the Marvellous Sayings of a Petral Portion of Fleet Street, London, to One Doctor Polyglott, Ph.D.* by Frank Baker, D.O.N., London – Robert Hardwicke, 1865.'

Kayal was handed a slim but elegant book, got up in contemporary binding: Green levant morocco, with the spine ruled and lettered in gilt. This was the *Pictorial Pilgrimage*. It was, she noted, a signed Sangorksi and Sutcliffe binding.

Whitehead was saying, 'I plumped it up, because it was such a waif of a thing, more pamphlet than book. Let me read a bit to you about what Burton's first bibliographer, Norman Penzer, said about this little thing.'

From the table Whitehead now picked up a more substantially sized modern book – the Penzer she could see from the spine title – and read aloud from it. '"I have already stated the great rarity of this little pamphlet. I only know of six copies in existence, including that in my own library. There is no copy in the British Museum."

'It's possible,' Whitehead went on, 'that the British Library does possess a copy now. Penzer was noting this decades ago. I still think my copy is, perhaps, more singular than even the Keynes copy that went up for sale at Christie's in 2004, because mine has the elusive errata slip which the book was originally issued with and that most copies subsequently lost. You'll appreciate how precious my volume is when I tell you that even Burton's own copy apparently lacked the errata slip!'

As Whitehead caressed the little volume in his hand, Kayal waited for the other rare Burtoniana to materialize, but after a while it looked like Whitehead had nothing more to offer her.

'Ah, you are waiting for the other thing I mentioned,' he remarked, reading her mind. 'The rarest of all

Burtoniana, *Stone Talk*, is an even tinier pamphlet, bound just in wrappers. And this is something I don't have with me at the moment. I've given it to our Pandian to do a little restoration work on it.'

Clement Pandian was Biblio's in-house fine binder, who sometimes freelanced for collectors, undertaking complicated book-restoration jobs.

'Still, if I may,' Whitehead went on, 'I'd like to read a bit again from Penzer. He describes it as "one of the cleverest of all Burton's books, although it is practically unknown. It is very rare. Its scarcity is increased by the fact that Lady Burton bought up and destroyed a large number of the copies to save her husband from possible trouble with the 'authorities'." This would be a good time to mention what I lack by way of rare Burtoniana – the extensive correspondence between the explorer and numerous people in his life. I have a substantial number of Burton letters and documents, but there is someone who remains unrivalled in his collection of Burton manuscripts.'

'Viscount Pilkington?' Kayal offered helpfully, knowing full well it would set Whitehead off.

Whitehead sighed. 'Yes, Pilkington, damn him. So you can see now how unearthing a hitherto unknown Burton manuscript – something this fellow, Kenton Selvaganesan, says is truly unique – will put me on par with Pilkington, perhaps even make me Burton's most pre-eminent collector.'

'I take it you didn't come by the *Pictorial Pilgrimage* through the Keynes sale?'

'Alas, no. It would have been superb to have had Keynes's own copy, but that was snapped up quickly by the Huntington, I think, or perhaps it was the Lilly Library – anyway, one of those well-funded, rare-book institutions in America. My copy, you will be thrilled to know, Kayal, was obtained for me by Neela at a fraction of its market price. Your boss was on one of her yearly book-scouting trips to that well-known antiquarian bookshop in Simla, Maria Bros – which, sadly, has now shut down – and chanced upon it there. Maria Bros had no idea of its rarity, but still asked for a stiff price, knowing Burton first editions usually go for anything between $500 to $800 in the antiquarian market. They asked for $400; Neela surprised them by saying she would pay $3,000, because it was one of the scarcer Burton items. She decided not to tell them it was the rarest. Finders keepers, she said to herself, grabbed it and ran for her life.

'It was only after she was back in Chennai and was looking through it at leisure that she spied the errata slip stuck deep inside the page gutter and realized she had struck bibliographic gold. A complete copy had not been seen since the Keynes sale, making it the only other known copy. Neela described her transaction at Maria's in full to me and asked if $10,000 was a fair price. A bargain, I replied, and paid her right away.'

'What would it go for if you put it up?'

'Copies lacking the slip – and thus considered incomplete – have gone for anything between $9,000 and $12,000. My copy, being complete, should fetch $20,000–$25,000.'

Whitehead gathered the Burton material into a pile and rose to put them away. 'Come, shall we go? I've kept you too long as it is.'

Kayal protested, saying more than once what a privilege it had been to spend even an hour with these extraordinary editions.

Stepping out of the room, the collector said, 'Oh, before you leave, let me burden you with some homework. Let's see now... I think all my Burton biographies and bibliographies are on this little shelf by the armchair. Here you are... I'm afraid they are going to be quite an armload to carry. I'll make it easier for you by having Inba drop you off at home or at the bookshop, wherever you like.'

There were a total of six books, two of them particularly large and heavy.

'I'd recommend the Godsall biography, which some would probably say is the definitive one.'

The Godsall biography was one of the fat ones.

'And, of course, the second bibliography by Casada is extremely useful if you want to focus sharply on everything Burton wrote, translated and published, along with the material written *on* Burton – until at least the nineties. Would it be okay if I don't see you out? Down one floor in the elevator, and my driver will have the car waiting for you.'

Part Two

6

A Bibliographical Study

Back at Biblio, Kayal found Neela deep in conversation with a patron of the bookshop. She discreetly signalled to her boss to indicate that she had returned and could be summoned if needed, and proceeded to the inner room. Neela silently acknowledged her gesture and turned her attention once more to the work of ringing up purchases at the checkout.

Working in a bookshop, Kayal had learnt soon enough, wasn't only about bibliophilic pursuits – a large part of it involved physical labour. Either the heavy lifting of cartons tightly packed with books bought from auctions or private collections; or the careful packing and shipping of books when fulfilling online orders. Daily, it meant packing and unloading books, shelving them, pricing and cataloguing, getting the bookshop in order each evening after a string of browsers had been through the shelves, and readying the bookshop again the next morning for the day ahead. 'The first casualty,' she remembered Neela telling her on her first day on the job, 'will be your back. If you stick around, you'll have to learn to live with a bad back and calloused palms and fingers. It's the lot of every second-hand bookseller, an occupational hazard.' There were the slow days, of course, when no one visited the bookshop for hours together, or only a trickle of customers came through in a week. You also had to be prepared for the mild boredom that took over at these times.

Kayal ticked off the regulars in the bookshop this afternoon: Hip college student aka amateur book thief, faking the rituals of browsing while studying the perfect moment to tuck a book into his jacket; the young freelance book illustrator who could never get enough of the limited-edition books at Biblio (for every book she bought, she first contemplated a dozen, and where fine books were concerned that was exactly what every decent bibliophile ought to do, Kayal strongly felt; after all, wasn't *that* the artefactual pleasure to be derived from well-made books?) and finally, the unscholarly-looking, pony-tailed book historian, who never bought anything and treated Biblio like a reference library. Such patrons were the browsing variety, looking more than buying, but browsers, Kayal had learnt, were important to the ecology of a bookshop.

The bookshop had been around for a little more than a year now and yet Neela and Kayal continued to get baffled queries from those who happened to chance upon Biblio and strayed in.

'If you are not a second-hand bookshop, why are all the books old and not new?'

'A bit pricey, aren't they, for old books?'

'Why are most of them inside bookcases or wrapped in...what is this, anyway? It's not polythene; I know polythene when I see it... It's what? Mylar? Aiyo, what's that?'

The signboard – BIBLIO: ANTIQUARIAN, FINE AND RARE EDITIONS – seemed to largely go unheeded.

Neela and Kayal were, of course, prepared to field all queries. More than that, the two bookwomen took pleasure in explaining to those who were willing to listen why Biblio was different from other bookshops in the country. Neela's vision was to coax an antiquarian culture from these exchanges – inspire Indian bibliophiles to embrace the book arts; identify serious collectors; involve book scholars; initiate a pukka antiquarian book fair and form a bibliophile club along the lines of the Roxburghe Club in London or the Grolier Club in New York. Her high standards for the bookshop had made it possible for Biblio to become a member of the International League of Antiquarian Booksellers (ILAB) within a year of its existence. However, it took a little more than a year for the bookshop to turn profitable and find its true patrons: Dedicated, knowledgeable collectors. They were pleased and grateful that from now on they would no longer have to depend solely on online antiquarian book dealers or bookshop-hopping trips abroad to acquire rare books. Biblio itself now had a vibrant online presence, both through their own website and on AbeBooks and ILAB, managed by Pokisha, Neela's tech-savvy niece.

Much as all this high-end buying pleased Neela, she was happier when a young bibliophile or a modest collector with limited resources showed a passionate interest in Biblio's books. Straightaway, she offered them a 15 to 20 per cent discount. As she proclaimed firmly, and often, she had set up an antiquarian bookshop to give anyone passionate about the printed book a chance to browse through and handle beautiful and rare books, even if they didn't always have the means to buy them, or could afford them only occasionally. More than half the stock was modestly priced, making it easy for any browser to leave the bookshop with an uncommon edition or two. Colin Franklin, a scholar-book dealer in private-press books whom Neela and Kayal admired, was convinced that 'the dilemma of those who desire, but cannot afford is more interesting'. If you could walk in and afford anything, where was the fun in collecting, the thrill of the chase, the anticipation and the sweetly delayed gratification? After all, every collector knew that the moment you possessed a book, your interest had already turned to the edition you didn't have.

From the tea-and-biscuit *kadai* a few buildings down the street, Kayal parcelled vadai and chutney and returned to the bookshop to put the kettle on; she would make some black tea. When it was ready, she carried it into the garden, away from the glare of the afternoon sun. The Burton biographies lay in a neat little pile next to her on the garden bench. She left them alone for a bit, content to just sit by the books, gazing, instead, at the legendary banyan tree in the gardens of the Theosophical Society just across the street. It was 450 years old, perhaps the oldest and thickest banyan tree in India and one of the world's most ancient. In its shade, for nearly a century, had sat many illustrious teachers, discoursing for hours with their pupils. Among them were Annie Besant, Madame Blavatsky, Maria Montessori, Rukmini Devi and J. Krishnamurti.

Quickly devouring the vadai and the strong black tea, Kayal rose to her feet and washed the oil off her hands at the little tap in the garden. She wiped them clean as she returned to the garden bench, waited until they were dry and then carefully placed the Burton biographies on her lap. What exactly did she have here? There was Edward Rice's *Captain Sir Richard Francis Burton: The Secret Agent Who Made the Pilgrimage to Mecca, Discovered the Kama Sutra and Brought the Arabian Nights to the West*, 1990. Whew! The title on that one, thought Kayal, as she turned to look at the rest of the books: Fawn M. Brodie's *The Devil Drives: A Life of Sir Richard Burton,* 1967; Byron Farwell's *Burton: A Biography of Sir Richard Francis Burton,* 1963; Frank McLynn's *Burton: Snow upon the Desert*, 1990; Mary S. Lovell's *A Rage to Live: A Biography of Sir Richard and Isabel Burton,* 1998; Jon R. Godsall's *The Tangled Web: A Life of Sir Richard Burton*, 2008. And the two bibliographies: Norman Mosley Penzer's *An Annotated Bibliography of Sir Richard Burton*, 1923 and James A. Casada's *Sir Richard F. Burton: A Biobibliographical Study*, 1990. She opened the Casada bibliography to make a start and then stopped, letting it lie on her lap unread.

Before she plunged into the biographies, Kayal felt she had to ask herself what she really thought of Burton. Not so much who or what Richard Francis Burton was, but about his place in popular imagination. Somewhere in her own imagination, he seemed to have always been one of those romantic intellectual heroes, real and yet mythical, that one grew up wanting to know more about. Who, after all, could resist the idea of this dashing Victorian figure of soldier, scholar, explorer, ethnographer and translator, all rolled into one?

Her own encounter with his exploits had been in high school, when she borrowed William Harrison's *Burton and Speke* – an absorbing fictionalized account of Burton's quest in Africa of the true source of the White Nile – from her school library at the Church Park Convent. It was only several years later, when the movie version, *Mountains of the Moon,* was released, that Kayal would discover that Harrison's account had been more speculative than factual. The revelation hadn't bothered her; the book had been a rousing read that she hadn't forgotten even after so many years.

It was here in this book that she had met the people close to Burton's life for the first time: His friend John Steinhauser, his rival John Hanning Speke, his wife Isabel, his guide Sidi Mubarak Bombay and, of course, all the characters at the Royal Geographical Society in London. But what Whitehead had said earlier was also true; even people with a lifelong fascination for the man knew little about his years in India. And this, no doubt, was what she had to dig up from these books. She herself had forgotten about Burton over the years, perhaps because he had seemed too much like a fictional hero to haunt her adult years. The biographies, at least the better ones, would, she hoped, set her straight about the highly romanticized idea of Burton she carried in her head.

Surprisingly, popular culture hadn't made too much of him. Kayal knew this not because she had been following how novelists and film-makers had been portraying Burton over the years, but from working in the bookshop – from the odd novel or short story that featured him or a patron with an interest in this most unusual explorer-translator. The oldest and most substantial reference to Burton in a novel was in the Hugo Award-winning sci-fi thriller, *To Your Scattered Bodies Go* by Philip José Farmer, the first book of the Riverworld series. In this novel, Burton passes away in our earthly world only to discover, as he regains consciousness, that he has been transported to a new planet, an alien world, where he embarks on a fresh set of adventures. In his second avatar he appeared, interestingly, in another sci-fi series – the steampunk novels from Mark Hodder, beginning in 2010 and featuring Burton and the poet Swinburne in six adventures: *The Strange Affair of Spring Heeled Jack*, *The Curious Case of the Clockwork Man* and *Expedition to the Mountains of the Moon*. Burton was also the focus of John Dunning's bibliomystery, *The Bookman's Promise*, which was about, among other things, a journey Burton makes to Salt Lake City. There were some scattered, half-hearted references to him in a few television serials and short stories (like Jorge Luis Borges story, 'The Aleph'), but nothing really notable or significant that Kayal could think of. In literary fiction, he had made a sudden reappearance just when the world had almost forgotten him – in the acclaimed novel in 2006 by Ilija Troyanov, *The Collector of Worlds*, a subaltern reworking of Burton's story, told through the eyes of his Parsi servant in India and Sidi Mubarak Bombay in Africa. A novel Kayal had been meaning to read for a long time at Neela's urging, but had not got around to.

But that was that.

Burton's story – or what little she knew of it – brought T.E. Lawrence to Kayal's mind. She realized suddenly that Lawrence could have been another reason why she hadn't plunged into Burton during her college years. It was a few months into her first year at college that she had discovered that Lawrence was not just *the* Lawrence of Arabia, but the Lawrence of literature, of books, of fine printing; and from that moment, she had been in thrall to his literary prowess. Lawrence's adventures in Arabia were but a small part of his life; books and writing had dominated it. They were, in fact, the only things he had cared about passionately. Like Burton, Lawrence too had been a man of action on the one hand, and a man of words on the other. Had one explorer supplanted the other in her mind? It occurred to Kayal that Lawrence too had been in India – and in Karachi as well. Yet, people had made very little of those years, of the fact that he was Lawrence of India, too!

Neela stepped out into the garden looking for her associate and found her, quite obviously, struggling with her new assignment.

'Hey, that's far too much reading!' she called out, chuckling.

Kayal looked up smiling, and handed her the Burton bibliography from her lap. 'They are all good biographies, Kayal, except the Rice,' Neela said, looking over the books. 'Rice's is a bestseller but it's more fanciful than scholarly. For now, I'd say, go with Lovell's bio. It's my favourite – beautifully written and, I think, the most balanced. Perhaps fairer than most biographers in her treatment of Burton's wife, Isabel. You probably know that she was reviled after Burton's death by his friends and colleagues for burning some of his manuscripts and letters. Lovell tackles it head on and sets it right. And when you're done with that one, you could look at Jon R. Godsall's biography for an objective, exhaustive account. For the others, perhaps, instead of digging into all the biographies, read just the chapters dealing with Burton in India. And the bibliographies will be most useful, of course, particularly the Casada. In terms of Burton studies, the most recent is *Paths without Glory: Richard Francis Burton in Africa* by James Newman, an important book on Burton's years in Africa. I wish someone would do as impeccable a study of his years in India one day.'

'I know. That would have simply been the go-to book for me!'

'It's a pity that Burton himself didn't write an autobiography after he had semi-retired. Instead, he chose to write, over the period of his life, short accounts that were part scholarly, part travelogues and occasionally revealing the personal.'

'Oh, then for a more direct account I should read *his* own books, isn't it?' said Kayal, getting up from the bench, gathering the books to carry them in.

'Absolutely. For the India period it would be primarily two books, *Scinde; or the Unhappy Valley* and *Goa, and the Blue Mountains*. I think I have copies of both somewhere in my apartment.'

'Thanks, Neela, I'll dig them out myself.'

'Come along then - our chatty customers have left, and we can now get some work done.' They headed inside.

'Hey, have you had a chance to meet Cheran yet, to finalize the catalogue design?' Neela asked. Cheran Perumal, a gifted graphic artist, was not only a collector of fine-press books, but was also that rare thing in India – a private-press printer. Kayal was excited to be working on the catalogue design with him.

'Actually, as soon as I've finished up here I'm headed to his letterpress shop to go over those details. Neela, I'm hoping to get a start on building up an inventory of fine-press books for Biblio using his antiquarian book dealer sources.'

It was the first time Kayal had voiced her dream for the bookshop, though from the twinkle in Neela's eyes and the gentle nod she got as a response, it seemed to her that the older woman had been expecting her to say exactly these words for a while now.

7

The Catalogue

Once inside the shop, Neela and Kayal hastened to finalize the last set of details for the catalogue. Quite apart from modern Indian first editions, Biblio was also offering in its first catalogue a sumptuous collection of scarce, out-of-print and antiquarian editions dealing with the book arts, a collection that Neela and Kayal were especially proud of. It was a collection of uncommon books on books that they had put together over the years, drawing from their personal collection. Only now, when they had succeeded in acquiring multiple copies of most of these editions, were they able to put them up on the antiquarian market. An attractive listing here was a pet focus of Kayal's: Vintage bibliomysteries. Like many fans of this bookish sub-genre in mystery fiction, Kayal's introduction to the world of bibliomysteries had begun with the modern works of Lawrence Block and John Dunning, which then led to the surprising discovery that this genre wasn't new; not only had it been around for a long time, much before Dunning or Block came on the scene, but the best bibliomysteries were also the old ones, known in the book trade as classic vintage bibliomysteries.

Three of the best vintage bibliomysteries, displaying an intimate knowledge of rare-book dealing, were also three of the most sought after in their dust-jacketed first editions: Carolyn Wells's *Murder in a Bookshop* from 1936, set in an antiquarian bookstore; Marco Page's *Fast Company* from 1938, featuring an attractive and charming couple who also happened to be book dealers trying to crack a case; and Bernard J. Farmer's *Death of a Bookseller* from 1956, where a clever London bobby adopts collecting rare books as a hobby and unexpectedly finds intrigue among the city's fabled book runners. Biblio had all three titles with dust jackets in unusually fine conditions and Kayal had managed a further coup by unearthing an even more uncommon paperback edition of *Murder in a Bookshop*, not usually listed by rare-book dealers.

Being both a book dealer and someone keen on building her collection, Kayal hadn't been able to resist delving deeper, bibliographically, into bibliomysteries, becoming curious about the genre's origins. And anything that turned up which dealt with bibliomysteries – dealer catalogues, pamphlets, bibliographies and other ephemera – she stocked, along with the fiction titles, feeling they were just as valuable to a collector pursuing bibliomysteries. One of her first bibliographical findings that contained some information about the genre's origins had been John Ballinger's pamphlet, *Collecting Bibliomysteries*, published in 1985, a witty account by the book dealer of how he was, perhaps, the first to coin the term 'bibliomystery' for the genre, when he put out a catalogue listing about 313 bibliomystery titles for sale. Catalogue No. 42 had been offered by Ballinger and Oak Knoll Books in 1982, but Kayal would stumble on another catalogue, Catalogue No. 3, offered in 1981 by a dealer called Sarkis Shmavonian. It had a section titled 'Bibliomysteries'. So who had been the first to come up with that name for mysteries steeped in the world of books? There were no definite answers. A substantial work about bibliomania in literature and genre fiction had been explored by rare-book librarian Betty Rosenberg in *Bibliomania, Or Bound to Kill* and *The Letter Killeth: Three Bibliographical Essays for Bibliomaniacs* (Biblio had these in stock too), but the term 'bibliomysteries' did not figure there either. Both *Collecting Bibliomysteries* and *The Letter Killeth*, printed by private presses and signed by their authors, were nice little letterpress monographs to have. The most recent entry in the field was a comprehensive bibliography of bibliomysteries in their first editions, put out by Otto Penzler, the legendary owner of The Mysterious Press in New York City. But Penzler's long-awaited bibliography of the genre had turned out to be a disappointment; the entries for each title weren't annotated and it lacked a substantial introductory essay.

Neela's personal focus in the catalogue was an area that she enjoyed researching and collecting: Material about and by women collectors over the ages. It hadn't taken her very long, after she had turned collector and dealer, to see how little there was, biographically and bibliographically, on women bibliophiles and their collecting interests. Now she had pulled together a collection of material that covered book huntresses from medieval times to the present. The catalogue would list books, monographs, letters, pamphlets and various other ephemera related to Hrotsvitha, Diane de Poitiers, Catherine de' Medici, Frances Mary Richardson Currer, Abby Pope, Amy Lawrence Lowell, Belle da Costa Greene, Alida Roochvarg, Estelle Doheny and Viscountess Mary Hyde Eccles.

But perhaps the items both bookwomen felt the most pleasure in offering in the catalogue were a complete run of books hand-bound for the Writers Workshop. The Calcutta-based rare books connoisseur P. Lal's specially commissioned series had often been praised for publishing the early work of many gifted Indian English writers, but not celebrated sufficiently for its lovely physical qualities. While, alas, the Map Litho paper used to print on had no character, the text was handset and printed on a hand press and, most remarkable of all, the books were bound in handloom sari cloth, calligraphed and gold stamped – the unique work of a humble binder, called Tulamiah Mohiuddin.

Once again, Kayal eyed the big stack of modern Indian first editions on the floor, and let out a long sigh. Most of them were still waiting to be catalogued, described and priced. What they were attempting with the catalogue hadn't been done before: Creating a culture of collecting in India by raising bibliographical interest and curiosity for first-edition copies of books by Indian authors and, just as crucially, identifying copies of Indian editions (that is, printed-in-India hardcover copies, for the most part, but also some paperbacks, when they were the only editions issued) that could be bibliographically verified as a first printing for a fledgling, but promising collecting market. The ambiguous part was determining the antiquarian market value for each edition. If, for instance, they offered a fine copy of the Ravi Dayal Publisher, Delhi, 1988 first edition of Amitav Ghosh's *The Shadow Lines* for ₹2,000 or the paperback Indian Thought Publications, Mysore, 1943 scarce edition of R.K. Narayan's *Malgudi Days* for ₹10,000, another bookseller could, hypothetically, offer these for less or more. The market value of a collected book depended on how scarce or common it was and then, the specific edition, condition and state of the individual copy. Was it a first printing or a second? Was it pristine or flawed? Was there something extra-interesting about it, like a signed or association copy (inscribed by Ghosh to Ravi Dayal himself, perhaps?), and so on.

Kayal checked the time – if she didn't leave immediately, she would be late for her meeting with Cheran. After her discussion with him about the design and printing of the catalogue, she was hoping to enlist his help in putting together a stock of fine-press books for the shop. If there was one area their catalogue was lacking in, it was a listing of private-press books or finely printed editions. For Kayal, this was a serious lack in Biblio's book-arts stock. While they were well-stocked in trade editions on the subjects of private presses, fine printing and typography, there were no actual examples of fine-press books. She was raring to change that by assiduously seeking out as many booksellers and bookshops abroad as she could find that dealt in fine-press books and negotiate a substantial dealer's discount to make it possible for Biblio to gather an impressive stock of these editions.

Private-press books were considered expensive

even when you were paying in dollars or pounds; converted to rupees, the sum would seem so much more extravagant. They cost so much because they were expensive to print and produce – usually, a very limited edition of anything from fifty to five hundred copies, printed letterpress on handmade or mould-made paper, often in two-colours, and illustrated with wood engravings in decorative wrappers, paste papers or marbled boards. But Kayal knew that if Indian bibliophiles were given an opportunity to be near them, to see, feel and handle them, they wouldn't be able to resist wanting them and start building a collection. 'There's no substitute for handling books,' she had heard Neela say more than once.

Kayal had realized Cheran Perumal was the person who could help her stock the bookshop with the work of the very best fine-press printers, from the great private presses of the past to the most admired contemporary fine presses today. She had seen him a couple of times at the bookshop, in meetings with Neela, but hadn't really had a chance to chat with him. He had done some very fine letterpress work for them – letterpress business cards, bookmarks and brochures. And now he would, hopefully, print their first catalogue in letterpress.

8

Printer's Flowers

She watched him at work from a distance, not letting him know she was there. He was printing on an Albion iron hand press – or so she surmised from having seen photographs and illustrations of old iron hand presses in books and journals. She didn't want to distract him or stop what he was doing. Cheran was feeding the press, one page at a time, on the magnificent antique iron hand press, an enormous shiny black thing that seemed to dwarf everything else in the room.

Kayal had turned up late, having lost her way while trying to find his house in Georgetown. He had said on the phone, while giving her directions to where he lived and worked, that she would see the garage before she saw the house, because of the painted signboard

Cheran was feeding the press, one page at a time, on the magnificent antique iron hand press, an enormous shiny black thing that seemed to dwarf everything else in the room.

with the words 'The Handpress Studio' hanging high over the road, accompanied by, she would later learn, his press mark – a boy working on a hand press.

When he turned to dry the dampened sheet on a wire, he noticed her presence and called out, 'Hey, hi. Come on in. We've seen each other in the bookshop, but haven't actually met.' He was in his early thirties, slim, with a firm handshake. She couldn't help noticing his muscled arms and the way his long, elegant fingers held the handmade papers by their tips.

'I think every time you've been in the bookshop,' said Kayal, stepping in, 'I've been on my way out to run an errand or you were in meetings with Neela. I've been wanting to meet you, though – and not just for the catalogue.'

'You know, just before you walked in, I was wondering if Neela was purposely keeping me away from her lovely associate or if you were just late. But do tell me why you were so keen on us meeting.'

'For very bookish reasons, completely,' Kayal said, grinning. 'Neela said I could learn more about fine-press books and printers from you than from anyone else – including her.'

'She's just being modest.'

'No, really. I actually contradicted her and said no one here could possibly know more than her about finely printed books and she responded, quite emphatically, "Maybe bibliographically, but Cheran knows a book physically: About paper and typography and printing with metal type."'

'And that's a quote?' he asked, teasing.

Kayal laughed. 'I'm pretty sure I've remembered it verbatim.'

'That's really gratifying. I guess that's because there are only two or three fine presses in the entire country and even those are commercial-printing offices which also happen to do some craft printing. I, on the other hand, am a hobby printer; I print for pleasure. The fine press or the private press has, sadly, never been a movement in India. Such an irony, because the country was once dotted with mills making handmade paper... Much of that has been documented by Dard Hunter...'

'Dard Hunter?'

'Hunter is a remarkable figure in the history of modern handmade paper. He not only printed and bound his own books but also made the paper himself—first, in his house and then, on a larger scale, in his mill. Dard Hunter was also a paper historian, who travelled the world to write about different kinds of handmade paper. On returning home, he would produce a record of his travels, with photographs and samples of those papers, in a lovely limited-edition, printed on paper made by him. I mention him, because he came to India in the thirties to tour our paper mills and put down his observations in

1939 in a book titled *Papermaking by Hand in India* – an expensive book today. He met Gandhiji at his ashram after hearing of his efforts to keep papermaking alive as a livelihood. Gandhiji was very ill at the time, and bedridden, and Hunter apparently had to bend down to hear him whisper his blessings. In the last ten years, there's been a tiny revival in the making of handmade paper in India, some big changes, some small. And our paper, unlike much of the handmade paper available in the world today, is made from all-rag cotton –' He stopped mid-sentence, suddenly becoming self-conscious, and said with a grin, 'Clearly, it's a subject I can't resist.'

'No, no, go on. It interests me greatly. As you know, we, too, work in a bit of a void. There's really not been what you might call a culture of antiquarian and fine bookselling and collecting in our country – at least, not like the vibrant, pervasive and historically rich antiquarian culture in Europe, the States and Japan. So, as you can see, Biblio is now one of, perhaps, two or three – if that – brick-and-mortar antiquarian bookstores in India. The collectors are there, the money is there and, I think, even the knowledge is there, but not the bookshops, not the market, not even the odd, antiquarian book fair.'

'The catalogue is a splendid idea, by the way,' Cheran remarked. 'I'm sure it's going to put Biblio on the international map of antiquarian book dealing.

Did Neela have anything particular in mind, design-wise?'

'No, that's entirely up to us. She said we could splurge a bit, though, this being Biblio's first catalogue and all. So it can be a richly illustrated, lavish affair.'

'Yeah, she mentioned that to me as well and, right off, I thought of something: To split the print run into standard and deluxe editions. Say, a total run of six hundred standard copies on Somerset paper – five hundred offset in Fabriano wrappers and hundred deluxe copies printed letterpress in quarter cloth and marbled paper sides.'

'Sounds wonderful!'

'That way anyone picking up the catalogue will have a taste of something finely printed. Somerset, though machine-made, is a really fine mould-made paper and Fabriano covers...let's see if I have a sample of it here somewhere; it makes more sense if you actually feel one rather than just look at it, because it has a beautiful texture.'

Walking over to a chest of drawers, Cheran removed a slim, attractive-looking pamphlet in green. Handing it to Kayal, he said, 'Feel those green wrappers.'

Even before she had brushed her hand over the green covers, she could make out that the wrappers had texture on them. To the touch, they were grainy, toothy and yet felt pliant and silky. And, amazingly, the paper was thick, without being cardstock-stiff.

'Fabriano wrappers are often used in fine-press printing as a soft-cover wrapper for a slim volume of anything – keepsakes, poetry, an essay. But I'm thinking, why not use it as the cover for the larger run of the catalogues?'

'Sounds fabulous to me.'

'Your first catalogue covers primarily modern Indian first editions, so you'll want to make sure your books are fetchingly displayed and described. You'll want to show off the bright jackets, emphasize the crisp condition, single out signed copies, zoom in on the signature or inscription or association – if it's an association copy. In other words, a slightly dazzling affair is what you want. So we'll highlight your most interesting editions by showcasing their title pages, jackets or bindings on a full page. And I guess each bibliographical entry will be accompanied by a photo of the book?'

'Yes, we have the images already – nice, sharp close-ups of each book, with the dust jackets. Cheran, before we get into a more detailed discussion of the catalogue, can I ask you something else that I've been dying to know?'

'Sure. What?'

'I was watching you print on that hand press – that *is* an Albion hand press, isn't it?

'Yes, a cast-iron Albion.'

'And, of course, I was surprised. I thought when I walked into your workplace that I would see a MacBook Pro and an editing suite.'

'The workstation you're describing is very much here, but it's in the house. The garage is just my private press. I print the things that strike my fancy in a printing process that totally engages and fascinates me – letterpress, which is the bite of metal type on fine paper. Occasionally, I take up some letterpress jobbing work for a friend or colleague – broadsides, invitations, announcements and so on – and for these, I use a small Adana Press or a Vandercook.'

'And choosing to print on a hand press – is that a private-press tradition too?'

'One of the traditions – certainly the oldest and, for some, the most sacred. The few who print on a hand press use hot metal founts, handset the type and print on dampened handmade paper – or ought to! – often, only a few pages at a time. Which means the going is slow, the work doubles and you can only print in small editions. However, most contemporary fine-press printers prefer to use a treadle or motor-operated press. The more famous private presses, like the Whittington Press, which issue a larger run of limited fine-press editions, can print several pages at a time on a large press, like the Heidelberg cylinder or a Wharfdale. What is important or essential in private-press printing is something all fine-press printers agree on: Printing letterpress.'

'I'm curious about how you came by the Albion.'

'Oh, it's actually something my father owned – he bought it from the India Office Stores. In 1940, they ordered four Super Royal Albions from, presumably, Hopkinson & Cope for the Jail Press in Bangalore. My father knew of them, because he worked as a type designer and punch-cutter at the Gujarati Type Foundry, GTF, in Bombay. His affinity for hot metal founts, antique presses and letterpress printing comes from having designed and cut some of the finest founts in the world for various international customers at this legendary Indian type foundry. GTF holds a unique and special place in the history of Indian type foundries, because at one time, it ranked among the best foundries in the world, supplying fine-press printers abroad with not only superb and varied hot metal-type specimens, but also an astonishing range of printer's flowers, ornaments, rules and borders.

'When the Jail Press – like so many presses around the world – stopped printing letterpress, they looked to discard the Albions. My father rescued this one, luckily, but we never found out what happened to the other three. When he retired from GTF and we moved back to Chennai, he started a small print shop, stubbornly printing letterpress when he found some jobbing work here and there, trying to convince the few clients he had that letterpress was still the best way to print. It never occurred to him to print just for himself, for his own pleasure. At some point, probably around the time even his dwindling clients completely turned to offset, he stopped printing. He seldom came into the print shop – which was right here in the garage.

'He could so easily have become a fine-press printer; he had all the skills and the right printing equipment for it. Apart from the hand press, he had quite a few wonderful typefaces, including Caslon Old Face, in different sizes – a farewell gift to him from the type foundry on his retirement. He also had a large stock of various fine handmade papers from famous English and Italian paper mills and a supply of the best black and red ink. I was only peripherally aware of all this while growing up, too absorbed with school and friends, but I can still remember with sharp clarity how it felt, each time, to enter the print shop back then – the dark lustre of the massive Albion, the cases of type racked against the wall, the smell of dampened handmade paper and printing ink.'

'Didn't you want to tinker around with all this stuff as a kid?'

'No. For me, it was just something my dad did for work. Once in a way, he would ask me to print with him and I may have got a feeling for it then, but I doubt it. You know how it is – what your parents do for a living bores you.'

'How did all that change?'

'As a graphic artist, I found myself drawn at once to book work. It was straightforward book work for the trade – jacket design, layout, some illustration work for brochures, pamphlets, books. And even after I had set up shop on my own and turned to full-time printing, it was all offset, using digital founts and smooth, machine-made paper. Not a single client asked for or enquired about printing letterpress. But something about the work, good as I was at it – surely something I must have imbibed from my father – felt slick, impersonal, cold. There was good money in it, but I felt jaded, unfulfilled.

'This was about two-and-half-years ago. Then one day something clicked when I wandered, rather distractedly, into the garage, looking for something, and couldn't leave; the whole thing hit me all at once – the smell I knew so well from childhood of printing ink, dampened paper and paraffin oil, along with the familiar sight of that slanted, rickety type-case rack, the shape and feel of metal founts and typefaces and the dark, looming shadow of the glinting Albion. There it had all been, under my very nose and in plain sight, and I had missed it: Printing by hand with hot metal type on fine, dampened paper on an old hand press. If the other thing was my job, this would be my vocation. From book work, I turned to press work. More than two years of printing this way has only made me thirstier for it. I suddenly went from being a bibliophile to a typophile. I began to immerse myself in the history of printers, printing and typography and that led me to the fine-press book and the fine-press printer.'

'May I take a peek at what you've just printed?'

'Actually, I was printing this sheet for you. I'd be very pleased if you took it back with you. It's a favourite bit of text on fine printing by a private-press printer I admire greatly – Leonard Bahr of the Adagio Press. I thought it would be fun to make a broadside of it, much in the spirit of the broadsides he issued.'

Cheran removed the sheet he had hung on the wire, lifting it at the tips and gently laying it down on a table top.

The sheet was twelve-by-eight square inches, beautifully printed in three colours – red, black and blue – the initial letters in red, the text in black and three little printer's ornaments in blue, decorating the sheet. The text was basically a quote on the pleasures of a private press, the peculiar joy of handling type, ink and paper. And below the printed text was a small colophon: 'Twenty-five copies on dampened Rives paper, handset in Palatino and Weiss Types and printed at The Handpress Studio, the Private Press of Cheran Perumal.'

'Go ahead, take it in your hand. The joy of letterpress is tactile.'

Kayal gingerly picked up the sheet; the paper felt delightful to the touch, feathery and sensuous. Running her hand over it, she could feel the text on the paper. Each letter had been deeply impressed onto the paper, making a raised surface from metal founts so absorbed into the paper, they felt etched.

'The whole thing is extraordinarily lovely,' she said reverently, putting it down with care.

'Thank you. I take very little credit for it. Good paper, the right typeface, a sturdy hand press, a fitting text and some delightful printer's ornaments account for its handsomeness. Even the finest private-press printers agree that most of the job is in the good materials you bring together when you set out to print. Make ready, inking and impression count only after you bring those together.'

'This paper – Rives? – is almost sensuous to the touch...'

'It's one of the finest French mould-made papers.'

'And is that how luxurious it always feels?'

'It is a laid paper, but the extra lushness you felt is from dampening the paper before printing. Dampened paper is perfect for letterpress, absorbing the type in a way that dry paper can't. There have been a small number of books on the aesthetics of printing damp but a fairly recent, wonderful fine-press book on the subject by Rollin Milroy of the Heavenly Monkey Press shows text printed on dampened and undampened paper. Rives is especially wonderful when dampened; so too are Johnnat and Fabriano papers and most handmade papers like Barcham Green, Hosho, Twinrocker and Amalfi.'

'So you import these papers?'

'Yes, I do. The problem with most Indian handmade papers is that they all seem to resemble each other: Either patterned or embossed or flowery, grassy nature paper – I think you know the kind I'm talking about. You keep running into them in those boutique showrooms. That's fine, I suppose, if it's just stationery – letters and envelopes and thank-you notes – but not for more elaborate letterpress printing. All our papers now seem to be geared for arts-and-crafts purposes. I'd like just cream, laid, internally sized or tub-sized handmade sheets. I've heard of one that seems promising: Khadi Papers from Hubli. Once upon a time, Mothers Paper or Meera Paper from Pondicherry was famous. Now, I think, it's called Sri Aurobindo Handmade Paper, but much of what they make seems geared for craft printing. Who can blame them? Since letterpress printers here are negligible in number, it wouldn't be economically viable to make paper for the needs of just a few. But coming back to the subject of papers that I source from abroad, here's a little keepsake I printed on Japanese paper that is a nice contrast to the more thickly grained European papers.'

From the same desk drawer, Cheran took out a buff folder and drew from it a four-by-six inch paper. 'This is very much in the fashion of another fine-press printer I adore – John Fass of the Hammer Creek Press. He printed delicate little things on a small hand press, combining type and ornaments to great effect.'

Taking it from him, Kayal couldn't help the small cry of pleasure that escaped her lips. She couldn't decide which of its features had delighted her so – the tissue-thin rice paper, the choice of type or the ornament wrapping the text.

'What did you call this border? Printer's flowers?' she asked.

'They're also called fleurons.'

'I can't wait to see – rather, touch – more! I'm also hankering to see your collection of fine-press books. Neela tells me you have a really impressive collection of press books.'

'My collection is very small and rather narrowly focused. I've had to collect that way, because I can't afford most of the best work from the great presses or the best ones. What I have from these presses are some examples of their best work, but not all of their work. The printers and presses and wood engravers that I have a personal preference for are well represented, but otherwise it's really a modest collection. But sure, I'd love to show them off to you!'

As the day wore on, Kayal and Cheran seemed reluctant to stop with the book talk and get on with the business of the day.

9

The Ziegenbalg Bibliophiles

There were exactly five book collectors of great significance in India: Tayeb Zafar from Hyderabad, Amartya Roy from Kolkata, Antara Ranadive from Mumbai and Nallathambi Whitehead and Arcot Manovalan Templar from Chennai. It was Kayal who had, half-jokingly, begun calling them the Famous Five, and the name had stuck. Though a collector of importance, Neela didn't include herself in this circle, seeing herself more as a scholar-book dealer than a collector. In her expertise in rare books and her knowledge of the book arts, however, she outstripped them all, as Kayal well knew.

What brought them together – what brought every impassioned Indian bibliophile together – was belonging to the Ziegenbalg Club, India's first and only bibliophile society devoted to the book arts. And on this humid Saturday morning, the Ziegenbalg Club was opening its first exhibit of rare and fine books at the Centre for Book Arts, a stylish, contemporary five-storeyed building in the heart of Triplicane in Chennai that had been purchased and refurbished with the financial assistance of the club's wealthier members.

The Ziegenbalg Club met once a month at the Centre for Book Arts, which housed an excellent book-arts library, with study carrels, a gallery for exhibitions, meetings and talks and modest-sized but comfortable rooms to put up visiting scholars and collectors (one wing of the Centre was leased by Arcot Templar's Heritage Auctions). The Centre was a not-for-profit resource for the book-arts community in India, offering workshops and exhibitions in papermaking, bookbinding, book restoration and letterpress printing. Similar to the book-arts centres in London and New York, this one too was focused on celebrating and studying the arts of the book and artistic practices related to the fine book. The Famous Five – that band of wealthy, knowledgeable collectors – along with Neela, formed the core of the Ziegenbalg Club. It was Neela who had set up this bibliophile society along the lines of the Roxburghe and the Grolier, two of the world's most illustrious clubs for collectors, curators, bibliographers, printers, graphic artists and book scholars dedicated to the book arts. However, unlike the Roxburghe Club, the Ziegenbalg Club was not exclusive; nor did it need references, like the Grolier did, before you could gain membership. It was sufficient if you proved your bibliophile credentials. It was also Neela who had named it the Ziegenbalg Club in honour of Bartholomaeus Ziegenbalg and his 1714 printing press in Tranquebar. The Famous Five, of course, were Ziegenbalg's most active members, meeting each month for book talks and organizing exhibitions related to the beauty and craft of the printed book.

Kayal had closely observed the minutiae of rare-book transactions between Neela and the five collectors and had realized where the pleasure of collecting lay. For collectors, it first came from reading about an individual copy in a catalogue or hearing about it from a bookseller or, if they happened to be lucky enough, actually seeing it in a bookshop. This was followed by a suspended period of waiting while they decided, and then the rush from knowing with certainty that they definitely wanted the copy, no matter the cost. Then came making the purchase and, finally, getting the book in the post or having the book dealer hand it to them. The ritual was repeated with each new buy. The bibliographical pleasure derived was not merely from the collector's emotions, but the feeling of ultimate satisfaction on the part of the bookseller who sourced the hard-to-acquire copy, described it, priced it and then offered it to an individual collector.

The Famous Five were collectors in the great tradition: 'They sought great examples of great books'. They went after the best copies of the rarest, the most beautifully printed and bound books. They collected what they loved, what their tastes dictated and not just what the market demanded. Their collecting passion matched their deep bibliographical knowledge of books, of specific editions. But each collector also had his own sharp focus and it was this individual, personal focus that distinguished them in the end. As with all such high-end collectors, their areas of collecting often overlapped. Indiana – an India focus – was one large area common to all of them. All five pursued antiquarian Indian material – books, maps, prints and ephemera printed in India (or about India) – from the late eighteenth century to the turn of the twentieth. The differences in each individual collection, if there were any, were differences in copies and variant editions.

In just a year after it had come into being, the Ziegenbalg Club was now curating India's first exhibition of rare books and prints, and there were plans already afoot to organize and host India's first international antiquarian book fair. The books, prints and broadsides on display this Saturday morning were from the personal collections of some of its most distinguished members, loaned to the club for this four-day exhibit. Many of the members had travelled to Chennai from various parts of the country to curate the collection, and Kayal and Neela had taken time off from the bookshop to spend time with them.

For now, though, Kayal decided she was going to be just another onlooker, like any other lay bibliophile or member of the non-bibliographic public, curious to check out the exhibit, free to wander or linger as they pleased. And what pleased her now was 'Minibibliomania', an exhibit of Antara Ranadive's personal collection of miniature books in exquisite bindings. In her early sixties, with a smallish frame and a head of elegantly greying hair, Antara was the collector Kayal felt closest to among the Famous Five.

'Miniature books,' Antara was saying to a little crowd gathered around her booth, 'are usually not taken seriously by collectors and bibliographers, who view them more as fanciful toys than fine books. But ask any fine printer – including the wonderful Henry Morris of the Bird and Bull Press, who said he disliked miniature books and then went on to enjoy printing one of the most typographically fascinating miniature books – and you'll discover that they all secretly long to create at least one miniature volume. The most recent private-press printer to do a finely printed miniature is Rollin Milroy of the Heavenly Monkey Press, with wonderful text by Anne Bromer. Titled *XI LXIVMOS:*

Memoirs of a Bibliomidget, it is a memoir of the eleven miniature books she and her husband produced. I have the deluxe edition on display, which we'll look at in a moment, along with Henry Morris's *You Can Judge a Book by Its Cover*.

'Their size – two-and-half to three inches – fools people into thinking they must be easy to print and make, but the opposite is true; because you work on the smallest of surfaces, your skills of printing and binding are put to the test. We also tend to think that they must be a modern publishing phenomenon, when you can actually trace them back to examples of incunabula – early printed books, from between 1455 and 1500. And, just as surprisingly, they have become an elegant form to construct a range of artistic bindings: Ornamentation, type, wood engraving, all manner of sumptuous onlay titling, designer bindings in leather, studded with precious materials and gold-stamped.'

From the exhibit display, Antara picked out one book housed in its own tiny clamshell case. She asked her audience to move in a little closer. 'A specialized focus I've pursued within my larger focus of miniature books has to do with those works dealing with the book arts. And here, today, I have examples of type specimen miniature books, papermaking and marbling paper, wood engraving, typography and miniature-book catalogues.

'This one,' she continued, gently removing the miniature from its Japanese cloth-covered clamshell case, 'is called *You Can Judge a Book by Its Cover* and in it, one of today's finest binders Bernard Middleton discusses his craft of bookbinding. Several renowned makers of fine books put it together.' She smiled at her audience. 'I can go on and on about the book and its printing details, but I'll shut up now and let all of you look on your own.'

Kayal decided she would return to the Minibibliomania exhibit once the crowd had thinned; there were far too many fascinating things in Antara's collection to simply skim over it. Midway down the exhibit hall, Kayal paused at the section of the exhibit featuring antiquarian Indian material, largely filled by the collection belonging to the Famous Five. Whenever she saw a complex bibliographical display like the one before her, demonstrating each collector's book-hunting skills and playful rivalry, she was reminded of the beloved Oxford bibliophile John Sparrow's witty reflection on the consummate collector: '"I rather think you haven't got a copy of this" is a remark one book collector will make to another when showing him round his library, and the note in his voice is not the note of compassion.'

For instance, Arcot Templar's 1873 copy, exhibited here, of *Pandurang Hari, or Memoirs of a Hindoo* in two volumes, published in London by Henry S. King and Co., was, possibly, the first ever novel published on Indian life. This copy, however, was the second edition. Scarce as it was, it could not rival the copy Nallathambi Whitehead owned: A first edition of *Pandurang Hari* from 1820. Both of them owned first editions of another scarce Indian item – *A Subaltern's Life In Madras: Being the Adventures of Ensign Blobbs*, printed in 1865 in Madras in maroon vellum quarter binding, with the title embossed in gold and lithographic plates. The condition of both copies was fragile, less than desirable, and high on the want-list of both collectors were finer examples of this edition. But until they turned up, Whitehead and Templar, sworn rivals, would continue to care for and cherish their prized copies of this nineteenth-century account of a soldier's life in Madras.

Kayal did a round of checking out their books and was, not for the first time, impressed by the kind of Indian material the Famous Five had dug up.

On display was Tayeb Zafar's copy of a fine illustrated Macmillan edition of *Deccan Nursery Tales* or *Fairy Tales from the South*, printed in 1914 in London in blue cloth, with floral design in black, title in gold lettering and illustrations and frontispiece by M.V. Dhurandhar. Amartya Roy's prized possession, displayed here, was a limited edition of *The Golden Book of Tagore*, printed in 1931 by the Golden Book Committee in Calcutta – a homage to Rabindranath Tagore on his seventieth birthday. On the title page, Tagore had signed and inscribed the copy to Satyajit Ray, then an eleven-year-old visiting Santiniketan. Also in Roy's library was a 1953 edition of Edward Lear's *Indian Journal* – watercolours and extracts from Lear's diary.

None of the Famous Five had any interest in the areas most Indians focused their own collections on – books featuring the British Raj, engravings, prints and albums pertaining to hunting and military accounts. The five collectors disdained this line of collecting.

There were many more exhibits to take in at the Ziegenbalg Club and many collectors and bibliophiles in the hall whom Kayal wanted to say hello to and catch up with, but she had to wrench herself away – she had promised to run a few errands for Paati before she returned to the rare-book exhibit to hang out with her friends in this small, intimate gathering of bookmen and bookwomen.

10

Lord Lubbock Das's Book Auction

Kayal hurried through the corridor offices of Heritage Auctions. She was late for the sale. She heard Lord Das's slick musical patter floating down the corridor. So the auction was already under way. Sampath Das, Heritage's especially imported auction crier, claimed peerage, reminding anyone who forgot to add the title when they addressed him that he was '*Lord* Das'. The truth was closer to something like his wife's cousin's husband being a baron. To rile him further, a few book collectors who ran into him here would call him Lord *Lubbock* Das, taking off from that popular running gag in Tamil cinema. But Das, a short, stout man whom you would never suspect of having a golden voice until he spoke, was kept in good humour by most of the regulars at Heritage Auctions.

What was truer about him was the way he could sound quite patrician, with his commanding presence and a rich baritone that transfixed listeners when he went into his slick auction patter. And he knew exactly how to coax higher bids from the room. When bidding was slow, he was known to pick a bid 'off the wall' – a bid that no one in the room could be quite sure they had heard, vaguely pointing his hammer over the heads in the crowd. It helped speed up the momentum, prompting someone else to top this 'anonymous' bid. Like clockwork, Heritage held their auctions once a month, usually on the first Sunday of each month; and these weekend sale dates nicely dovetailed with a Ziegenbalg Club meeting or exhibit, ensuring a solid attendance: Out-of-town collectors and bibliophiles attending a Ziegenbalg Club meeting on a Friday or a Saturday would linger on until Sunday to watch or participate in the auction.

Lord Das's skilled, sing-song patter was in full swing as Kayal ducked into the room.

'I've got a bid of hundred fifty. I need two hundred... two fifty! Three hundred on the floor – three fifty! I've got four hundred online. Now four fifty on the phone... Sold your way, sir! Lot Number twenty. Bird books; many colour plates, fine. Two boxes, one money. Two boxes, one money. Five hundred on the floor. Will you advance it to six hundred? Seven hundred there, eight hundred here. Nine hundred. Do I have a bid for nine hundred? No?'

At Lot 25, Lord Das slowed down, seeing the room thining out, the crowd looking less enthused.

'A set of ten Everyman's Library Classics. What am I bid?'

'Five rupees,' said a joker from the back, just to set Lord Das off-kilter.

'Come, come, let's not have any silly bids! Can I have a real bid?'

It seemed not. People were either chattering or yawning or texting. No one was going to help Lord Das out today. Some days were like this.

'Will you oblige, Mr Zafar?' Das looked at the collector from Hyderabad, a tall, thin man in his fifties with a slight stoop, who was always fastidiously dressed.

'Delighted.' Tayeb sportingly advanced the first bid.

The bidding progressed briskly once again.

When Das cried out, 'Lot 27!', Kayal sat up. This was the one she'd been hanging around for.

'A full run of *Civil Lines: New Writing from India*. Difficult to find in its complete run and scarce in this condition. What am I bid?'

'Five hundred,' Amartya Roy called out.

Though the youngest of the Famous Five, Roy, at thirty-five, was already balding. Waiting to see if there would be a bid against him, he was now furiously stroking his sharp, always well-tended beard. Kayal recognized this as his auction tic.

'I have five hundred.'

'Five hundred and fifty,' Antara piped up.

Kayal raised the stakes by calling out, 'One thousand!', in the hope that this would silence further bids. Just the other day, Rukun Advani of Permanent Black had phoned Biblio to ask if they happened to have a full run of *Civil Lines* – or if they could locate a set. Kayal planned to get it for him.

But Zafar raised it by another five hundred.

In the end, it was knocked down to a very determined Kayal for the hammer price of ₹2,500. She texted Rukun right away that a full run of the journal was now available at Biblio for an even ₹4,000.

'Lot 28. Modern Library Series. Fifty novels, various.'

Kayal fished her cell phone out of her bag and checked for messages and missed calls. Biblio had no interest at the moment in the Modern Library, having already overbought titles in the series. Earlier, she had viewed this lot and found too many duplicates in it. Several more lots went by that no one present seemed to show much enthusiasm for.

Looking around the sale room at Heritage, she spotted a few auction cranks for whom being present here was like an addiction. There was Jacob Tharoor, the impeccably attired and well-groomed tax consultant, who put his entire book collection up for auction every three months or so and then, under the pretence of wanting to find out what prices they went for, bought all his books back, outbidding every one in the room, because he could not bear to let his collection go. There was the smarmy retired civil servant Manikandan Iyer in white cotton veshti and bright Terylene shirt, who never failed to place exactly the same bid that someone else had already called. This inevitably raised laughter in the room, but Iyer didn't seem to mind. He was there to be seen and heard, not to buy anything, vigorously fanning himself with the auction catalogue and, just as vigorously, rocking his crossed legs. Oddest of all was Madhava Rao, the crotchety second-hand book dealer from Kundapur, who bought heavily at these auctions and secreted the lot away to his bookshop. This, in itself, was not strange but what came after was decidedly so. Rao would proudly welcome customers into his bookshop to browse through his varied stock, much of it obtained from auction sales, but when they brought over the books to pay for them, he would shake his head sadly and say, 'These particular books not for sale and all, okay? Please select others.' The words would be repeated with the same sorry shake of his head for whatever else they picked next. Finally, his temper surfacing, he would snap, 'We are not able to sell this, I say! Own use only.' And as the bewildered customers turned to leave, empty-handed, he would thrust his business card into their hands, saying, 'Please take.' The card, if they still cared to glance at it, would read: 'Madhava Rao, Rare-book Specialist.'

Kayal turned her attention back to the sale proceedings. The Famous Five were waiting for the next set of lots coming up at Heritage: Scarce Indian antiquarian material. One, in particular, was much sought after and when Lord Das called it out, Kayal too sat up, alert.

'Lot 9. Verelst's *A View of the Rise, Progress, and Present State of the English Government in Bengal: Including a Reply to the Misrepresentations of Mr Bolts, and Other Writers,* 1772, London. A fine copy of this bibliographical rarity, ladies and gentleman. That too in decorative cloth binding with gilt edges – '

'What's so rare about it?' asked the same joker from the back, riling up Lord Das again.

'Look into your catalogue – if you can read, that is!' Lord Das snapped back.

'Do go on and tell us, Lord Das. Sounds rarer in your grand auction crier's voice.'

'I shall; and I hope you'll shut up after that or else I'll have the porters chuck you out.'

'Yes, yes, careful! You'll be thrown out,' slurred the joker, as if someone else was being referred to.

'Not just a bibliographical rarity,' Lord Das went on, feigning nonchalance, 'but of great political interest for dealing with the subject of William Bolts, a trader notorious for attacking the East India Company, exposing how the Company and its officials despoiled and exploited Bengal. This is Harry Verelst – Governor of Bengal from 1767 to 1769 – responding to Bolts. Tragically, Bolts lost all the money he had made from trading in Bengal in trying to defend himself against the many lawsuits the Company would slap on him. This book is the only record of those developments. Now let's get on with the bidding. I open the bid at ten thousand.'

'Fifteen thousand.' Whitehead raised it with a tap of his cane.

'Twenty thousand.' That was Swaminathan, chief librarian at the Connemara Public Library.

'Twenty-three thousand,' called out Roy forgetting, in his impatience, where the bid stood.

'Five thousand advances only for this item, please.'

'Twenty-five thousand,' corrected Roy.

'Thirty thousand.' Two taps on the cane from Whitehead.

'Thirty-five thousand,' countered Roy

Whitehead raised it by another five.

'It's against you at forty thousand, Mr Roy.'

'Forty-five thousand.'

Tap-tap.

'I have fifty thousand.'

'Fifty-five thousand.'

Low murmurs spread across the room. Kayal sensed that the item must not only have exceeded its reserve, but the expected top hammer price. She had last seen a copy of this book, rebound in half leather, with a seller in Wales. It had been listed for £800. She had warned Neela beforehand that she was not going to get into the bidding for this one – she would rather spend the ₹50,000 on acquiring a few fine-press books than one more antiquarian rarity.

'Sixty thousand,' tapped Whitehead

'Sixty-five thousand,' threw in Roy.

Now it was just between them.

'Seventy thousand.'

'Seventy-five thousand.'

It did look like they were determined to drive up a ₹50,000 book into one that would go for a ₹1,00,000.

'Eighty thousand.'

'Eighty-five thousand.'

'Ninety thousand.'

'Ninety-five thousand.'

'No more for me,' grunted Whitehead.

Lord Das knocked it down to Roy, bringing the hammer down more loudly than he usually did.

Kayal anticipated more such feisty auctioneering for the lots ahead but felt a headache coming on, and called it a day. Before leaving she wrote out a cheque to a clerk adding the 15 per cent buyer's premium, with a note to deliver the *Civil Lines* set directly to the bookshop.

11

The Bindery at Luz Corner

The next afternoon Kayal took the 12B bus to Luz Corner in Mylapore. The pavement bookstall was abuzz with a noisy, clamouring crowd of bargain hunters falling over books. From across the road, Kayal tried peering through the thick wall of customers blocking her view of Clement Pandian, the owner of the popular roadside bookstall. She didn't relish the thought of pushing past them in the sweltering heat and waited under the cool shade of Luz Church, Chennai's oldest cathedral, built by the Franciscans in 1516.

When, after ten minutes or so, the stall looked emptier, Kayal crossed the street, clutching an ice-cold goli soda in her hand. Pandian didn't seem to be in, but his daughter was in attendance.

'Kayal Akka! Long time.'

'Hey, Sivakami. How're things here?'

'Total chaos, since we started keeping textbooks and computer manuals,' replied the slender bespectacled girl who physically resembled her mother but otherwise took after her father. 'We don't get any peace now. I miss the leisurely Sunday morning browser, hunting for Georgette Heyer and Wodehouse. Just passing by, or came to see Appa?'

'To see Appa. Is he in the workshop?'

'No, but he'll be back soon. I think he ran out of some binding material. But I don't think we have any books at the moment for you...or Appa would have called you, no?'

'I know, I know. It's a bookbinding job I came to see Pandian Annan about.'

'Why don't you wait inside, under the fan? I'll ask Amma to give you some lime juice, fresh out of a nice cool pot, not from the fridge.'

Kayal held up her goli soda. 'I'm taken care of, thanks. I think I'll just potter around, look at the books until your dad's back.'

'Okay, but if you get terribly thirsty, let me know; the juice shop next door makes great fresh-lime soda, best thing for dehydration.'

Kayal surrendered her initial resistance and joined the crowd in trawling through the mountain of books piled tower-high on the sidewalk. She made one find right away that pleased her enormously. In a pile of assorted magazines, she found six issues of *Marg* from 1946 in acceptable condition. Roswitha Jose, a book and art collector from Kochi, collected *Marg*, India's first quarterly art and architecture magazine edited by Mulk Raj Anand; its early issues from the forties and fifties were now in demand. Not many people had the entire first-run issues from 1946 and Kayal knew Roswitha had been looking for them to complete her set. She texted the Kochi collector right away, informing her about the issues she had found.

Kayal paid Sivakami more than the sum she quoted for the magazines, telling her they were worth more. The young girl would probably have let each of the *Marg* issues go for ₹30 or ₹50, at the most. A collector would pay up to ₹500 for each of these issues. Kayal gave her ₹200 for each copy, a little less than half of what Biblio would price it at. Among Neela's basic principles of fair dealing in the antiquarian trade that Kayal had imbibed, one was to pay good money for good material, not take it away for less than nothing. If you spotted a scarce item – a book or a pamphlet – in a second-hand bookshop or at a library sale, the right thing to do was to declare its true value and pay the owner half of what you could put it on the market for. Neela always said the antiquarian trade of such editions – already an idea with little currency in India – wouldn't be respected or valued otherwise. 'We should honour these editions,' Neela often told her associate, 'by paying the kind of prices they deserve.'

Waiting inside the bindery workshop was a better idea, Kayal realized, than being punished by the torpid afternoon heat. She drew Sivakami's attention to say she was going inside and would see her later.

'Right, pakalam!' Sivakami shouted out, waving back.

From browsing at the Luz bookstall for several years now, Kayal knew the place attracted the odd interesting or scarce book, sometimes from the boxloads of old books and ephemera that people brought here to sell before they moved house. One of the first things she had done after Neela had hired her was to persuade her boss to buy the more interesting material that floated through Luz from time to time. And, for over a year now, the Luz bookstall had been putting aside books – and other printed material – published up to the 1950s (but nothing printed after that) for Biblio to sort through and have first pick.

Much of it, of course, turned out to be junk; old without being antiquarian. For every hundred books that Neela and Kayal personally sorted through, only five or six would be worth something, what Kayal referred to as 'Biblio-worthy' items. Or if they made a decent find, the condition of the book or pamphlet – too soiled or tattered – would make it unfit for shelving. They would return the rest of the books to Luz Corner, even though Biblio always paid for them in full. Though Clement Pandian would protest against this, Neela always insisted that this was the deal. Pandian would gratefully take the lot Biblio had turned down and restock them at his stall.

When the women from Biblio were lamenting one day that all the best antiquarian items that turned up in second-hand bookshops like Luz or from en bloc estate or library sales and book auctions were in poor, unacceptable condition, Pandian had asked if he could take a shot at restoring them. And that's how Kayal and Neela discovered Clement Pandian's extraordinary gift for book restoration and binding.

Before he had set up the bookstall, Pandian had worked for several years at Easwari Lending Library – Chennai's oldest lending library in Royapettah – binding books on daily wages during the day and, in the evenings, working as a paper-scrap merchant on the pavements. He supported his family on meagre wages, and would have remained stuck in this groove as a daily-wage labourer if it hadn't been for a book borrower at Easwari who noticed his skills and hired him to work at his bookbindery-cum-printing shop. On Sundays, his day off from the printing press, Pandian would set up his roadside bookstall. When the business boomed, he let his daughter run the stall and began accepting more bookbinding assignments.

At the back of the bookstall was a small workshop that he used as a bindery. With the simple bookbinding tools in his possession, he had painstakingly restored a German 1823 edition of the *Bhagavad Gita*, the first known copy of this sacred text to be printed in the West. Neela had given up placing this copy on the market, so beyond repair had it been when she first acquired it from a German expat years ago. Impressed with the way Pandian had restored some tattered bindings in his workshop, she had taken a chance on him, placing the rare *Gita* edition in his hand and urging him to do his best. The result pleased even someone like Neela, who had seen enough samples of fine bookbinding in the antiquarian book trade to know Pandian's skill was exceptional.

Neela had wasted no time in getting him to be the best at what he was doing by enrolling him for an intensive professional course in hand binding at the Hyderabad Bookbinders Guild and setting up for his use a fully equipped bindery with the latest tools – all of it paid for by Biblio. Neela saw it as one of the best investments she had made. She also made sure Pandian was free to take up any other bookbinding assignment that he got. But Neela was the one responsible for providing Pandian with a steady source of work, from restoring books for the Connemara Public Library to taking up jobbing work for any bibliophile who needed his services.

But as far as binding and restoration work for Biblio itself was concerned, Neela and Kayal had drawn the line at using leather, whether for simple book restoration or for more sophisticated bookwork. They would ask Pandian to stick to cloth, paper and canvas. As much as these bookwomen admired the artistry of the great binders and the gorgeous examples of printing on vellum they had seen, they were saddened and troubled by another reality that lay behind it all: The slaughter of animals in the millions, a virtual holocaust of calves, goats, pigs and sheep over the centuries. The women knew, of course, that if the use of parchment and leather wasn't as rampant today, it was only because it had become far too costly to use skin instead of paper and cloth. The whole ethical issue of using animal skin for fine bookmaking was one that bibliophiles seemed to avoid speaking about or examining closely. Printing on vellum was unmatched, but it meant killing calves; if bound in morocco, then goats. This did not imply that as booksellers, they refused to deal with books or material in leather or parchment that came to them. The way they saw it, especially when it came to a sumptuously bound book, in the case of an illuminated vellum leaf or a finely printed parchment, the animal or animals had already been sacrificed; the best thing they could do was honour that sacrifice by caring for the book and extolling its beauty and the skill that had gone into transforming skin and hide into a fine book object.

Kayal was admiring some bindings on the table that Pandian had been working on when she thought she heard him speaking to his daughter outside. A few minutes later, Clement Pandian hurried in, wearing a red-and-white checked shirt and a white cotton veshti. He was a lean, gaunt dark man in his fifties, with a closely trimmed salt-and-pepper beard.

'Vanakkam, Ma. Sorry, if you'd told me you were coming I would have stayed in, not gone out.'

'No problem, Annan,' Kayal reassured him. 'I just came by to drop these books off and ask you if there was some way to keep the original binding and avoid rebacking them. The spines, of course, will have to be laid down.'

She had brought along three items – a psalter, a hymnal and the 1662 prayer book that Arulpragasam had duped the Heber Library out of.

'I'll see what I can do, Ma. In any case, I'll be calling you before I start work on them. Only thing is, I may not attend to them right away – our thalaivars want immediate delivery.'

Kayal giggled. He meant Whitehead and Templar, who had taken to burying him in book-restoration work and setting impossible deadlines for its completion.

'No hurry,' she reassured him. 'This is not for us – though the books are with Biblio right now. It's for Madras Christian College. It's a complicated story – '

'One minute, Ma. Just come this side and see these books.'

On a small table lay what looked very much like the books from Heber. Kayal looked through a few. Of exactly the same provenance, except these were even more brittle than the ones inside Biblio's glass cases. However, they weren't church-related. From what she could make out, they were first editions of English literary classics printed in the nineteenth century as triple deckers – exactly in the format they were published then. One took her breath away: *Pride and Prejudice*, in original boards, three volumes, 1813. Kayal checked the title page of Volume One: 'Printed for T. Egerton.' Good god, it was the first printing!

She raised an eyebrow, looking quizzically at Pandian.

'Librarian from MCC came here last week. He was asking the same thing – that I should somehow keep the original board binding. I saw at once that they were very valuable, Ma, and thought right away that I should call you or Neela Akka and ask if you could look at the books. But the librarian asked me not to mention them to anyone. He would be paying for the work himself, he said, because he wanted to surprise the college by showing them the books after they had been restored. Since it was for the college, I thought it was no point mentioning this to you.'

'Of course, Annan. You did the right thing. I mean, who would be suspicious of a librarian, no?'

'Correct, Ma.'

'If he drops by again, don't mention our conversation to him. He has been very clever about this. He actually looted the chapel library with the permission and blessing of the college! I'll explain it later – we don't know too much yet, but I hope to discover what happened by ambushing him at MCC when he returns from his vacation – a vacation *we* at Biblio seem to have funded!'

Part Three

12

The Man Who Loved Books Too Much

For the suburban commute to Madras Christian College in Tambaram, Kayal took the electric train from Mambalam. A little less than a month after her conversation with Reverend Satya at Biblio, she found herself strolling into the sprawling 365-acre college campus. Just the day before, the Reverend had rung up Biblio to let them know that Robert Arulpragasam, the chapel librarian, was now back from vacation and that this would be the right time for Kayal to pay a visit to the chapel library.

Kayal was familiar with the campus from visiting friends back in her student years at Stella Maris and from participating in Deep Woods, the college's annual cultural festival. She cut through the quadrangle to get to Heber Hall. Founded in 1837, the college had completed celebrating its 175-year anniversary, and everywhere she looked there were still signs of celebratory commemoration, though the actual event was long over. As she passed Anderson Hall, the college's old auditorium, she instinctively looked to her right for the Miller Memorial Library, which had now moved from its old premises to a new, impressive-looking building further inside the campus. She had fond memories of browsing in the library when it stood in its old premises, where it had been established in 1863.

An essential experience of being on campus at MCC was hostel life, spread across its famous resident halls, Heber being one of the oldest. Heber Hall was also unique in having its own chapel, which came with its own bell tower. Kayal crossed the warden's large, beautiful house and finally located the small path running alongside it that Reverend Satya had asked her to look out for. His charming little cottage was at the end of the narrow, wooded lane. The Reverend greeted her at the door and offered her the traditional campus drink: cold fresh-lime soda spiked with sugar and salt. She gulped it down gratefully.

'I would have asked you to meet me at the chapel straight off,' he said, taking the empty glass from her, 'but I know how thirsty the walk from the train station to the campus can make you.'

While she cooled off under a fan, he asked one of the student sacristans to bring him the chapel keys and, once they had been fetched, he led Kayal to the chapel. He gave her a quick tour of it, then pointed out the chaplain's office and an adjoining room which served as the chapel library. The library was a small room with four old glass bookcases. Three of them were bare; only one bookshelf was full. The Reverend suggested Kayal continue looking at the books on her own; if she needed him, he would be in his office.

Even peering through the glass doors of the bookshelf, Kayal could see how impressive the spines of the books looked. She swung open the doors and stepped back to view the whole shelf. The effect was undoubtedly fetching – with rows of gilt-edged leather – or, possibly, leatherette – spines displaying an array of decorative covers in deep blues and greens and reds that looked a little overwrought within this sturdy, plain bookcase. She knew what the books were even before she took them off the shelves. Not the faux-leather, cheap imitation deluxe editions that she had assumed they would be. These were respectable, if commonplace, fine editions, ranging from the Limited Editions Club (LEC) to the Folio Society to the Franklin Library editions to Heritage Press. Damn! This was supposed to be her little antiquarian trade trick and Arulpragasam had already thought of it and beaten her to it. A quick scan of the shelves told her they were mostly Franklin Library and Heritage Press editions with just a scattering of Folio Society and the LEC. As fine books went, the Franklins were at the bottom of the pile. They shone and glinted, but as far as fine bookmaking was concerned, they were shallow rather than sophisticated. The most sought-after fine editions were the LEC and the Folio Society editions. They had pedigree and artistry. After them came the Heritage Press and, more recently, the Easton Press books. The Franklins were the least desired, being more decorative than tasteful.

Looking further, she saw several more rows of Heritage Press books. And, in spite of herself, Kayal was a little impressed that the librarian had thought of this old switcheroo: Arulpragasam had cunningly replaced the superior editions of the LEC with the less desirable Heritage Press editions. They might look exactly like the same edition, but the differences were significant and intrinsic. George Macy, the maverick artist-publisher who founded the Limited Editions Club in 1929, had come up with the idea of printing fine limited editions of classics, to be produced by some of the greatest book designers, printers, illustrators and wood engravers of the twentieth century. The editions were usually limited to 1,500 copies on excellent paper and each copy was numbered and signed by the printer or the artist or both. Along with the Limited Editions Club, Macy began the Heritage Press, whose editions were basically reprints of the LEC editions, done on inferior paper and, of course, neither numbered nor signed. Unlike the LEC editions, Heritage Press copies had a large print run, were – and continued to be – inexpensive and were not especially known to be collected. From bitter experience, Kayal knew how common it was for online book dealers to mistakenly list a Heritage Press edition as an LEC one.

Curse those Heritage Press volumes, Kayal thought and giggled to herself. They'd given collectors of LEC editions such a headache over the years. What was George Macy thinking? You managed to get the best printers, typographers, designers and illustrators to make your books, printed them on fine paper, using illustrations made directly from the woodblocks, and issued them in limited, signed editions, only to reissue these handsome books, a few years later, in more ordinary editions that *resembled* the originals, but were not!

Now a worrying thought suddenly gripped her: If Robert Arulpragasam had replaced the original books that these shelves had once held with collected editions, how valuable, actually, was the library's antiquarian collection that had now vanished into Arulpragasam's private library? What sort of rare or fine editions were those books? She had some idea, going by the lot Arulpragasam had sold to Biblio –

there was that 1662 prayer book and then, at Pandian's bindery, the Austen in original boards. They had all been in a state of disrepair, needing restoration. If Arulpragasam had not brought the rest in to Biblio or the bindery, there must have been a reason. But what could these rarities possibly be? If only she could see what Arulpragasam had stowed away in his house!

She took an armload of the Franklin and Heritage editions from the shelf, stacked them on a little reading table and began flipping through them hurriedly. Someone getting their first look at such luxury editions wouldn't be able to just rifle through them, the need to stop and gaze at the books would be paramount. But Biblio's specialization in fine books meant that Kayal handled such volumes on a daily basis, allowing her now to just cut to the chase and confirm her growing hunch about this collection that the librarian had so carefully put together. She was forming a clear impression as she moved from row to row, examining the books. And when she had finished, she grinned broadly and exclaimed so loudly, it brought the Reverend rushing in.

'Bad news?' he asked, looking at the tall stacks of books on the floor and the table and then at the empty shelves.

'Shocking,' said Kayal.

'That bad?'

Kayal selected half-a-dozen books from the lot

and placed them on the table. Next, from her bag, she took out two fine-looking books, placed them alongside on the desk, and began to elaborate.

'When you first described the books Arulpragasam had given the library as beautifully bound leather volumes and richly illustrated editions, I didn't suspect they would be Franklins or Heritage Press editions. I thought they would be the cheap, garden-variety leatherettes you so commonly see nowadays on the shelves at bookshops. These books here are, however, certainly fine editions, especially when you place them next to trade editions, but they pale before truly fine books. The Limited Editions Club editions are, perhaps, the only ones that qualify as typographically fine editions.'

Kayal picked up two books from the table, one of them an edition she had brought along, and asked the priest to examine the two. 'How do they seem to you at a glance?' She stepped away from the table, allowing him to examine them.

'Strange,' he remarked, turning to her. 'The cover – the bindings? – look different, but they seem like the same edition inside.'

'Yes, exactly. Arulpragasam's gifted copy is Heritage, the Limited Editions Club copy is the one I brought along.' She showed him the colophon for the Club, signed by the illustrator, and pointed to the difference in paper and binding. 'Many online booksellers, who aren't bibliographically familiar with Club editions, list the Heritage editions as Limited Editions Club. You're happy to buy them, because they are sold at bargain prices. "Wow," you think, "I've just bought a book signed by Valenti Angelo or Fritz Kredel or Edmund Dulac for a few hundred rupees!" And when the book arrives, several weeks later, you open the parcel, riffle though the pages and take in the stunning hand-coloured Angelo illustrations. But when you finally, eagerly, turn to the limitations page to view the artist's signature, there's nothing there, except a note saying, "This edition has been reprinted with the kind permission of the members of the Limited Editions Club."'

'So Heritage retains the format but just reprints the contents without all the features that make the Limited Editions Club books special?'

'Yes! I couldn't have put it better myself. I should add, however, that often Heritage editions, though inferior in quality, look as pretty as many Club bindings, with marbled or patterned boards. And in some cases they are just as coveted, like the ones hand illuminated by Valenti Angelo just for Heritage.' She placed two books with patterned boards side by side. 'With these, for instance, you can hardly tell which is which, though they both look lovely. But only one of them is printed on finer paper, illustrated directly from woodblocks and signed by the illustrator or printer. Half the editions Arulpragasam lined your bookshelves with are all Heritage Press.'

'Is the Limited Editions Club still around?'

'No, but for a brief time it looked like it might continue after Macy. Around the late seventies, a retired businessman named Shiff revived it but decided to take as his model the few artists' books Macy had commissioned in the early days: *Lysistrata,* illustrated by Picasso and signed by the artist, or *Ulysses,* illustrated and signed by Matisse. He began issuing books illustrated by famous contemporary artists in a more limited fashion and priced them at several hundred dollars each. I think the Club folded up around 2012. But I'm digressing. Let me get you to look closer at the other set of "sparkling books" that the college and you were so impressed by: The leather-bound Franklin books. The Franklin editions are not the most desired among fine bindings, but still, some of their deluxe editions of classic titles were nicely done and even signed by the author. And the leather binding was sewn, not glued, the edges of the books were gilded and the spines fitted with raised bands – actually, false bands – to give them that antiquarian flourish. Each title had such a large print run that copies are easy to find online, with several booksellers on eBay listing them routinely. However, some of these Franklin editions are more than just pretty editions; they are also signed limited first editions. But here's the thing: While some of the editions put out by the Franklin Library are actually quite sought after and can be expensive – in the range of $100 – $150 – several are quite common and lack a market, going for as little as $10 or $20 dollars, because not all the Franklins are full leather or signed by the author or fully deluxe. They put out editions in imitation leather – leatherette – and quarter leather as well.'

'And these books, I'm guessing, are the more common editions?'

'Yes, quite clever of your librarian – and, by the way, the exact stunt I had wanted to pull on him.'

'And you are quite certain about this?'

'It's easy and simple enough to make out, if you know what to look for. The librarian, of course, calculated quite correctly that you wouldn't know. The full-leather editions would have had silk markers in them and the endpapers would be silk moire.' Kayal picked up a book from the pile that had come out of the bookcase: *The Maltese Falcon*. 'The leatherette edition, like this one, for instance, does not come with the silk bookmark and the endpapers are decorative paper, not moire. And, of course, this is not a first, and neither is it signed by Hammett. We have a box full of the less desirable Franklins at Biblio, as well as a whole bookshelf of Heritage Press. We got the whole lot for very little; so we are selling each book for as little as ₹300. My little trick would have been to entice your librarian with a boxload of them; persuade him to take all those shiny leatherette books, swapping them for the chapel's antiquarian books. Once we had them, Biblio would have returned them quietly to the chapel. It would have all been done discreetly, after the librarian had retired, without fuss or embarrassment to either the college or to him. But Arulpragasam has already made his own switcheroo.'

'I don't think I still fully get it...' responded the Reverend.

'I know, I know. It's a little twisted. Remember when you dropped by the bookshop you said how impressed you were with the sumptuous leather-bounds the librarian had replaced your old books with? Okay, so, my guess at the time was – though I didn't say anything then – that Arulpragasam must have used fake fine editions with imitation leather to replace the library's antiquarian collection. They are shiny and look luxurious but are actually inexpensive and common. My plan was to lure the librarian with genuinely fine editions such as the LEC, Heritage Press and Franklin Press books that we have extra stock of at the bookshop in the hope that he would grab them and let go of the antiquarian editions he took from here. But now that I am here and am actually looking at them, I see the books he used to make the substitution are just the kind of fine editions I had in mind to tempt him with. Which makes it all the more worrying – because if he has parted with all these lovely editions in order to have what you have, those books must indeed be very desirable. In all these years of serving as the custodian of these books, Arulpragasam must have watched over the library's antiquarian collection carefully, protecting it like a hawk, biding his time until retirement. And now that he is about to retire, and none of you seem to have realized how valuable these editions are, he has come up with this simple plan to persuade you that these "old" books could go out the door and that he will, in his munificence, part with his beautiful-looking books to furnish the chapel library.'

The Reverend took a deep breath, then queried, sounding a little weary, 'And now what? How do we rescue our books from his clutches without accusing him?'

'Neela suspects that the books from the chapel are not only very valuable, but also special. If Arulpragasam has gone to such lengths of deception, he knows something about those books that the college did not. Neela has a hunch about what they could be, but first I need to get close to the books to see for myself.' Kayal then told the Reverend about the books she had seen at Pandian's bindery, how they had come to be there and what Arulpragasam's instructions to the binder had been. 'Even high-end, specialist antiquarian dealers seldom come across a Jane Austen in original boards. Such copies in good condition are often auction material. The copies we have seen, so far, offer a tiny glimpse into the extraordinary quality of the books that the chapel library seems to have had in its possession. If Neela thinks they belong to a special collection, then you – and the college – should not bother being discreet any more about this whole affair. You have to confront the librarian and simply demand the books back. We have to act quickly, because we don't know at this point whether he intends to sell them off to a collector, pack them off to an auction house – possibly, Arcot Templar's Heritage Auctions – or keep them in his private collection.'

'Then let's go to his house right away and see what's happened to the rest of the books.'

'That will scare him off,' Kayal cautioned the Reverend. 'At this point, I need to get a quick look at the books and find a way to take a few back with me for Neela to verify her hunch. At the bookshop, it was Pokisha, who works part-time, who dealt with him. So he's not likely to recognize me. But on what pretext can I get in?'

'That's easily done. I'll just introduce you as someone who is helping me with researching and writing a history of the chapel's library – which, in any case, is long overdue.'

13

The Bibliomaniac at Madras Christian College

The librarian's house was set deeper inside the campus, well beyond the MacPhail's Arts Centre. When Reverend Satya rang the doorbell, it was answered almost at once by Robert Arulpragasam, who seemed unable to hide his surprise. Kayal panicked; had he recognized her? In his late fifties, the man didn't in the least look like a librarian – more like a body builder, with oiled hair slicked back, oil-shined skin, tight-fitting pants and broad shoulders that his chest-hugging T-shirt seemed to emphasize.

In the brief, tense silence that followed, Reverend Satya persisted with his plan, but his introduction sounded unconvincing, even to Kayal. Luckily,

Arulpragasam responded effusively, inviting her to look through the bookshelves in his large study. Relieved that she hadn't been recognized, Kayal guessed that, like many old-world Indian bibliophiles, Arulpragasam had assumed that no one else could possibly know as much about these books as he did (later, Neela would remark to Kayal that he had missed the most important thing about these books: their true provenance).

Arulpragasam led them past the living room to a larger room crammed wall to wall with heavily stacked bookshelves. The young antiquarian feigned an air of mild interest in the bookshelves until Reverend Satya tactfully led the librarian back to the living room and kept him distracted with faculty gossip. As soon as she had the room to herself, Kayal began to scan the shelves. She stopped short when she realized what the shelves contained. Even to a seasoned bookwoman, exposed to innumerable book treasures, the contents of these shelves were a marvel. For the first time, she was looking at an antiquarian collection that few would have had the privilege to be in the presence of; even the rare books that the collectors of the Ziegenbalg Club had in their possession, high-end as they were, were not this completely or emphatically antiquarian. Here were incunabula. Kayal thought she spied one with a printer's device that could have come from Fust and Schoeffer; perhaps in here was a Ratdolt, too, or even something from Sweynheym and Pannartz! There were certainly plenty from the sixteenth and seventeenth centuries, many in large paper-copy editions, and even an Aldine in blue paper, which was rarer than a copy on vellum. Some of them seemed to be in Jean Grolier bindings, carrying the famous arms of the iconic French bibliophile – three gold bezants accompanied by three silver stars with the instantly recognizable ownership inscription: 'IO. GROLIERII ET AMICORVM', meaning 'Of Jean Grolier and friends'. Sweet, Kayal thought to herself.

Other rarities were present too: Elseviers, Bodonis, Baskerville – and, just as remarkably (unlike the prayer book and the Austen first), all in good condition. To think that these had been in circulation at the chapel library! For once, Kayal was thankful that the students of the college had shown no interest in the library. These books hadn't been borrowed in decades, even though they had sat on open shelves. Some of them, like the incunabula, had survived for centuries! But that still didn't answer the question of how editions of this calibre could have found their way here. Scarce as they were, she knew anything that was ex-libris immediately brought down the value of a copy. But Neela had said, quite strangely, that in this case, it wouldn't matter; that, in fact, it would be their strength, their glory. What had she meant by that, Kayal wondered.

She picked out four volumes from Arulpragasam's shelves and called her boss, relaying as much bibliographical information as she could about each copy. They were in varying editions, sizes and printed dates, from a folio to a duodecimo, from an incunabulum to something in a fine binding.

'Astonishing!' Neela remarked over the phone. 'To think these copies have just been floating around in some corner of Madras! And now for the most important detail, Kayal: You told me they all have bookplates. What do they say?'

'*Bibliotheca Heberiana*,' whispered Kayal.

She heard Neela's sharp intake of breath at the other end, and then, silence. From somewhere inside the house, Kayal could hear Reverend Satya and the librarian talking. Outside, a few students laughed loudly on their way to class and, in the distance, the chapel bell tolled sweetly.

'These extraordinary copies, Kayal,' said Neela finally, 'probably once belonged to none other than Richard Heber.'

'Good God! The great bibliomaniac?'

'That's the one.'

Kayal knew enough about Heber to realize that Neela was referring to one of the most remarkable book collectors the world had ever known. In fact, the word 'bibliomaniac' had become synonymous with him; Thomas Frognall Dibdin had dedicated his treatise on book collecting, called *Bibliomania*, to Heber. And Dibdin had even modelled a character after Heber in his finest paean to book collecting, *The Bibliographical Decameron*.

'Richard Heber, I have since discovered,' Neela continued, 'was the half-brother of Reginald Heber, once Bishop of Calcutta. Bishop Reginald Heber died in Trichy in 1826. A college was named after him – Bishop Heber College in Trichy – which moved its campus to Vepery, Madras, and eventually merged with Madras Christian College. Heber Hall is named after Reginald Heber. It's entirely possible that some part of Richard Heber's famous library somehow travelled with his brother when he took up his post in India – perhaps, Reginald carried some of those books with him. At first, I thought Richard Heber may have left part of his library to Reginald, but the bishop brother died *before* the bibliomaniac brother. These books in themselves are very valuable, but as copies coming from *Bibliotheca Heberiana*, Richard Heber's private library, their worth assumes legendary proportions. Collectors from around the world will queue up just to *look* at these copies, let alone wanting to touch or possess them.'

'Oh my God! Okay. The thing is, they are, at the moment, about to turn into *Bibiliotheca Arulpragasiana*. What should we do, Neela?'

'Reverend Satya will have to get the college to intervene immediately, declare these books as heritage and prise them away, once and for all, from the chapel librarian. But right now, while you are still there, have the Reverend round up some students to help you carefully and safely move the books back to the chapel library, preferably back to their bookcases.'

'Will do. And you'll come by later to properly appraise them?'

'Biblio can step in soon after to figure out the provenance of these copies and, if we can confirm that the collection was a part of Richard Heber's library, we can triumphantly announce this monumental find to the antiquarian book world.'

Neela arrived at Madras Christian College a couple of hours later, made a quick sweep of the books and emerged with a wide grin.

'I think this is it!' she announced. 'If I'm not seriously mistaken, we are looking at a small portion of Richard Heber's famed library. And what's just as remarkable about this lot is that some of these books even carry a date and place scribbled on the flyleaf in what must be Heber's own manuscript hand!'

Earlier, Reverend Satya had had a quiet word with Arulpragasam: If he turned in all the books, the

Reverend would not mention a word of this to the college; he would even ask the college to commend the librarian for recognizing the collection's true value and offering it back to the institution. Arulpragasam seemed neither scared nor contrite, and instead acted as though he had been instrumental in unearthing the lost books of Richard Heber all along. Neela had to admit that if the dubious librarian had not tried to sell these books, they might never have surfaced and would probably have perished entirely from further neglect or simply languished on these shelves, undiscovered for years.

Now, seated in Reverend Satya's study, Neela told him and Kayal a little more about the significance of this discovery. 'The book label or book stamp of ownership in some of these books that says *Bibliotheca Heberiana* does *not* denote Bishop Reginald Heber's books, but his half-brother's, the famous book collector Richard Heber, whose bookplate that was. I'm guessing that after the bishop died suddenly in Trichy, his library in Calcutta, too, must have become part of the Trichy Heber library as a memorial to him.'

'But there's a Bishop Heber College now in Trichy, isn't there?' Kayal asked.

'It was revived again in Trichy as Bishop Heber College in the late sixties and flourishes now,' replied the Reverend.

'Our interest isn't in the college at all,' Neela reminded them, 'but in the bishop's bibliomaniac half-brother.'

'I can't get over Bishop Heber having a bibliomaniac brother. Amazing, isn't it?' The Reverend was shaking his head in disbelief.

'Oh, and he wasn't just another bibliomaniac, but one of the two most famous bibliomaniacs in book-collecting history.'

'And the other?'

'The vello-maniac Sir Thomas Phillips.'

'Vello-maniac?' asked Kayal, amused.

'Phillips collected manuscripts; if Heber aspired to have three copies of every book in his library, Phillips wanted one copy of every significant manuscript in the world – and most of them were printed on parchment.'

'Fascinating! Does Thomas Phillips have an Indian connection as well?'

'No. But Thomas Frognall Dibdin, who inspired both these collectors with his writings on bibliophily, did – he was born in Calcutta!'

'Oh wow! Really?'

'Fantastic, isn't it? And that's a part of Dibdin's biography that usually seems to be ignored by most bibliophiles in the West. His father, who had been in the Royal Navy, moved to India in the 1770s, earning a living ferrying passengers from Calcutta to Madras.

When he married in 1775, his marriage licence was, apparently, the first to be issued in British India, and T.F. Dibdin was born in 1776.'

'Imagine,' murmured Kayal, 'the patron saint of book collecting, born right here!'

'Another interesting bibliographical point that has puzzled collectors and scholars regarding Heber's library can now be cleared up because of these very books from your chapel, Reverend: The controversy over when Heber's books came to have the ownership bookplate or stamp of *Bibliotheca Heberiana*. Some think it was added only after his death, most probably by Dibdin or the booksellers Payne and Foss, before the books were auctioned off, while a few have maintained that like every first-rate collector, Heber must have had the stamp put in while he was still living. And now these copies seem to indicate that Heber did use a book stamp after all. How else do we explain its presence in these books which were never part of the Heber sale? What it doesn't change is how unadorned the stamp is; most collectors of his stature would have had an elaborate bookplate with a coat of arms. Indeed, his family had a coat of arms, but Heber was clearly private, not only about his personal life, but also in the way he collected, taking pleasure only in the ritual of collecting, not in its public display.'

'Did you say Richard Heber wanted three copies of every book?' Kayal asked.

'That was his ideal,' Neela replied, smiling. 'As a result, his collection grew to occupy several large houses in England and the Continent. Five houses, if I remember, all of them filled with nothing but books.'

'So, what now?' Reverend Satya asked Neela, looking overwhelmed by all the book talk.

'I have an idea,' she replied, 'but I don't know if it will meet with the approval of the college. Once we've catalogued them, we could hold an exhibit of the books right here on the campus, jointly curated by the college and our bibliophile society, the Ziegenbalg Club. We'll use that opportunity to urge the college to think of creating a special-collections section for its library, using the Richard Heber collection as its first acquisition of a great rare-book collection. That's the beauty of it... They don't have to spend a fortune in creating the first collection, since this magnificent set of Heber's books has just fallen into their laps. It will make MCC one of the few colleges in the country with a special-collections section for rare books.'

'That's a splendid idea. I'm sure the college will be grateful and lend you support. Let me know what I can do personally.'

'We need a little time to see what exactly we've got here. Perhaps a month. Can the books be isolated and housed somewhere safely for the next couple of days?'

'Yes, I think I know the perfect place for it. Leave it with me,' said Reverend Satya confidently.

They took the Reverend's leave soon after and as she drove Kayal back to the city, Neela said, 'What an extraordinary find! Occasionally, a lot or two from the original library of Richard Heber is known to turn up at auctions, but the books we saw will fill several lots.'

'I imagine they are terribly valuable.'

'Maybe not,' replied Neela thoughtfully, surprising Kayal. 'Not, at least, in terms of individual or significant editions. Since Heber bought any edition, any imprint, many of them large lots that he probably never even looked at, his collection was legendary for its volume. There's no doubt that his library was full of collecting high spots, since he bought from – and, in many cases, personally attended – every auction in England and on the Continent. So it's entirely possible there are some rarities among the books we've found here. But the thrill, I feel – the frisson any collector would feel – is simply from coming into contact with books from Richard Heber's own library. With luck, you might be holding a book that he once held in his hands. After a point, some collectors don't read, but they do like to handle their treasures.'

Giggling, Kayal asked, 'So how do you propose working on this collection?'

'We need to go deeper, beyond the books collected by Richard Heber alone; we have to look at the entire circle of collectors around at the time, because the events connected with Heber, Dibdin and Phillips are watersheds in bibliophily that lead us right into the modern age of book collecting.'

'What happened back then? I mean what were these watershed events?'

'I think you'll enjoy finding out for yourself. I was thinking, in any case, that in the light of your discovery, it would be instructive and fun for you to know a bit about the background of bibliophily in the mid-nineteenth and early twentieth centuries, often characterized as the golden age of book collecting.'

'I'd love that,' replied Kayal.

'I know you will. And I thought we could produce a little brochure to accompany the exhibit, a bibliographical listing of the collection at hand, a biographical note on Heber, a little background to his book-collecting world and the significance of this discovery for Indian bibliophily.'

14

Ootacamund

The Nilgiri Express, known more popularly as the Blue Mountain Express, left from Chennai Central station at 9 p.m. and reached Coimbatore early in the morning, at 4.50 a.m. To connect to Ooty, you had to stay on board until Mettupalayam, a little junction at the foot of the hills, which the train reached a few hours later, at 6.15 a.m. You then hopped off to board the Nilgiri Passenger.

Luckily, the Express wasn't crowded that evening and Kayal had the entire berth to herself – always an unexpected luxury on Indian trains. She had never been much of a sleeper on overnight journeys, and when the train pulled into the Mettupalayam junction, she felt groggy as she got out, having slept fitfully through the night. But she was looking forward to the next part, the point at which this journey always got interesting for travellers taking the Nilgiri Passenger.

The Niligiri Mountain Railway, of which the local Nilgiri Passenger from Mettupalayam to Ooty was a part, was one of the few heritage mountain rail routes remaining in India. Travellers in a hurry preferred to take the faster route by hiring a cab or boarding a bus to the top, but there was nothing to rival the sight of the toy-like train leisurely snaking its way up (and taking five hours to reach its destination, as opposed to the two hours that it took by road) through hillsides shrouded in mist, stopping at quaint little stations – fetching relics from the British Raj that Kayal was not only grateful were still standing, but pleasantly surprised by, since the government had actually made an effort to restore them. The cream-and-blue wooden carriages of this train had large windows and, for the best view, you had to grab a window seat in First Class, ensuring that you were in the very first carriage, with an unfettered view of what lay ahead.

If this had been summer – the peak tourist season in Ooty – Kayal would have had to race ahead to get hold of a good seat, but this morning the Mettupalayam platform was half-empty and Kayal could take her time boarding the train, which was already on the track, puffing steam. She strolled along the platform, trying to work out the kinks in her back and legs, bought some bottled water for the journey and, before getting on to the carriage, dug into her strolley and pulled out a sweater which she then put on. The train wasn't sufficiently heated and it could get cold as the mist clung to the carriages, fogging the windows and permeating the interiors with a damp chill that seemed to seep through to the passengers' bones.

With a loud, shrill whistle, the train lurched forward. As it chugged out of the station, passengers continued to amble alongside, in no hurry to jump on. The cold had made Kayal hungry for a hot breakfast. She avoided the bread-omelette and the jam sandwiches the railway canteen was serving and, instead, bought some soggy vadas from a hawker who guaranteed that the chutney, at least, was really fresh and spicy. It was. Her lips burning, Kayal settled next for tea from a teabag to dodge the decoction that passed for black coffee on the train. She coaxed one of the canteen vendors into sneaking her a wedge of lemon that she squeezed into her cup of strong, steaming Red Label tea. After she had had her fill of eucalyptus trees, tea estates, tunnels blackened with soot, little stations named Hill Grove and Wellington and the rolling hillsides, all of them more shrouded in mist this February than she ever remembered, she fished out from her strolley the first volume of Mary S. Lovell's biography of Burton, which she had carried along for the journey. A few minutes later, soothed by the hypnotic chugging of the train and its gentle motion she drifted into a deep sleep, the volume still unopened beside her.

She was woken up at Coonoor, where several passengers got off. Coonoor was probably the prettiest station on this metre-gauge line, the rack section ending here and the track levelling out from here on. Kayal resisted the impulse to jump off with the other passengers; Coonoor was a little more secluded than most hill stations, with a panoramic view of the Nilgiri valley, with its ravines and waterfalls. It was also quieter than the township of Ooty, which became unbearably crowded by tourists in the summer and was only just a little less crowded in winter. When Lovedale Station arrived, Kayal saw school kids in various uniforms get on and off; this was the station for students, teachers, parents and visitors wanting to access Ooty's premier boarding schools – including Beardsley, where Kayal was headed – scattered through Lovedale. Ideally, this would have been the station to have got off at, but the Ootacamund Gymkhana Club, where she was booked in, courtesy of Whitehead, was in downtown Ooty, which meant she would have to stay on till the very last stop.

When she finally got off the train, Kayal looked around for a stall or a cart selling the kind of fruits you hankered for when you came to the hills – pears and plums and strawberries. Before bagging them, she washed a pear and some plums with bottled water and sank her teeth into their juicy flesh as she looked around for a taxi to the club.

An hour later, she had checked in, showered and ordered breakfast. Afterwards, Kayal called for a taxi and, on the way to Lovedale, asked the driver to return for her at 7 p.m, leaving her sufficient time to catch the train back. The previous day, Kayal had spoken to the librarian at Beardsley to inform them that she was on her way to look at the books. Meanwhile, Neela had made the important call to Kenton Selvaganesan,the history teacher with the mysterious Burton manuscript, asking him if her associate could meet with him to discuss the Burton material in his possession, primarily to decide if Biblio could help him make up his mind about what he wanted – or did not want – to do with it. Kenton hadn't hesitated; he would be grateful, he said, for any expert counsel he could get.

Kayal felt a little guilty about neglecting to read up sufficiently on Burton but it was too late now. Before leaving on the trip, she had planned to take some time, while in Ooty, to retrace Burton's footsteps in this hill station, but both Neela and Whitehead had pointed out that, frustratingly enough, there were no markers to where he had stayed and the places he had visited. Hearing this had been a disappointment – to actually be here, in the very place where Burton had spent time, and not revisit the neighbourhoods he had lived in and frequented, seemed like a missed opportunity.

The Beardsley School, predictably, had a picturesque campus. The library was a vast, dark hall, with little pools of light bouncing off computer screens and reading lamps. The bookstacks, as in every other school library Kayal had ever seen, were few, arranged on a dozen old, dusty wooden bookshelves along the walls. At the checkout desk, a bright-eyed young librarian, who introduced herself as Afsana, showed her the shelves that held the books for sale. Kayal cast a quick, expert eye over them and saw that they were mostly without worth. Just as Neela and she had feared, they were common reprint editions of classics, charming to own if you were simply looking for old books, not collected editions. The paperbacks seemed mostly popular fiction. Nice cargo for a second-hand bookshop and had Biblio been one she would have hauled the whole lot away with her. Biblio's interest in paperbacks was strictly vintage pulp or out-of-print titles. Still, here she was with several hours to kill before her meeting with Kenton Selvaganesan. She could indifferently browse through the lot or go for a nice long walk across the beautiful campus. But how would that look? Probably like she was goofing off in the name of work. So Kayal pulled up a chair and began taking out the books for a closer, second look. Finally, she spotted some things she could happily take: out-of-print paperbacks of Billy Bunter, William Brown, Tom Swift and Biggles. She was grateful for another little find – three hardcover first editions of the Alfred Hitchcock and the Three Investigators series; one of them, *The Mystery of the Green Ghost*, had cover art by Harry Kane, one of the finest illustrators of the time. The cover art here was, indeed, a nice little job and Regina Desai, a book collector from Baroda who was fond of children's mysteries, would certainly want to get her hands on it. Beginning a second round of inspection for anything else that could turn up – unlikely as it was – Kayal suddenly thought of something and stopped.

She hurried to the librarian's desk. 'Sorry to bother you, Afsana,' she said, 'but I was wondering if the school is also selling books from the junior-school library?'

'Selling? No, I think they're just being given away – you know, it's mostly children's picture books that nobody would really want to *buy*. But give it away for free and people will, maybe, pick a few. So whatever hasn't been taken away by teachers or parents will be dumped with the paper-scrap merchant tomorrow.'

'Hey, do you think I could take a quick look at those books?' Kayal asked. 'Biblio is very interested in children's picture books and if I found something we want, we'd buy them, not cart them away for free.'

'Really? Okay, let me go find a student who can walk you there. The junior library is at the other end of the campus.'

'Thanks! And I'm done here, actually. Can I put away the books I've picked in some corner where they won't be disturbed?'

'Let's leave them behind the circulation desk,' Afsana suggested. 'That way, they won't get mixed up with the others. Just make sure you collect them before school's out – which is at 3.30 p.m.'

15

The Scruffy Little Book in the Blue Mountains

It was bracing, stepping out in to the cold again. It had become a little too toasty inside the library. As Kayal walked along with the chattering student, she felt lucky. She hoarded children's picture books. So even if there wasn't anything really interesting there edition-wise, she knew she would always find some nice reading copies to keep her happy. The times she couldn't get on with reading anything, these were the books she'd pull out from her shelves to keep her company.

She sensed the presence of the library even before they approached its doors. Children were reading aloud, singing, chattering noisily as they sat with dozens of picture books scattered around them. Afsana had called ahead and told the junior-school librarian what Kayal was looking for. So she was taken straight to a little storeroom piled high with discarded books, precariously balanced because of all the different sizes and shapes picture books usually came in.

A welcome mess, Kayal concluded, rubbing her hands in glee, and set to work. When she'd got on the train last night, she had secretly hoped to find a first edition of a Milne or Beatrix Potter book. A hundred-year-old school, with an equally old library, was just the place to have something like the Methuen & Co. 1928 *The House at Pooh Corner*. She sorted the books into two piles: The larger one contained the ones that didn't interest her – they were either too mediocre or too soiled; the second pile looked interesting and, condition-wise, ranged from acceptable to good, if not excellent or fine. She packed them into two boxes, got the librarian's permission to take the books out to a little bench in the garden where it was sunny, and began looking at each of them carefully.

The box of books didn't yield any finds, but there were several delightful picture books in them – some that Kayal had been searching for in bookstores without much luck. There were at least three Ludwig Bemelmans books that were not *Madelines* – *Fifi*, *Quito Express* and *The Castle Number Nine*. Mostly reprints, but handsome editions. Equally unexpected and charming were the early editions of three Winnie-the-Pooh books that had turned up in the lot. The moment she spied Christopher Robin and his toy bear on the spine of the book, she knew it would be an out-of-print edition from the 1930s or 1940s.

When she had finished sorting through them, she carried the books back inside.

'Would you like some boxes for that?' asked the librarian.

'Yeah, please. Just for now. I have a strolley, you know, that I left in the other library. But if you can tell me where I can find the cartons, I can fetch them myself.'

'Come with me, then. It's just at the back, in the stock room.' The junior-school librarian opened the door to a little room crammed with register books and files. 'Our library loan records before we digitized,' she explained, smiling apologetically.

Kayal helped herself to some cardboard boxes. The last box at the bottom of the pile wasn't empty.

'Looks like this one is still full of books,' Kayal observed.

'That's probably a box of books discarded from a previous year that they missed clearing out. You can bring it out if you like and take a look at it. We are sending all the stuff here to the scrap market tomorrow anyway,' the librarian said and left her to her discoveries.

Kayal dragged the box outside; it was too dusty to carry without getting her clothes soiled. A mid-sized box that had been overstuffed – the work, probably, of some school peon too lazy to split it into two boxes. The flaps, at least, had been tightly taped shut; so too much dust wouldn't have reached the books inside. She began emptying the box, sorting through a jumble of cheap reprints of several girls' classics: *A Little Princess*, *Anne of Green Gables*, *The Secret Garden*, *What Katy Did* and so on – all of them a little mildewed and musty, even under sealed flaps. And then she saw it, buried at the bottom of the box, the simple book bound in green cloth, with its plain cover bearing the title and the author's name.

With quickening excitement, Kayal carefully drew it out. But how old was it? What edition? Even in its first year of publication, the book had gone through several impressions. With her hands suddenly feeling a little unsteady, Kayal gently pried the frail little book away from the other heavies. She was pleased to see it was plain, with no frills, no adornments, nothing deluxe – which was a good sign, because later editions had decked it up. The starkness of this copy could mean that it was, at least, one of the early editions.

She moved the book a little more into the sunlight, quickly turning the pages, looking closely at the pictures of what could be the rare first edition of the most controversial children's book in history: *The*

As far as she could make out, it was bibliographically sound, with all the points of a first impression intact.

Story of Little Black Sambo by Helen Bannerman. Not many people were aware that the picture book, as one knew it today, was invented with *Sambo* and that it was conceived, written and illustrated on a train journey that its author, Helen Bannerman, had made from Kodaikanal to Madras in 1898.

At first, Kayal didn't dare look at the imprint; what if it was one of the many pirated editions of the book that had swamped the market from the thirties to the fifties, or even some poor Indian reprint? By the time she finally examined it, Kayal already knew what it was – the style of the illustrations had told her enough: Grant Richards, 1899, London. Green cloth cover, with vertical stripes and ruled border. Across the title page, she looked for the advertisement. Yes, 'Number Four in the Dumpy Books for Children'. Twenty-seven full-page illustrations by the author, engraved on wood and colour-printed by Edmund Evans.

A first printing of one of the scarcest children's picture books in the world. Perhaps, even scarcer than the suppressed 1865 *Alice in Wonderland* edition or the privately printed 1901 *The Tailor of Gloucester* by Beatrix Potter. On the antiquarian market, this would fetch around $12,000, less than what an 1865 *Alice* or a 1901 Beatrix Potter would command, since *Sambo* had never become a collecting high spot. But in bibliographical terms, the Bannerman picture book was, in some ways, far more significant.

Kayal re-examined the book carefully a few more times to dispel all doubt. As far as she could make out, it was bibliographically sound, with all the points of a first impression intact. The condition of the copy was more than acceptable; it was very good. For a copy that was over a hundred years old, it was clean and tight. No crayon markings and, best of all, it didn't warrant repair or restoration. It could be auctioned as an unsophisticated copy that would exceed its reserve easily. Kayal hurriedly dug her cell phone out of her handbag and speed-dialled Neela.

'Let me describe the book I'm holding,' she began. She went into the details, then waited until she heard Neela give out a little cry of pleasure from the other end, before she finished with, 'And the bloody thing still has a jacket!'

The jacket was slightly torn along the corners, with some edges fraying, but it was still intact after all these years. Neela asked her several questions, running through its first-edition points so that there was no mistaking what Kayal had uncovered. Satisfied, she asked her to set up a meeting with the school's principal and the librarian and explain to them why this was a very valuable find, something the school could benefit from hugely.

After she hung up, Kayal held the book for a while, gazing at it fondly. It had been sitting for all these years, packed away in a cardboard box, waiting to be taken to its rightful home at Biblio, where it would receive full recognition and be celebrated with bibliographic intimacy. One more night spent here and it would, most likely, have been used as wrapping paper in a tea *kadai* to parcel oily samosas. Kayal shuddered at the thought. She couldn't find the librarian when she went back to the library, but there was a message waiting for Kayal, inviting her to join the librarians for lunch at the cafeteria.

With *Sambo* tucked under her arm, she went looking for the school cafeteria. She hurried through the cool, dark corridors, grinning at all the schoolchildren, smart in their red ties and blue blazers as they tumbled out of classrooms. Over lunch, Kayal showed the two librarians what she had found. It drew a complete blank from them, which didn't surprise her; *Sambo* was so much before their time. Kayal tried to impress upon them why it was an important and valuable find and asked if she could meet the principal to persuade her to put the book up for auction. Afsana told her that the principal was at a school conference in Bangalore, but Kamala Menon, the senior English teacher who made the library purchases and who had the authority to deal with this sort of thing, would be available to meet her in the staffroom. Afsana said she would join them, just to be in on the whole thing.

To Kayal's surprise, Kamala Menon knew the book right away. 'This is that children's book that was banned, because it was meant to be racist or something, isn't it?' she said, peering at the book through her spectacles.

'A lot of controversy surrounded the book for a long time,' agreed Kayal, 'and I'm not sure it has really gone away. Some school librarians in America still refuse to keep the book.'

'What was it all about, Kayal?' asked Afsana, growing more curious now.

'I'll come back to the racism charge a little later. *Sambo* has an interesting, but complicated publishing history and I'd like – while I still have both of you here – to establish how long and since when the library has had this 1899 edition in its possession. I'm guessing this copy has been here in the school for more than a hundred years, probably since it was first published.'

'From what I can make out,' replied Mrs Menon, taking the little book from Afsana and holding it up for Kayal, 'this probably belonged to one of the Scottish missionaries who taught at this school around the twenties. The inside of the front cover had a... what? Label...?

'Bookplate,' prompted Kayal.

'...a bookplate stuck on it that has been peeled off, as you can see from the bits of paper still sticking to the inside cover board. And I've seen these only in the books that belonged to the missionaries.'

'And when they left or died, their books automatically became school property?'

'Not just their books, but most of their household things, like furniture and so on.'

'Thank you for helping out with this. That's sufficient provenance for us to put it on the market. Later in the week, my boss Neelambari Adigal can talk to the principal and come to an agreement on how the money from the book's sale can be shared between the school and the bookshop. I can assure you the school will get the larger percentage.'

'It's kind of funny for us to think a book that has been lying around here, discarded, is suddenly so valuable,' Mrs Menon remarked. 'What kind of a price will it fetch?'

'At a conservative estimate, at least ₹5,00,000. But it will probably be more.'

'Arre, what are you saying?' Mrs Menon exclaimed, her eyes widening behind the spectacles. 'When Afsana told me earlier it was apparently something valuable, I thought it was worth some ₹1,000 or so. How can a book sell for so much? Are you sure it's this scruffy little book that we are talking about?'

'Scruffy and little is right,' said Kayal, smiling, 'and it disappeared from sight, making it scarcer and scarcer. With fewer and fewer copies from the early editions being sighted, they became hotly pursued rarities. But it's not how elusive the first edition of *Sambo* is that makes it such a desirable book in children's literature. To know why it is also an important book, you should know a little bit about its publishing history and who its author, Helen Bannerman, was.'

The staffroom attendant had brought in tea and biscuits and as Afsana poured out some black tea for Kayal and passed the biscuits around, the young antiquarian bookseller told them the little-known story of an unassuming British housewife in Madras, who created a picture book that would become the first of its kind, and then suffer the misfortune of not only losing her copyright to it but also seeing it become one of the most reviled children's picture books in history.

16

A Bibliographical Rarity

'For the longest time,' began Kayal, 'there was little information about Helen Bannerman's background, leading to widely accepted biographical details that were inaccurate. It wasn't until Elizabeth Hay's biography *Sambo Sahib* was published in 1981 that the record was set straight on several details about her life and writing career. Largely from her biography and from the research undertaken by more recent scholars of children's literature, we know now that Helen Bannerman wrote *The Story of Little Black Sambo* on a train ride from Kodaikanal to Madras. She had arrived in Madras with her husband in November 1889 from Edinburgh. He worked as a public health officer in the Indian Medical Service. They lived initially on Harrington Road in Chetput in Madras and, when he became the Civil Surgeon, moved to a large bungalow on Cathedral Road. Helen was an Evangelical, but not a missionary or a typical memsahib. She was deeply artistic and a naturalist who closely observed insect- – she called them "poochies", you know, the way we say it in Tamil – and bird-life around their house. Her children studied in Kodaikanal at a missionary school and Helen divided her time between Kodai and Madras. Every time she left the kids to join her husband in Madras, she felt torn.

'On one occasion, saying goodbye to them had been particularly hard for her and it was on this train ride back from Kodaikanal to Madras that Helen began sketching and writing what would eventually become *The Story of Little Black Sambo*. The plan was to keep writing stories about this clever little boy and his adventures in instalments, accompanied by her illustrations, and send them to her children in Kodaikanal, along with her letters. This way, she felt, they wouldn't miss her or home too much. And then she had a better idea: To turn the story into a little book. She had a wooden book press and bound the book herself. She made sure it was small enough for a child to hold comfortably in her hands. As a child, Helen had never found books that children could easily hold and carry. And now she had a makeshift book, about the size that you see before you. She sent it off to her children, Janet and

Day. They loved it right away. And thus was born the default format for the picture book!'

'And how did it get published?' asked Afsana. 'The original wasn't exactly in the same form that we see here, right?'

'It was very close. Helen's friend Alice Bond saw the manuscript of the bound book and offered to show it to publishers in London. Mrs Bond happened to be making her annual trip home anyway, and felt the booklet had potential. Helen was totally indifferent to its publishing prospects and left it to Alice to do with it what she thought best. She only had one condition: That if the book was accepted for publication, she would keep the copyright.

'Bond took it to a big publisher, a friend she knew: Grant Richards, who would go on to publish H.G. Wells and A.E. Housman. Richards offered to pay £5 and keep the copyright and asked if the author would be interested in such a deal. Alice wrote to Helen right away, asking for her decision on the matter. Letters despatched from London obviously took ages to reach Madras and when a reply was too long in coming, Richards said he couldn't wait; Alice had to decide on her friend's behalf. And Mrs Bond did so, telling him he could keep the copyright and publish the book. When Helen heard about it later, she was very upset, but she resigned herself to it. This eventually led to the appearance of spurious editions, some of which didn't even have the author's name on it. All Helen got out of her invention was the £5.

'*Sambo* was published by Grant Richards in October 1899 in a simple hardcover, with an even plainer jacket of vertical stripes, like wooden picket fences. The book was an instant success. Children loved the story and adults enjoyed the tale of a little boy in a forest who uses his wits to trick tigers. The illustrations, Bannerman's biographer Elizabeth Day points out, were direct, using primary colours; not many children's books looked like that then. And, of course, it was the first small book to fit easily in a child's hands. Maurice Sendak has always considered *Sambo* a great picture book, he said more than once that it was the earliest example of words, colours and pictures synchronizing perfectly in a children's picture book.

'The Grant Richards edition would set the norm for children's picture books. In its first year alone, *Sambo* went into three impressions. In the following years, there were numerous British and American editions. Later editions feature a little boy on the cover, holding an umbrella, the key edition, after the Richards, being the 1900 American version published by Frederick Stokes. As the years went by, the 1899 copy became obscure, lost to time. Even today, high-end antiquarian dealers and auction houses seldom come across a copy. And that's what you hold in your hand now: One of the most uncommon children's books in the world. Remember that the book we are looking at – specifically, this copy of the first printing from October 1899 – came two years before Beatrix Potter's first Peter Rabbit book, which was printed in 1901.'

Mrs Menon and Afsana eyed the scruffy little book, now placed between them on the tea table, with a new reverence. Kayal picked it up from the table quickly She couldn't risk getting tea stains on it.

'And what about the racism charges?' asked Mrs Menon.

'Given what you know now about *Sambo*, what do the characters in the pictures – mainly, the mother and the little boy we see a lot of – look like to you?'

'I know! That's just what I was going to remark on!' exclaimed Mrs Menon. 'They don't look very Indian. Rather, they look surprisingly African.'

'And yet,' Afsana observed, 'through the story, there are references to tigers, ghee, chatti, sari, bazaar, mangoes!'

'That's always been one of the oddest things about the book: African-looking characters with Indian elements.'

'Now I remember!' Mrs Menon interjected with a little cry. 'The mother and her little boy were seen as racist caricatures of Africans – bulging eyes, thick lips and with names like Black Mumbo and Jumbo Sambo. And didn't the name Sambo itself come to become a generic, demeaning label for black slaves in America?'

'But that's the thing – it wasn't from *this* edition that we have here. Within a few years from when it was first published, the book became so popular that several unauthorized editions began popping up in Japan and America. The original edition, as written and illustrated by Helen Bannerman, was forgotten. And it was the pirated editions that dropped the Indian references and *redrew* the characters as exaggerated caricatures of African-American slaves on plantations, reinforcing hateful racial stereotypes.'

'But even in this edition,' pointed out Afsana, 'the boy and the mother look slightly distorted, don't you think?'

'Yes; enough for both of you to identify them straight away as being exaggeratedly African, though there were tigers and saris and bazaars in the story. Bannerman said she wasn't very good at drawing people and that the best she could do in quickly sketching these characters was to end up heightening expressions and faces. She wasn't – and nor was her family – racist, as far as we can tell, though the general colonial mindset could be a factor here. It's possible that her original illustrations had simplified and distorted Africans enough for the illustrators of the unauthorized editions to exaggerate and distort their features further.'

'When was it actually banned?' asked Afsana, looking more carefully at the picture book.

'In the seventies, I think, when some librarians noticed how false and ugly and grotesque the characters looked in those pirated editions. They felt the book shouldn't circulate and began a campaign to pull it off the shelves.'

'But you said it was also popular, no?' Afsana asked, looking puzzled.

'The story Bannerman was telling was such a classic one that it appealed deeply to children and parents alike. It had instant appeal. A little boy sets out into the world alone, only to be stopped again and again by danger – tigers that come after him, one after the other – but he bargains for his life, tricking all of them. And he finds his way back home. That last image of all the tigers stuck in ghee will always remain a classic illustration, a classic idea. Over the years, fifty different editions of the book have come out. Some of them fairly recent and by African-American illustrators and writers too! *Sam and the Tigers*, *The Story of Little Babaji* and *Black Sambo* are all inspired by and adapted from the original Bannerman edition, of course. Some contemporary versions deliberately set them in India, with distinctively Indian-looking characters and places.

'Older black artists have expressed a fondness for the book, describing their happy memories of reading it as one of the few children's books to feature black characters in a literature peopled almost exclusively with white child protagonists.'

'I wonder how she came to mix up Indian and African elements in the story...' Mrs Menon mused.

'That,' said Kayal, sighing, 'will remain a mystery. Her publisher actually wanted to remove the Indian references in the sequels to the first book, but Bannerman was stubborn about keeping them and fought for it. In the later books – she wrote several after *Sambo*, though none were as successful – there were even more Indian words. My boss Neela has always felt that in spite of the names – Sambo, Jumbo, Mingo – which aren't remotely Indian or Tamil, Helen had Tamil children in mind. The kids from the streets of Madras, the children of the servants who would come play with her children in their house. She knew that if not anybody else, her children, at least, would recognize the family she was drawing and telling stories about. She was caricaturing Tamil children!'

'Caricaturing Tamil children!' exclaimed Mrs Menon. 'Why, yes, of course. It makes total sense.'

'So what happens now with the book?' Afsana asked. 'What would you like us to do?'

'If the school will trust me – that is, trust Biblio – with it, I'll take it back so that Neela can begin the process of letting collectors know it is on the market. We need to accurately describe the copy, condition, provenance and so on. While it is in our safekeeping, Neela can talk the details of the sale over with your principal.'

Kamala Menon saw no problem with that and twenty minutes later Kayal was back in the senior library, collecting the other books she had reserved and packing the lot of them into her strolley with care, wrapping each of them in glassine wrappers. She slipped *Sambo* into her handbag, after placing it inside a solander box that she had brought along, just in case she actually made an unexpected find. The book's small format made it lie snugly inside.

When she finished, it was 4.30 p.m. and school was over. Her meeting with Kenton Francis Selvaganesan was at 5 p.m. He had left a message for her at the library, saying he would come and fetch her from the reading room, so that's where she settled down to wait. She contemplated her haul with considerable pleasure. Even discounting the discovery of a first printing of the little book, the day's find was not without some interesting items. She thought of how unpromising the books had looked at first, and now she had one huge find and some lovely old editions of the Pooh books.

After the overnight journey and the day's excitement, the wait made her sleepy. Before she knew it, Kayal's eyes shut and she settled into a catnap.

Part Four

17

The Schoolteacher's Secret

'Kayalveli? Kayalveli Anbuchelvan...?'

Kayal awoke with a start. Her blurry eyes registered before her a wiry physique, a round, moonish, bespectacled face, curly brown hair and coal-black eyes that stood out on a pale face.

'I must have dozed off,' Kayal murmured apologetically, sitting up straight. 'Mr Selvaganesan?'

'Kenton, please,' he said pleasantly, coming around the strolley, smiling. They shook hands and she noted that his palms were slightly moist. 'Don't worry. The cold mountain air does that to you. Did you have a good trip?'

'Yeah, it was lovely, thanks. By the way, everyone calls me Kayal... This is quite a campus you have here.'

'Isn't it? It's been my home for nearly twenty years. If you're all done here, shall we go get some tea?'

'I've just had some. But I wouldn't mind another cup.'

'Can I get that for you?' Kenton pointed at the strolley.

'Thanks, but it's easy enough to wheel along.'

'I thought we could sit in my cottage and talk. It's not very far out of campus.'

They walked out into the darkening cold.

'You must have a lot of family here, then?' Kayal asked, turning to him.

'My family has been here for a few generations, right from the time of my great-grandparents. But no, I don't have much family here any more. I'm an only child. My father died when I was twenty-two. My mother lives with me. The aunts and cousins have all moved to Australia. And I'm not married.'

'Do you like it here? The school, teaching?'

'I'm sort of good at it, I think. But it wasn't out of choice – I mean, hanging on here at Ooty, at Beardsley. My father was the school's bandmaster. Everyone here knows him as Selva – at some point, Selvaganesan became Selva and that's how most people in this town know me – Kenton or Selva. My mother, Lorraine, was a nurse at the school infirmary before she retired. I studied here and then got a Masters in history from the Arts College, Coimbatore. After that, I wanted, quite badly, to go abroad for a PhD, but that's when my father died. My mother found it hard to cope and I decided to stay put. The school very graciously gave me a job, even though I didn't have a B.Ed. I have, since, got a teacher's training degree. I enjoy it now, though there are times when Ooty and the school feel very provincial. A small world. Which it is, I guess. That's the charm and the curse.' He smiled.

'Believe me, you don't want to be down there in the burning plains.'

Kenton's cottage was cold and damp. Even after turning on several lights, the history teacher couldn't dispel the gloom. The furniture looked very old and uncomfortable. Kayal eyed a large rocking chair and made a move to drop into it, but Kenton cautioned her against it with an apologetic gesture, pointing out that it was broken. He indicated a divan as the best thing in the room to sit on. The upholstery had long faded, but it was surprisingly comfortable. A rickety cane bookshelf held what looked mostly like school textbooks and a few comics.

'Not very cosy or bright,' Kenton said, 'and you must be wondering why we had to come here. But I needed to check on my mother, who's recovering from a really bad stroke that happened a month ago. Also, I didn't want to carry the Burton material with me. Let me put the kettle on, quickly look in on my mother and then we can talk.'

He placed a tray of ginger biscuits and homemade chocolates before her and went into an adjoining room. Kayal took a biscuit, but not the chocolates. She was craving something hot and spicy to warm her up, some spicy, crunchy, deep-fried snack. While she waited, she called the taxi service and asked to be picked up from Kenton's home, rather than the school, as had been decided earlier. Restless, she got up to look at some old family photographs on the wall. They told her what she had guessed: Kenton was Anglo-Indian – at least, on one side of his family. She could hear him talking softly with his mother in the other room, switching from Tamil to English and back to Tamil again.

A short while later, Kenton emerged from the room with his mother, supporting her as she stumbled forward awkwardly, even though she was using a walker to move. Kayal turned towards them in polite greeting, but the pair of them went past her, crossing the living room to what was probably the bathroom. In a while they crossed her again towards the interior of the cottage, but this time Kayal remained immersed in the photographs.

Kenton finally returned with the tea, apologizing again for making her wait. Observing her interest in the wall of family photos, he pointed out his parents and then a large number of uncles, aunts and cousins. As she sat down again, Kenton encouraged her to tell him more about the bookshop. She explained as swiftly and precisely as she could what kind of bookshop Biblio was, and the world of collectors it interacted with.

'What brought me around to calling Mr Whitehead,' Kenton told her, 'was coming across a snippet in the papers about some fantastic sum he had paid for a rare Burton book. His wealth didn't interest me, but it told me he would be curious and passionate about things related to Burton.'

'Why didn't you pursue it with Whitehead after that call? You're right about how seriously he has taken it. It's been the only thing on his mind for some weeks now.'

'He seemed a little sceptical, if not dismissive, and that put me off a bit.'

'Indian collectors seldom allow for the possibility of something rare or desirable turning up here,' Kayal said, sighing. 'They think – as the rest of the antiquarian world does – that all the good stuff is abroad, either in private hands, libraries or with the big rare-book dealers. They forget what that character in Larry McMurtry's book says: "Anything can be anywhere."' Kayal grinned self-consciously and confessed, 'That was mostly Neela I was parroting. Neelambari Adigal, that is, my boss. I've heard her say these things so often that it's become part of my spiel.'

'Oh yeah, the one I spoke to on the phone. It's reassuring to know all of you take me seriously,' Kenton said. 'Coming into this Burton material has really put me in a strange position. And I hesitate so much because it might turn my life upside down here at the school.'

'Can you tell me more about it?'

'For this to make sense to you, I first have to tell you a little about my family – well, my mother's side of the family, that is – and how I came to possess the Burton material. But I don't feel like getting into all that just now. The best thing, perhaps, is for me to make that trip down to Chennai, when I can manage it. I can then bring the Burton stuff with me – it's basically a couple of books that belonged to him, a letter, some stationery and a file with some loose papers. What I can let you have now is a photocopy of the Burton letter.'

Kayal hid her disappointment as Kenton got up to fetch the photocopy. She had hoped to find out just a little more to take back with her.

He came back with a large envelope. 'Just something for you to read on the train,' he said, smiling.

She got up to leave, wrapping her shawl around herself, adjusting the handle of her strolley.

He opened the door for her and said, 'I'll see you to the car.'

She thanked him and they walked to the car in silence. Though it was still early evening, it had already become dark. She got into the cab.

'Wait!' he called out, rushing back into the house, and emerging with a folder in his hand. 'You didn't think I'd bring you all this way for nothing, did you?' he said, leaning into her window.

'I *was* wondering...' she said, smiling uncertainly.

'The Burton letter is to a woman named Parvathy, a Tamil nurse who looked after him when he was recovering from a severe eye infection here in Ooty. They had a brief affair. For Parvathy and her family, it meant a scandal. For Burton, it was just something to kill his boredom in a place he had come to loathe. Parvathy had his child – a daughter. Burton never knew about her. He had, by then, left Ooty and had taken up his new posting in Sindh. Their daughter, whom Parvathy named Francesca Kalaiarasi, is my great-great-great-grandmother. I'm a direct descendant, Kayal, of Richard Francis Burton.'

He was, she could see, completely serious.

'Burton returned to India in 1872 and visited Ooty again. Parvathy rushed to meet him, to show him his daughter, but discovered he was married now. And his bride Isabel had accompanied him. Parvathy never contacted him again. If he made any attempts to find her, she, at least, never knew about it.'

While Kayal was still trying to take this in, he leaned in closer.

'I trust you,' he said. 'I'll tell you what I have and you can share it with Mr Whitehead. You can tell him the Burton manuscript I have is not a manuscript at all, that it is something better, a fragment of something he wrote – the notorious Karachi Report.'

'The Karachi Report?'

'Yes – also known as the Karachi Papers. What I have is a *fragment* of those lost papers. You just go on and tell Mr Whitehead that. He'll know what it means. Goodbye, now. Have a safe trip back.'

The car shot out into the cold, blue night.

18

The Unholy Grail of Burtoniana

'Impossible!' spluttered Whitehead. 'The Karachi Report is a fiction. A Burton myth. Everyone knows that! Whoever has gone looking for it has come away empty-handed, looking like a bloody fool. Who does this Kenton Selva think he can trick with this stunt?'

Kayal was going to say something further, but Neela brushed her arm, warning her not to say more until Whitehead had calmed down. They were at Biblio. It was late afternoon and they had the bookshop to themselves for a while. *The Story of Little Black Sambo* was safely tucked away in a safe in the bookshop's office. Kayal had barely had the time to show it to

Neela properly. Whitehead had demanded to see her the moment she got off the train that morning. She had given her report of the trip to Neela just fifteen minutes before Whitehead arrived at the bookshop.

When Whitehead had bustled in, she had given him an account of her meeting with the history teacher. But Kayal hadn't managed to get very far; when she brought up the matter of Kenton claiming to be a descendant of Burton, the collector had looked astonished, even amused. Her boss had also looked shocked and then sceptical when Kayal shared Kenton's startling double revelation. And then the very mention of the Karachi Report had caused Whitehead to erupt with outrage. Kayal wished she had read up more on the significance of the Karachi Report before the meeting, but she just hadn't had a chance to do very much since she'd returned. She had a feeling, though, that she was about to find out a whole lot about this now from Whitehead and Neela, the Burton experts.

No one said anything for a while. Kayal waited for one of them to speak.

'There's something to that story, I have to admit,' said Whitehead after a while, now considerably calmer. 'There being a nurse in Ooty who may have taken care of Burton when he was ill is not unbelievable.'

'It's plausible, isn't it?' said Neela, looking at the collector for some confirmation.

'So there was a nurse in Burton's life?' Kayal asked finally.

'Well, not exactly in his life,' Neela answered. 'He was packed off on sick leave to Ootcamund. He had developed an eye infection. It required constant attention, but I don't think there's anything anywhere about a nurse looking after him. It's plausible, I suppose. If Kenton's account – that they had an affair which produced a child – is true, it's extraordinary. Because Burton and Isabel never had children. And now, after all these years, the world will learn that Burton had a child, after all. One he didn't know about.'

'But none of this explains how this woman could possibly have the Karachi Papers in her possession – if, indeed, that is what they are,' said Whitehead, his tone impatient. 'I'm assuming that Kenton has the papers now, because they somehow stayed in his family. But if Parvathy meant little to Burton and he did not keep in touch with her – and even Kenton admits that for Burton the affair had been no more than a frivolity – how would he have left behind something so controversial with her? Besides, there had been, you'll recall, several women in his life during his years in India; perhaps, many more than there would be later, during his stay in Arabia and Africa. He became engaged to Isabel soon after his return to England but during his years in Baroda and Karachi there had been many mistresses. There was even one, in particular, he would become obsessed with. Burton had enthusiastically embraced the common practice among British officers of taking a morganatic wife – an Indian woman whom an Englishman married with the understanding that the marriage would automatically dissolve when his wife came down from England to join him, or when he left the country – whichever came first. Burton liked variety.'

'What next, Nallathambi?'

'I'm tempted, Neela. Seduced. I'll have to explore this further. So let's invite the man here and see the damn thing first with our own eyes. And then get what he has authenticated by experts and rule out the possibility that it's just some bit of regimental duty report or personal scribbling Burton had left behind or misplaced. Then there's the possibility of forgery. There's no turning back now.'

'I've been meaning to ask,' said Kayal, speaking up, 'what *is* the Karachi Report?'

'Only the holy grail of Richard Burton's writings,' Whitehead replied, perking up. 'Or should I say, the *unholy* grail? Even the former Pakistani Prime Minister Zulfikar Ali Bhutto had his people look for it, though the search didn't turn up anything.'

'Bhutto!' Kayal exclaimed.

'Apparently, yes – or so a Pakistani official had once claimed. Bhutto was similarly intrigued by Burton and heard rumours that the Karachi Report could still be unearthed in Karachi. Sir Christopher Ondaatje mentions this in his *Sindh Revisited: A Journey in the Footsteps of Captain Sir Richard Francis Burton*.'

'There was a time,' explained Neela, 'when every Burton scholar, collector and biographer went in search of what came to be called the Karachi Papers. There were tantalizing references to it in different places – Burton's own memoirs, Isabel's biography of her husband and, of course, the biography that made it so well-known: Edward Rice's *Captain Sir Richard Francis Burton: The Secret Agent Who Made the Pilgrimage to Mecca.* The notion that Burton was part of the Great Game was made popular in the book; and it doesn't seem to have ever faded away, though it is probably false. The Great Game, you'll remember, Kayal, was the rivalry that existed in the nineteenth century between Britain and Russia over Afghanistan, as they fought for dominance over frontier roads in India. Rice picked this up from Burton himself, who first mentioned it. Later, Burton's wife would also bring it up. The Karachi Report is apparently something that got Burton into a lot of trouble with his superiors, ultimately even leading to his failure and downfall in India.

'As he and Isabel have told it – later embellished by others – some two years before he returned, dejected, to England from India, his commanding officer, Sir Charles Napier, had been using spies from time to time to get a feel of what was happening around him, especially when it came to interactions between the locals and his officers. Aware of Burton's linguistic skills and penchant for disguises, Napier sent him out on a secret mission. He had heard reports of a sudden upsurge of male brothels in Karachi, which his officers were frequenting.

'Brothels springing up around military cantonments were commonplace, but what disturbed and outraged Napier's Victorian sensibilities were the reports he received of his officers' preference for bordellos offering the services of male prostitutes. He was equally incensed by rumours of the exorbitant sums these establishments charged. So Burton set off in disguise to visit these brothels undercover. He then discreetly turned the unofficial report over to Napier, stipulating that it would have to be kept between them. Napier promised Burton to keep it confidential, then carelessly put it away somewhere, only for it to turn up later at the Government House in Bombay. However, he did act on the report promptly, identifying three male "lupanars" – brothels – and closing them down. The report was subsequently forgotten.

'Then Napier returned to England and his successor, who had little or no knowledge of Burton, stumbled upon the report in his predecessor's office. Burton was due for another promotion as interpreter to his regiment, but despite his knowledge of Punjabi, Marathi and Gujarati, in addition to Hindi, he was passed over and the job, to his shock and dismay, went to a junior whose language skills were limited to Hindi. Burton was disgraced. He asked for sick leave and fled to England.'

'Except,' growled Whitehead, 'no such report has turned up anywhere, especially where it should have. And the whole thing is seen today as possibly a Burton fabrication or embellishment.'

Neela nodded in agreement and continued. 'Fawn Brodie, a Burton biographer, sent archivists to look for it in the India Office Records at the British Library in London, but it couldn't be traced. Burton's most recent biographer Jon Godsall checked every possible source, before arriving at the definitive conclusion that there had been no such thing. Godsall, as well as other scholars, now agree that Burton had invented it – not a surprising thing and not for the first or last time: He would invent stuff from time to time and Isabel simply took his word for it, embellishing it further.'

'I can't imagine Burton making things up about himself,' said Kayal, looking troubled. 'He had accomplished so much. Why would he have wanted to invent?'

Whitehead chuckled. 'You'll get used to that side of him. Everyone has to, eventually. Ruffian Dick loved a good tale and his opulent imagination couldn't resist spicing up stories. In his accounts, Burton gave the impression that it was extremely dangerous to enter Mecca as a white man and, if caught, it meant certain death. But not many know that he *wasn't* the first white man to make the Hajj pilgrimage to the holy cities. Someone else got there first.'

'No, they didn't!' Kayal gasped, hardly believing what she was hearing, and turned to Neela to see if the collector was teasing her.

Neela corroborated the collector's statement. 'Johann Ludwig Burckhardt, a Swiss traveller and adventurer – who stumbled upon the Petra ruins – also went to Mecca in much the same way as Burton: dressed as a Muslim merchant. Except, he did it forty years before Burton. And the journey is no secret; he wrote numerous books about it. But Burckhardt didn't make it sound as theatrical as Sir Richard Francis Burton eventually would.

'The chief culprit who gave the Karachi Report weight and credibility,' Neela eventually continued, as Kayal tried to absorb all that she was hearing, 'was Rice. More recent biographers agree that his best-selling book made the report officially a part of

Burton's biography. By recording the Great Game as part of Burton's adventures in India, Rice established it as fact. A piece of information that Burton fans and readers were delighted to believe in and celebrate was that the translator of the *Kama Sutra* – the white secret agent who penetrated the holy city of Mecca, the daring explorer of Africa – had begun his exploits as a young soldier in India. It seemed to fit. Burton began his long, daring career as a young spy in India, not Arabia.

'Today, nearly all Burton scholars and collectors agree that the Karachi Papers are Burton's own invention, calculated to make his years in India look more exotic than they actually were. What had happened, at least in his eyes, was that he had simply failed. The India years had been a source of shame to him. In recalling them later, Burton invented the Karachi Papers as the reason for his fall from grace with the 18th Bombay Native Infantry. Except for Burton, not a single one of his friends, colleagues or superiors seemed to know of such a document. You see now, Kayal, why it's hard to believe that Kenton has it, or even something like it?'

'Let me see that photocopy again,' said Whitehead, reaching out to take it from Neela.

The letter, written and signed in Burton's hand, was addressed to Parvathy, telling her that his eye was healing well, thanks to her, followed by some news of what he had been up to since being back with his regiment in Karachi. And here the letter ended, somewhat abruptly. Though there was nothing intimate in it to suggest they could have been lovers or any hint of the Karachi Report, the letter did, at least, lend some provenance to the Burton material Kenton alleged he had.

'It looks convincing enough,' Whitehead said. 'This is Burton's handwriting and signature, which I know as well as any Burton collector or scholar, and it is written, apparently, on Company or Regiment stationary. And if there is something to this schoolteacher claiming he has the Karachi Papers, it will be the first ever sighting of it, shaking Burton scholarship to its very roots.'

'If Burton wasn't lying about this the whole time,' Neela said, 'then his first account of it – the one that says he submitted the report secretly to Napier, asking him to either destroy it or not keep it in his office – how does that affect this finding? Shouldn't the report be lost somewhere in Napier's Bombay offices? How was it still with Burton? Had he then made another copy, his own copy? And knowing what a stickler he always was for taking notes and recording even less sensational details of his life at this point, it would make good sense for him to want his own record of it.'

Heaving himself out of his chair, Whitehead addressed both of them. 'The best known Burton collector, Quentin Keynes, was once invited to be part of a Burton conference at the Huntington Library. When the audience asked him if he had turned up any new material pertaining to Burton's career in India, he replied, "I haven't got the Karachi brothel report." The room had echoed with knowing titters. And then Keynes added, "There is very little extant, as far as I know, of his time in India." This is what fills me with both foreboding and excitement now: Keynes himself didn't find it and now I get the privilege to see it, perhaps even *own* it? It's unthinkable, fantastic, but it's also why I became a collector, dammit! And to think that with a single, unique Burton acquisition like this, I can topple Pilkington in one move! The Viscount will simply have to bow out.'

Whitehead left a short while later, after Neela assured him that she would do what she could to persuade Kenton to agree to a meeting with them soon, perhaps get him to make a quick trip to Chennai with the alleged Burton manuscript fragment and encourage him to reveal more about Parvathy and Burton. Kayal and Neela lingered in the bookshop for a while longer, examining the *Sambo* copy. Neela backed her associate's finding, that it was, indeed, the true, scarce first edition of the Bannerman book. They decided not to put it up for auction and to offer it, instead, to a collector who would treasure it: Antara Ranadive, who collected children's picture books and would pay top money for it.

After Neela left, Kayal made herself some tea and sat down to work on the catalogue, but found her mind wandering instead to the first time she'd met Neela, and how that had led to Biblio.

19

A Fine Movable Type

Kayalveli Anbuchelvan had met Neelambari Adigal for the first time on a Friday evening in May 2015 during her internship at the Roja Muthiah Research Library (RMRL). The RMRL, located in Taramani, just west of Adyar, is a one-of-a-kind library and research space for Tamil studies. It houses an extensive collection of printed books, ephemera and journals in Tamil, several dating back to the middle of the nineteenth century, including a few examples of palm-leaf manuscripts. It had started out as the collection of one man. The story of its origins was one of those rare instances in India of bibliomania, a true story that sounded more like a cautionary fairy tale for bibliophiles. And it was the passion of Roja Muthiah Chettiar that had brought

Kayal to this library, to this place which had made her lucky meeting with Neela possible.

That November, the RMRL had held a week of seminars on book conservation. And on that particular Friday evening, Neela had been the speaker, addressing a gathering of librarians, book scholars, collectors and bibliophiles. The title of her talk was 'India's Antiquarian Book Culture – What's Missing?' The talk had made a deep impression on Kayal: Up until then, she hadn't heard anyone talking about the book world in India the way this speaker did, and years later she still recalled the excitement and awe with which she had taken it all in.

'My bibliophile friends, who know how deeply the book as a physical object interests me, sometimes wonder how I feel about digital books,' Neela had begun, 'and always look a little disappointed, when I tell them that I think it's possibly the best thing that's happened to the printed book. Digital books have freed the traditional book from being merely functional, from being objects carrying information and text. Now, the book can go back to being what it used to be in its infancy: A finely printed, finely made object. It can now focus on its form – the paper, typography, design, illustration and binding. The Ideal Book or the "Book Beautiful" that William Morris and Cobden T.J. Sanderson spoke of. Not to be confused with the garden-variety deluxe edition, but a book that is typographically handsome, with all its elements – paper, ink, type, presswork – in harmony.

'But typography in India,' Neela had continued, 'indeed, in South Asia itself, has never taken off or had much of an impact on our printing and publishing history, even though it arrived here in the 1550s, when Portuguese and Indian blacksmiths cast founts of Tamil in Lisbon, Goa and Quilon, or Kolam, to print Christian pamphlets. Interestingly, the introduction of lithography to India in the 1820s had a bigger and immediate effect in its first ten years than typography ever had in its two hundred and fifty years. Printed in 1578, *Doctrina Christom, Thambiran Vanakkam*, a translation of a Portuguese catechism, became the first printed book in India. This book was not only the first to be printed in Indian type, but the first anywhere in the world printed in non-Roman metallic type. The Tamil type was prepared by the Spaniard Juan Gonsalves, a former blacksmith and clockmaker, with assistance from Father Pero Luis, a Tamil who had entered the Jesuit order in 1562. The second instance of movable type in India was also, incredibly enough, of Tamil letters, when in 1717, the missionary Bartholomäus Ziegenbalg set up his press in Tranquebar, now Tharangambadi.'

Neela had gone on to identify more remarkable printing instances in Tamil Nadu: A type foundry set up in Porayar – again, the first such in India – and in 1715, the first modern paper mill in the country. After this, printing had remained a sporadic coastal phenomenon in India. As a result, there was little or no development of Indian typefaces, no attempt to design and manufacture types in Indian scripts. Tamil, by circumstances, fate or history, had the lead, becoming the first Indian script in movable type and it was a pity that nothing further had happened to make Tamil printing more vibrant, so that it would blaze a trail, making printing a strong, prolific tradition in India.

Listening to Neela, Kayal would learn that while these developments were taking place in India, in Europe and England, typography was flourishing with great creativity, producing type designers of real genius, thriving type foundries and gifted scholar-printers. In India, though, typography would remain stagnant, until Charles Wilkins, an East India Company civil servant and librarian, enlisted the help of an Indian blacksmith named Panchanan Karmakar and took up the challenge of making a fine typeface for Bengali. Wilkins set the standard for fine metal type and it is he who was really India's William Caxton, though William Carey at Serampore has often been given the credit for reviving Indian typography and printing. 'But that honour, as typographic scholars Fiona Ross and Graham Shaw have clearly shown,' Neela had reminded her audience, 'belongs to Wilkins'.

However, with the discovery of the lithographic process in Calcutta around the same time, printing with movable types was again sidelined, as lithography became the preferred way to print.

Neela went on to explain that the reasons for the typographic book – that is, the well-printed book – fading into insignificance in India actually went further back, before the printed book, to our poor manuscript culture. Its roots lay in the Hindu manuscript book or codex, which had been, for the most part, pedestrian, utilitarian and lacking in the arts and graces of the beautiful manuscript book produced in the same period by Muslim calligraphers, illustrators and binders.

Kayal recalled how beautifully Neela had explained this. 'Our long oral tradition had kept us away from nearly a thousand years of development in the book arts. And when the manuscript book finally began to emerge, it paled before the beauty and sophistication of Islamic calligraphy and miniaturist painting. A page with text and illustration, say, from a Rajasthani manuscript, placed alongside a similar page from a Muslim manuscript, was, in every way, less appealing; the calligraphy was plain, the human figures were flat, the colours were dull and the paper not as fine.

In contrast, the Islamic codex was unrivalled in its artistry. The colours were vibrant, the human and animal figures were two-dimensional and the writing was accomplished in an elegant calligraphic hand. The same artistry was apparent in those Jain manuscripts influenced by the book-arts tradition in the Muslim courts that, in turn, had probably absorbed a great deal from Persian-Iranian manuscript makers of the time.

'In Europe, movable type had arrived fully fledged at birth, because the early printers had drawn their type from the great calligraphic models of the manuscript hand-developed by scribes in monastic scriptoriums over several centuries. If only our manuscript tradition had flourished, our printing culture too would have flowered.

'So, you see,' Neela had continued, 'when print came along, we seemed to have missed the bus, indifferent to exploring its finer typographical aspects.

'But what Charles Wilkins did with his Bengali movable type is, for our purpose – which is to look at the art of the printed book – more relevant, more important and more exciting than any of these fledgling instances of Indian movable type. Because Wilkins was the first to create a truly fine typeface for Indian scripts, beginning with his success with Bengali.

'In 1778, he printed Nathaniel Brassey Halhed's *A Grammar of the Bengal Language* at Hooghly. He used movable type, having designed the letters himself after a careful study of Bengali calligraphic and cursive manuscripts, and then had a goldsmith or a blacksmith punch-cut them. The India Office Records at the British Library in London has material belonging to Wilkins that shows the process he followed: Drawing letterform first in pencil and then with ink. Often, he is single-handedly credited with the achievement of designing the type, cutting the punch and casting it. Wilkins was not trained in the complete process of casting – from taking metal in its crude state to the point of engraving and founding. Even a master printer and typographer like William Caslon expressed doubt that the former could have accomplished this so quickly. In a report prepared by the Royal Society of Arts in 1819, Caslon stated that it would be impossible for one person to complete a fount of letters from the first to the last. Wilkins must have had Indian assistants, and evidence points to the blacksmith Karmakar. He assisted the printer in punch-cutting and in striking the matrices and probably took on the task of actually casting the type. But after these first movable printing presses, attempts at designing and cutting type for Indian languages waned as lithography firmly took root.'

Neela had then gone on to make a sharp and unsparing critique of India's long indifference to print culture, drawing attention to the way books as objects had counted for very little here. Kayal had nearly risen to her feet when Neela began speaking of the importance of pursuing, collecting, preserving and cataloguing important Indian editions, both antiquarian and modern. 'If we've neglected to take care of our physical books in the past,' Neela had emphasized, 'let's not make that mistake again in the present. God alone knows – and, perhaps, even She may not – why antiquarian bookselling never became an ingrained tradition in India, the way it did in Europe.'

Kayal remembered her audience groaning and chuckling along with her.

'Several charming and dusty second-hand bookshops – a few dabbling in antiquarian British Raj material, books on hunting and so on – may well have made some effort to perpetuate the tradition,' Neela had continued, 'but it's hard to think of a string of fine antiquarian bookstores, devoted entirely to rare and fine books. The paltry few antiquarian bookshops were all from the fifties – Thacker Spink and Nirmal Kumar's in Calcutta come most to mind. Some of you would be astonished to know – as I was – that between 1884 and 1889, the venerable E.M. Dring, Bernard Quaritch's right-hand man, had actually worked at

Thacker Spink! And Quaritch himself, possibly, had a small sideline going in India in the sale of trade editions. But the rare bookshop in India may as well have begun and ended with them.

'Today, there are only two or three antiquarian bookshops serving the whole country. Baffling, don't you think, in a literary and publishing culture that has been so rich, varied, brilliant and fêted? Even its authors and literary critics, sharply and passionately attuned to literature, are indifferent to print culture and bibliography. Engaged rigorously with the content inside a book, they show no interest in the material book: Its physicality, typography, edition, printing history and condition. Lost in a kind of bibliographic naïveté, the literary community here didn't bat an eyelid when the reality of digital books set in; there was little reflection or criticism of e-books, nothing like the furore one witnessed in the West over digital books as opposed to printed ones. I can't recall a single Indian author or literary critic offering a paean to the printed book or even coming out in its defence. There has been, instead, a kind of warm, rising anticipation of e-books, a restless impatience over the fact that they haven't yet arrived full-blown and quickly enough here.

'At least, authors and critics have an engagement with the text inside. What's the excuse of Indian "book collectors"?' Neela had asked, expressing her irritation with the breed she had just referred to by hooking her forefingers to suggest the quote-unquote marks framing the term 'book collectors'. 'A mostly eager, misguided lot,' she had continued, 'who think collecting means *volume*, when it should be *edition*. Passionate collecting in our country is misconstrued as the indiscriminate collecting of as many books as possible; the more the number of books, the bigger the collector. And what *are* these books? Reading copies – mostly new books and used ones, not first or fine or rare editions. The Indian book collector, with his collection of reading copies, doesn't realize what he has is a large private library, not a fine collection of valuable editions.

'But who can blame anyone in India, really? There is simply no established tradition here of book collecting, in addition to the complete absence of an antiquarian book market and an utter lack of keen book collectors and their community of shared knowledge. You have to have a space like an antiquarian bookshop to walk into and see and handle these books, these *editions*, or walk the floors of a first-rate antiquarian book fair, where you can experience, in one place, a gathering of rare-book sellers, book collectors and the best copies of high spots in collecting.

'Our narrow circle of genuine Indian book collectors, with an exquisite collection of high spots, acquire their choice items from international online antiquarian dealers or, when travelling abroad, browse and buy from the multitude of stores specializing in rare books to be found there.'

This is exactly how she herself had got started, Neela had informed her audience: A brief stint of living and working in London had turned her into a book collector and a rare-book dealer, after she had been lucky enough to stumble on to the city's famed antiquarian book trade. She had illustrated her talk with examples from her experience as both Indian collector and book dealer of rare and fine books.

Neela's impassioned presentation had set Kayal thinking. As far as Kayal knew – and she had looked far and wide – there wasn't a bookshop in India like the one Neelambari Adigal had just described.

At the reception afterwards, held in RMRL's A.K. Ramanujan Reading Room, Kayal had gone up to Neela to tell her how much she had enjoyed the talk. And that she had been stunned – delighted – to learn that Neela ran a shop that specialized in rare books.

'I'm delighted that you're delighted,' Neela had answered, laughing. 'The whole thing has been very low-key,' she'd explained, 'and even people in the book trade don't seem to know of it, because it's a by-appointment-only bookshop. It's been reasonably profitable, but I've been thinking more and more of a brick-and-mortar antiquarian bookshop. This means, I can throw it open to bibliophiles and readers who might want to walk in and browse. It's been challenging and fun to fulfil the want-lists of rich book collectors, but I've been feeling that it's a shame that bibliophiles don't have an antiquarian bookshop to walk into and explore its treasures – to handle these books, examine them up close. It doesn't matter in the end if they look more than they buy, but they must first get a chance, at least, to be near such fine books, such fine bookmaking.'

Sensing Kayal's interest, Neela had said they should talk more, but somewhere quieter and more comfortable. And that had turned out to be at Neela's Adyar cottage (which would go on to become Biblio) two days later, on a Sunday morning, with Neela pouring both of them cups of aromatic coffee (Monsoon Malabar beans, ground fresh) and talking about how she had got started in the rare-book business.

20

The Taste and Technique of a Bookwoman

'Next to love, book collecting is the most exhilarating sport of all,' Dr A.S.W. Rosenbach had declared, after all, and when Neela's five-year marriage to a textile industrialist with businesses in London ended suddenly but amicably, she found herself diving deep into the city's famed rare-book world, ecstatically exploring its historically rich, energetic and colourful antiquarian contours. The divorce settlement had been considerably large, amounting to a small fortune in shares, an apartment in central London and an impressive art collection. Art didn't do much for her; it wasn't her thing. Books were.

After she discovered the world of rare and fine books, the first thing Neela did was to sell off the art collection that had come to her to generate the funds she needed to start collecting books. It had begun quite simply, with the long walks she would take during her lunch breaks at The Nehru Centre, the cultural office of the Indian High Commission in London – where she worked part-time as Programme Assistant – wandering into the little byways and side streets of central London. On one such drizzly afternoon, she found herself walking through Cecil Court, a pedestrian-only thoroughfare, with a row of bookshops with Victorian storefronts.

As the drizzle threatened to turn into a downpour, Neela ducked into the nearest bookshop. After some twenty minutes or so of browsing, she realized that she had, possibly, never been inside a bookshop like this one. Though it was stocked entirely with old books, it wasn't just another second-hand bookshop. Over the years spent in London, she had done the rounds of the used bookshops located in and around Charing Cross Road (at Foyles, she had bought with pleasure a Helene Hanff-inscribed and signed copy of *The Duchess of Bloomsbury Street*) and couldn't help but notice how many of them had a rare-book section, consisting mainly, it seemed, of modern first editions – several of them made more special by the fact that they were signed. But the bookshop she now found herself in appeared to have only rare books or special editions. The books were shelved immaculately, with none of the pleasant disorder you usually saw in second-hand shops and with the sections clearly demarcated and defined: Fine Bindings, Private-Press Books, Early Printed Books, Illustrated Editions, Colour-Plate Books and Prints, and so on. They were old, more than used, and it wasn't the condition of the books that made her think of them as old; on the contrary, most of them were so fine that it was like looking at second-hand books that had never been used! Suddenly, something she'd read once in a bibliomystery by Dunning came to mind about what a well preserved rare book looks like: *It does not look like a new book – it looks so wonderfully like an old book that's never been touched.*

Someone had evidently gone to great trouble to keep these old books looking new, as if shining and polishing them every morning. There were shelves stocked with books that had no dust jackets, books printed when wrappers were uncommon; and yet when you turned their pages, they looked bright and clean, while the shelves with dust-jacketed books had jackets that looked unfaded, if not pristine or in mint condition. Then it hit Neelambari – each book mattered here; every copy was special. The books, row upon row of them, couldn't be lumped together, even if all twenty copies were of the same book: Each copy had its individuality, uniqueness, something to distinguish it from its companions. They were *editions*.

There it was. It was the edition that mattered. So it was a bookshop that sold particular editions, not just second-hand books, thought Neela, who had also begun to notice that just below or above the price of each book, which was lightly pencilled on the flyleaf, there were tiny, loopy jottings, varying from copy to copy, things like: *op, 1sted, rp, 1st thus, sg/in, w.e.f*. It must mark the edition, she concluded. She had looked only fleetingly, while entering the bookshop, at its signboard outside and was now curious to learn more. So she crept up to the counter and plucked a business card off a stack that read: *Old Editions. Uncommon Books at Common Prices. Antiquarian, Rare and Fine Books. Martin Treevis, Proprietor.* She was, perhaps for the first time in all her long browsing life, inside an antiquarian bookshop.

Browsing feverishly, Neela felt herself fatally drawn to these antiquarian editions. She couldn't think of them as just books any more. And the editions she was most powerfully drawn to were her long-standing personal favourites. It was to these that she now turned, touching each edition with a rising, visceral desire to possess them. Neela gently put her little pile of books on the floor and picked up the one she wanted badly. But would she be able to afford it, she wondered, opening the book. A beautiful trade edition of Lewis Carroll's *Alice's Adventures in Wonderland*, with illustrations by her favourite Alice illustrator – Arthur Rackham (whose work she preferred to the original Tenniel illustrations) – tipped in colour plates with black-and-white drawings. A 1907 edition, published by William Heinemann.

The beauty of this copy was that it wasn't one more of those ubiquitous contemporary deluxe *Alice* editions you saw in bookshops; just plain cloth boards, with the gilt-stamped Gryphon and Mock Turtle. The bookseller had slipped in a little typed note describing the copy: *V.G. Quarto in original boards; cloth lightly soiled, scattered foxing on pages, spine and endpapers toned, corners of upper board bumped, top edge gilt slightly rubbed. Lacking the called-for signature.* The price said: £200. She had no idea if £200 was low or high or just right for what must surely be a much-sought-after out-of-print *Alice* edition, but she wanted it.

She placed it to her left and picked up from the floor on her right another book – a private-press booklet: *Farewell to True Bookshops* by Rocket Press, with fetching bookshop illustrations by Pamela Franklin. £15. Fifteen! Sold! The press book, too, was put aside. The last in the pile was something she had been meaning to read for a long time: Robert Curzon's *Visits to Monasteries in the Levant*, a fascinating account of Curzon persuading and bribing monasteries to sell him some of their illuminated manuscripts. This particular copy, a first impression from John Murray, was an uncommonly well-preserved one, and at £45, it seemed like a bargain.

She started to approach the bookseller, but held back from addressing him. He seemed preoccupied, stooped over a cluttered work desk that glowed orange from the light of a lamp nearby; with the overcast afternoon sky outside, there was very little daylight in the room. From a transistor, with the volume turned low, came the faint murmur of cricket commentary. Treevis, if he was indeed Treevis, was a frail man in his seventies, with a prominent hooked nose. He was almost completely bald, but for an uncharacteristic shock of thick snow-white hair growing at the back of his head. The desk he was working at held envelopes, letters, papers, invoices and stock lists, a few catalogues and two neat piles of books flanking a half-eaten apple on either side. Maintaining a steady pace and unwavering concentration, he was examining a pile of books on his table, bringing each book closer to the light, inspecting the binding, thumbing the pages and then carefully pricing it with a pencil stub. The pencil scribbles were not just about pricing the books, Neela figured, but also about noting edition and condition – it explained the close inspection of the spine, boards and jacket. She couldn't interrupt him now, she decided, and was about to turn away, when he looked up and smiled.

'Afternoon. So sorry to have kept you waiting.'

Neela was embarrassed at being caught in the act of watching him at work. 'I don't wish to bother you if you're busy,' she said apologetically. 'My question can wait until later, or even until next time – and there's going to be a next time. I can't wait to come again.'

She laughed self-consciously at her eagerness, but he seemed to understand. He had kind eyes, she noticed.

'The afternoons are slow – gives me time to catch up with a little shop work,' he said, pointing to the books on the table. 'But it's always nice to have someone come in. So please ask away.'

'Perhaps you should bill me, Mr Treevis, before I do any more damage to my purse.'

'Martin, please. And I'll accept a cheque, if that makes it easier.'

'I'll keep that in mind for the next time! Oh, and is this really £200?' She handed him the Rackham *Alice*.

'Something like this would cost much, much more, so you're right about questioning the price, but you must have noticed its poor condition. That's one reason for the low pricing. And here's the other.'

Stepping away from his desk, Treevis opened one of the four glass cases that Neela had peered into earlier and removed another copy of what looked like the same book. Turning to the half-title page, he pointed to a signature.

'Heinemann printed just over eleven hundred copies in 1907 and Rackham signed all of them – or thought he had. But there were a few copies in that print run that went unsigned. Now look at the half-title page in your copy.'

It wasn't signed.

'There was, in fact, a limited edition of five hundred and fifty copies that followed the trade copies, but they weren't signed by Rackham, because he was apparently travelling when the book was in production. So it's mostly the trade edition that carries the signature, which is interesting, because it's usually the other way around.'

He handed her the signed copy. The condition of this copy was far better; it had been nicely preserved. So now she was actually holding a copy that Rackham had signed. She peeked at the price: £1,200. Running her hands over the half-title page, she stopped just before the signature, feeling goosebumps. She stared at Treevis.

'I'm holding a book that Rackham once held,' she murmured.

He laughed. 'That's the way it goes,' he said.

Neela handed it back to him and picked up the unsigned copy. 'This is still such a lovely copy,' she said, turning the pages, admiring the illustrations, unwilling to let it go.

'Isn't it, though? That's why I keep them. And

they are still scarce, you know. If you're interested in that sort of thing, I have some very nice children's illustrated reprints for much less.'

'I've been looking for some children's illustrated books that I used to own as a child,' she told him. 'I would gaze at the illustrations in them long after I had finished re-reading the stories. I must have lost interest in them or just forgotten about them when I grew up, in the sad way we do with most things from our childhood. But I've never forgotten the illustrations; one was a book of fairy tales and one of the stories in it was "The Princess and the Pea", with a full-page illustration of an enormous bed, with mattress upon mattress piled high on it in exotic, iridescent colours.'

'Ah, Dulac!' he exclaimed in recognition. 'I know the one. And you're in luck, because I think I have one lying about somewhere. Let me dig it out.'

He continued talking as he pottered around his bookshop, looking for the book.

'That's fantastic!' Neela said. 'I've asked around at so many second-hand bookshops, but none of them seemed to have a clue what I was talking about.'

'Some think Edmund Dulac's illustrations were superior even to Rackham's. He was absorbed in studying Indian and Persian miniatures and their influence was strong in most things he illustrated, highlighting them with a touch of Oriental mystery. His colour plates were "a cornucopia of Eastern fantasy, colour feasts for the eyes", I recall one critic saying. He did his best work for Hodder and Stoughton. There's a 1909 *Rubaiyat* he illustrated that is a classic. It marked the birth centenary of Fitzgerald. I used to have the original edition once. Now even reprints are hard to find. Let's see, I think I have the Dulac you want. *Stories from Hans Andersen*, a kind of gift book he made in 1911, with twenty-eight colour plates. What's the other one you're looking for?'

'Well, all I can remember is that there were these extraordinary pictures of wild animals – they were lifelike, detailed and yet with mythic qualities to them.'

'Ah! I don't have that one, I'm afraid. I could keep an eye out for it for you.'

'But you know the book?' Neela asked.

'I know the illustrator – E.J. Detmold. He's fascinating, totally fascinating. He illustrated so many fables with animals in them; I don't know which one you had. There was a 1909 Aesop's *Fables*, *Birds and Beasts* and Kipling's *The Second Jungle Book*, from 1910 or 1911, I forget now. At his peak, he turned a recluse and eventually committed suicide. A great artist of fantasy.'

'Thank you so much for the Dulac and for taking the time to talk.'

'If you can drop in another time, I'll keep the

other reprints aside for you to look at. Remember, there's no obligation to buy any of them just because I put them together for you. It'll be a pleasure to have someone looking at them. That was the golden age of children's illustrated books, you know, 1905 to 1920 – Cruikshank, Tenniel, the Dalziel brothers, Lear, Crane, Greenaway, Caldecott, Pogany, Detmold, Dulac, Nielsen, Potter, Shepard...so many more I'm forgetting.'

Neela resisted the impulse to take the afternoon off from work and simply linger there for the rest of the day, perhaps coax the owner into some more shop talk or even check out the other bookshops on the street to see if they were antiquarian too. She settled the bill, thanked Treevis as she left, saying she would return.

'Oh, yes, please *do*.'

Walking back to the office with a broad grin on her face, clutching her bag of antiquarian loot, Neela passed several rare and fine bookshops on the street and wondered how she could have missed coming there before – Cecil Court cut through St Martin's Lane and Charing Cross, streets she knew well from frequent second-hand bookshop-hopping in the neighbourhood. But none had the antiquarian charm of Cecil Court. And it was only later that Neela would discover, to her utter delight, that Cecil Court happened to be one of the most celebrated antiquarian bookplaces in London, a street apparently haunted by

English bibliophiles for centuries for its legendary rare-book shops and knowledgeable rare-book traders. For fifty years, it had been Graham Greene's favourite place in London to go book hunting. When the West End and Charing Cross lost their charm for him, he is said to have cried out gratefully, 'But thank God! Cecil Court remains Cecil Court.'

The next afternoon, Neela returned – rushed, in fact – to Treevis's bookshop and lingered there, picking up more antiquarian editions. She devoted her weekends now to combing Cecil Court. Treevis told her it was a great pity that she had missed out on H.M. Fletcher Books and David Low, two of the street's most admired rare and fine-book dealers who had moved now. Away from Cecil Court, she began spending a great deal of time at Bertram Rota, one of the first to specialize in modern first editions and private-press books. She left till the last the antiquarian heavies of London: Quaritch, Maggs, Sotheran, Pickering, Harington. They dealt mostly with museum-quality editions and the highest of the high spots, though Neela also realized quickly enough that some books on the shelves of even the most high-end antiquarian bookshops weren't always very expensive or forbidding; if you left the high spots alone in their locked bookcases and their strong rooms, some of the stock was temptingly affordable. Book-hunting in London now became a weekend obsession. Is it to be Rota or Treevis, Neela would ask herself and then set off.

Neela's book-hunting trips also took her out of London to the provincial bookshops in the country, where she acquired a few personal favourites (much, much later, after she had left Britain, she would regret not stumbling upon the first bookshop in the world to deal exclusively with in-print, contemporary-press books – Charlene Garry's Basilisk Bookshop, still a legend, though now no more). However, she was able to hook up with other bookshops that continued the Basilisk tradition of focusing on the book arts, stocking in-print contemporary private-press books such as Claude Cox Old & Rare Books, Sophie Schneideman Rare Books and Prints, and Collinge and Clark (whose storefront had doubled as the bookshop in the cult BBC comedy, *Black Books*).

Neela was rapidly soaking it all in; she could never have enough of the antiquarian book world which, she was discovering, meant more than rare-book shops and rare-book dealers; it was studded with all kinds of other marvellous and brilliant characters. Just as exciting to discover was the parallel world of the scholar-book dealer, book runners, private-press printers and auction houses; the learned catalogues of E.P. Goldschmidt, the witty bibliophile writings of A.N.L. Munby and John Carter, the highly charged atmosphere at Sotheby's under Christopher de Hamel and the charming essays of Carter, Muir, Munby, Sparrow and Sadlier, known, sometimes, as the Biblio Boys (but why no Biblio Girls, she couldn't help wonder), which fetchingly expressed the joy a modest collector felt in building up a particular collection and accurately described the pleasures of the hunt. What these modern bookmen, contemporaries at Oxford and Cambridge in the twenties and thirties, had accomplished was to replace the much-caricatured, fusty image of the antiquarian book collector and bookseller as the near-sighted, absent-minded, stooped antiquarian with a vivacious new image of the bookman (and the bookwoman) – sharp-witted, with elegant and dashing personalities.

And then you had Driff, the fascinating and mysterious Driff or Dryfield, London's most famous – or perhaps infamous – book runner along with Martin Stone. Their knowledge of rare books, uncommon editions, and where they could be lying hidden, undiscovered and underpriced, was legendary. The book finds would later be sold to collectors or dealers at their true market price. However, there was also some mystery surrounding Driff – he had suddenly disappeared. Vanished, without a trace. Occasionally there were rumours in the book trade that he had been sighted for a minute somewhere before he vanished again; or that he had vanished in India. Driff, Neela learnt to her astonishment, was a vegetarian with a love for Indian food and women (especially those in sarees). On his long book-hunting trips all over Britain he would just as single-mindedly search for Indian restaurants to feast on a vegetarian thali as look for obscure bookshops. It would be most interesting, Neela thought, to run into Driff, but where was the man? He was simply not to be found.

When her knowledge of bibliophilic culture expanded to include Europe, she stumbled upon an even more radically new image of the modern bibliophile in the writings of the French dandy Octave Uzanne and his circle of book collectors who deplored the idea of the passive collector, a materialistic hoarder of books. Their idea of a collector was someone who actually took part in the production of a fine book. A true collector in this New Bibliopolis had to participate in the making of at least one finely printed book. Uzanne, the prince of bibliophilia, called this 'creative bibliophily'.

Neela began to feel a growing sense of book connoisseurship in her. Something the stylish bookman John Carter had said – 'Book collecting is the orchid in the hothouse of connoisseurship' – suddenly made sense to her.

One day, a staffer at Maggs, a friendly soul who had always had a welcoming smile for her, told her about the London Rare Books School and its intensive five-day seminar in book connoisseurship. Neela looked it up and was pleased to read what the school had to say about the course: 'Close encounters with some of the rarest books and manuscripts in the world, access to the collections at the British Library, a deep appreciation for the materiality of the book, a study of bound structures as cultural artefacts, renowned international book scholars for teachers and, perhaps, best of all, a reception hosted by major London antiquarian booksellers who might be persuaded to take you on as an intern.'

Neela lost no time in enrolling at the London Rare Books School. Thirteen seminars held on Monday and Friday afternoons, with the rest of the time given to visits to rare-book libraries and museums, where you could actually handle the usually hands-off material. Armed now with a certification, Neela resigned from her part-time gig at The Nehru Centre and took the plunge by responding to an advertisement for a cataloguer at Cavendish Rare Books, another distinguished rare-book seller in London. She got the job and, in less than a year, was heading one of their sections, buying heavily for her department, bidding at auctions and walking the floors of antiquarian book fairs.

Her flat was now crammed with her own rare-book purchases. She had begun buying and investing heavily and was a well-known customer now, not only on Cecil Court, but throughout England's antiquarian book trade, which flourished even in the countryside. Treevis, with his old network of dealers and runners, helped her source good books and avail of the best trade discounts. She was specializing now, focusing sharply on antiquarian Indian material, fine bindings, illustrated books and children's literature. It was during those yearly visits home to see her parents and friends that she became acutely aware of the scarcity of good antiquarian bookshops in India, and it was at this point that the idea of starting one of her own back home began to take root.

She put her central London apartment on the market and when she got an irresistible offer, sold it, left Cavendish (not without feeling a pang, though) and returned to India. She had already shipped out her books (which now numbered over 10,000) months before her actual departure. They were stored carefully and securely at her Adyar home. Once she felt more settled in Chennai, Neela finally opened a by-appointment-only antiquarian bookshop and ran it from her flat in Besant Nagar, which she had bought to work out of, preferring to make the Adyar cottage her home.

It was at this time that she was introduced to Arcot Manovalan Templar of Heritage Auctions, an Indian auction house that dealt solely with books, eschewing art and antiques. She persuaded Templar to part with Heritage's list of client-collectors, and one of the most promising and distinguished from that list turned out to be Nallathambi Whitehead, who then went on to become her best customer, buying heavily from her, offering her many commissions. By then, she had accumulated a large inventory of British and American books – antiquarian, rare modern firsts, signed copies and fine editions, but like nearly every other antiquarian dealer in the world, her stock too had only a less-than-modest inventory of Indian material. The occasional antiquarian Indian book that turned up at auctions or at the odd second-hand bookshop was invariably in poor condition and had to be restored, decreasing not only its value, but the pleasure of owning a book, printed in India, from the eighteenth or nineteenth century still in its original cloth binding, with clean pages. The more sophisticated the restoration, the less charming the copy.

Neela was determined to make up for the lack of Indian antiquarian material by building her inventory of modern Indian material. She focused all her energy, knowledge and resources on finding first editions of modern Indian authors, signed and association copies, thus forging an entirely new path of collecting for Indian bibliophiles – modern first and signed editions of Indian authors, a line of collecting not previously imagined or pursued.

They had finished their coffee a while ago. Now, Neela brought out two cans of cold beer and handed one to Kayal. The morning had gone by quickly, and all this book talk had made them both thirsty. A bottle of wine, too, was proffered. And now, said Neela, it was Kayal's turn to talk about her own communion with books as artefacts.

21

A True Instance of Tamil Bibliomania

Kayal had just finished up her master's degree in history from Stella Maris and the usual route of studing history at Jawaharlal Nehru University, New Delhi, had suddenly begun to lose its appeal after she discovered that the School of Cultural Texts and Records at Jadavpur University, Kolkata, offered short-term courses in book history and print culture. She jumped at the chance and enrolled without wasting too much time. Here, students were taught to prepare bibliographies, compile bibliographical catalogues, edit manuscripts and printed texts, investigate the history of publishing and printing, collect all sorts of ephemera and street literature and archive documents and manuscripts of modern writers. One of the professors here, Dr Abhijit Gupta, had worked in and published extensively on print culture, and was even working on the history of the book in Bengal.

The city, then Calcutta, had been home to some of the first bookshops in India dealing in antiquarian material. Cambray, and Thacker and Spink came first, and just when they were sizing down, Kumar's sprang up in the mid 1940s to keep antiquarian bookselling alive. Kumar's was owned and run by Nirmal Chandra Kumar, the city's most magnificent antiquarian and rare-book man who had never been sufficiently remembered, celebrated and honoured outside Bengal. His son Aloke Kumar had kept his father's memory alive through various blog posts that Kayal had read with pleasure and surprise. From 1945 until his death in 1976, Nirmal Chandra Kumar had run a rare-book shop from his home. He was probably the first Indian bookseller to publish a rare-book catalogue in the long tradition of all accomplished antiquarian booksellers around the world, especially the legends Kumar had done business with – Quaritch and Maggs.

The city's bibliophiles, artists, luminaries, antiquarians and bohemians all frequented Kumar's. Satyajit Ray, a regular browser here, consulted Kumar when he was directing *Shatranj ke Khiladi*; at a London book auction, Kumar had bid for and won a priceless scrapbook on the 1857 Mutiny. Ray went on to pay his own little tribute to Kumar in the character of the encyclopaedic 'Sidhu Jetha' in the Feluda stories.

Kayal spent a good part of many weekends in the city eating phuchka and book-crawling through Free School Street and College Street. Inspired by what she was hearing in class about the city's bibliophile history, she trawled the wares of the book hawkers on these streets for something unusual, a find she could make. But if these streets had once been home to hidden print treasures you could ferret out, there was little now that seemed scarce or rare – or even remotely antiquarian. It was, disastrously, mostly all textbooks! But here and there, a few second-hand bookshops still gave off a whiff of the old bookselling tradition, prompting Kayal to ask herself: What was it *she* wanted to collect? After considerable pondering, she concluded that she wanted to focus on what she knew best and loved, and what was also within her resources to buy: Interesting editions of modern literature. First printings of hypermoderns to start with – the easiest to find in bookshops or with pavement hawkers and then, when occasionally chancing on some deluxe or special edition, grabbing it even if it cost her a pretty paisa, like the set of *Griffin and Sabine* books by Nick Bantock that turned up at a Free School Street book stall. From this, it wasn't difficult to make the jump to collecting editions printed in India.

Kayal now became relentless in her search for modern Indian editions with an interesting print history. She began scouring second-hand bookshops for Jaico paperbacks from the forties and fifties, Hind Pocket Books from the sixties, the Indian Thought Publication paperbacks R.K. Narayan had issued from Mysore from the late forties (she found a ratty, but fairly scarce copy of *The Bachelor of Arts* with a 1952 copyright). She hunted for Indian hardcover editions with book jackets that looked like they might be first printing. She came away with a bunch of interesting editions, many firsts with dust jackets intact, from that ground-breaking new period in Indian English fiction: The 1999 India Ink *The Trotter-Nama,* the 1996 Ravi Dayal *The Calcutta Chromosome* and the 1994 *Beethoven among the Cows*, the 1980 Penguin *The Householder* and the 1964 *Sunlight on a Broken Column*, the 1936 Orient Paperback *Coolie* and the 1968 *The Foreigner*, the 1954 Jaico *Nectar in a Sieve*, the 1965 Hind Pocket Books *The Cat and Shakespeare* and the 1988 Vision Books *The Chessmaster and his Moves*.

Two exceptional finds were the G.V. Desanis: the 1968 New Delhi Arnold-Heinemann copy of *All about H. Hatterr* and the fragile 1967 Calcutta Writers Workshop's *Hali*, each picked up for ₹65. Out of print and hard to find. But her best book-hunting coup she considered to be something else – G.V. Desani again, but an honest-to-God find, even as Desanis went:

A bound set of the *Illustrated Weekly of India*, which just happened to contain his short stories as they appeared originally for the first time in these issues.

Kayal didn't know too much about regional pulp fiction, but found so many Hindi and Bengali paperbacks with such striking cover art that she couldn't resist getting the lot of them. She would later discover to her delight that several of these had cover art by Mustajab Ahmed Siddiqui, better known to readers as 'Shelle', one of the last great pulp cover artists, who was now beginning to be collected.

During several lectures by Professor Gupta at Jadavpur, she would hear of Bengali collectors in Kolkata who simply collected everything in print form they could get hold of, from booklets to pamphlets to *heto* books or street literature – regional pulp sold on trains and buses. The last thing Kayal collected before she left Kolkata was as many pamphlet titles as she could find from P. Lal's Writers Workshop. Rightly assessing that one day they would be collected, she particularly sought out those beautiful hand-blocked textile covers stamped in gold.

Kayal now became more curious to discover possible instances of such bibliophilia in Tamil Nadu, her home state, and shifted her focus there, with three possible places to begin a new line of research: The Maraimalai Adigal Library, the RMRL and the famed Sarasvati Mahal Library in Thanjavur. She divided her time between the three book centres, but for her thesis Kayal finally homed in on RMRL, which had begun with the core collection of the bibliomane, Raja Muthiah Chettiar. Here she worked on the methods and forms of collecting as displayed and exemplified by this maverick collector, with a particular focus on the bibliography of cinema and theatre handbills in the Roja Muthiah collection.

In their website note on their collector, the RMRL said that it was sometime in the fifties that Muthiah left the little Chettinad town of Kottaiyur to start a small business in Madras as a signboard painter. He called it Roja Arts. His father had already instilled in him a love for books and now, when he did the rounds of the bookstalls in Moore Market (a kind of booksellers' row in Madras near the railway station that was later destroyed in a suspicious fire), Muthiah began buying heavily; each week would see a large number of book purchases. Newspaper scrap dealers had standing orders to comb through the papers they hoarded to put aside for him any printed material that seemed interesting. His particular focus in collecting was gathering ephemera: Tamil songbooks, theatre and cinema handbills and devotional chapbooks – forms of print that libraries usually ignored. A large part of his family fortune went into acquiring palm-leaf manuscripts, whenever such rare items crept into the market.

There seemed to be more than one version about his book-collecting days and Kayal found it difficult to get all the facts straight. Some had his collection numbered at 50,000; others claimed it was not quite that high. And, one day, apparently, they were all gone – stolen! But he began collecting all over again, starting from scratch and building up his collection to the volume he had once achieved. The story went that the entire collection was stolen yet again, though a particular historian Kayal met would claim that neither of the thefts had taken place. Whatever the truth, Muthiah apparently began collecting furiously now, more than ever before, and the collection grew larger than anything he had had earlier. Meanwhile, his signboard business had suffered and he didn't feel safe in Madras any more.

Muthiah moved his family and business back to Kottaiyur and, with them, his monumental collection, housing it in his ancestral home. He now pursued book dealers beyond Madras, searching far and wide across Tamil Nadu. His collection outgrew his ancestral house and he had to rent two concrete sheds nearby to store it in. He collected obsessively and, in the best tradition of bibliomaniacs, indiscriminately. He spent up to sixteen hours with his books at times, taking them off the shelves, dusting them and replacing them. He periodically sprayed the shelves with insecticide to keep silverfish and cockroaches at bay. It's probable that some of the poison from the insecticide affected him, for he became very ill. He knew the insecticide wasn't doing him any good, but he never stopped working with the books, indexing and cross-referencing them with the help of his children. He allowed scholars to browse through and consult the books. He charged a token fee of ₹10 to use his collection on a daily basis and this included coffee and lunch, which he plied them unfailingly with sustenance.

In perhaps one of several such instances, a Tamil scholar from Malaysia wrote of his hunt for *Varai Mallai*, an out-of-print book from the nineteenth century, which was basically a sheaf of palm leaves. He was told that if anyone had it, it would be Roja Muthiah. When the scholar finally tracked him down to Kottaiyur, he found it in Muthiah's collection. He asked to borrow it, but Muthiah said he couldn't possibly let it out of his sight. However, as the scholar prepared to leave, Muthiah pressed the copy into his hand, insisting over the feeble protests of his visitor that the book belonged to someone who knew its true worth, someone like him who had come from far away in search of it.

Towards the end, Muthiah became too ill to manage the collection and began looking for a buyer, someone who could buy the collection en bloc, not separately. The Tamil writer Ambai, who had once consulted the books in his library, mentioned it to the department of South Asian Languages and Civilizations at the University of Chicago, which immediately raised the funds to buy the collection. The books, packed in waterproof boxes, were transported in five trucks to Madras. They formed the nucleus of the RMRL collection. Muthiah was sixty-six when he died on 4 June 1992 of suspected exposure to insecticide poisoning.

Kayal's interest in the RMRL collection earned her an internship at the research library. And it was here that she met Neela and abandoned her plans to continue her doctoral work at Jadavpur University when Neela asked her if she would come work as an associate and help set up a brick-and-mortar antiquarian bookshop in Chennai to be called Biblio.

Part Five

22

The K Fragment

On a rainy Saturday morning, unusually damp for March, Kenton Selvaganesan turned up at Biblio with the alleged Burton material. Being the weekend, things were busy, but Pokisha had volunteered to be at the desk for the day. Earlier in the week, Kenton had called and agreed to a meeting with them. He would travel down to Chennai on Friday, he had confirmed, and meet them on the following day at the bookshop. He would bring along the Burton material. A rare bookshop would give the history teacher a sense of the antiquarian world he was about to enter, the world of collectors and dealers that would, perhaps, impress him enough to trust them with his Burton discovery.

Nallathambi Whitehead made it a point to arrive at Biblio quite early on that Saturday, impatient and anxious. While they waited for the history teacher to show up, Kayal tried to keep the collector distracted with Biblio's recent acquisitions but, contrary to his usual eagerness to know about any addition to Biblio's treasures, he barely glanced at them.

By the time Neela arrived with Kenton fifteen minutes later, having picked him up from the Book Arts Centre where they had put him up for the night, Whitehead was furiously pacing the bookshop muttering, 'Where are they? Where are they?'

As he caught sight of Kayal in the store, Kenton smiled broadly in recognition. Neela introduced him to the collector and Whitehead shook Kenton's hand vigorously, murmuring, 'At last, at last,' before ushering them into her office.

Kenton looked a little intimidated and whispered, 'Thank you for meeting me.'

Inside the office, even before they had all taken their seats, Whitehead thrust out his hand towards Kenton, asking to see the Burton papers. From a rather weathered leather valise, the schoolteacher removed two books in attractive bindings, an envelope and a folder and placed them all on the table.

'The books, the letter in the original postmarked mailing envelope and the folder with the Karachi Papers were all found in this beaten-down valise which, in all probability, belonged to Burton,' Kenton said. He caressed the books a little, before gently nudging one of them towards the collector. 'I've already told you that the books contain Burton's ownership signature and manuscript annotations, but I haven't yet said anything about what these books *are*. Take a look, Mr Whitehead. You'll be pleased.'

The collector picked up the first book and looked at the fading gilt spines. 'Good God, Burckhardt! *Travels in Arabia*!'

Neela gave a low, appreciative whistle and said to Kayal, 'That's one hell of an association copy. Burton used Burckhardt's notes for his Hajj trip and had found the Swiss explorer to be a great inspiration.'

'Are you telling me that if I open these books now, I'm going to be looking at Burton's scribbles in the margins?' asked Whitehead, excitement palpable in his voice.

'In *Travels in Arabia*, yes. Now this one...' Kenton slid the second book across to the incredulous collector, '*Travels in Nubia*...is Burckhardt's own copy. It contains *his* ownership signature and date, *and* Burton's marginalia.'

'Burton was using Burckhardt's own copy? Extraordinary!'

Kenton then handed the envelope with the Parvathy–Burton letter to the collector, explaining, 'You've already seen a photocopy of this.'

After a quick study of the manuscript hand in the books and the letter, Whitehead declared he was in no doubt that it was Burton's own. Though not as familiar with the autograph hand of the Swiss explorer, he was simply ecstatic at the idea of such a highly desirable association copy being available. The books were passed around for everyone at the table to look at. Both books were in their original boards (most copies of this explorer's early editions were usually found rebound in quarter leather and marble boards) and still had the author's frontispiece and half-title page. They were both second editions from 1822 and 1829, John Murray, London. It was a thrilling experience for Kayal to see the two at one go and in such close proximity, as they lay next to each other on Neela's table – not just Burton's manuscript hand in the books, but that of Burckhardt's as well, a scarcer hand to find and, in some sense, that of Burton's true master.

'I *must* have both copies now!' pleaded Whitehead. 'I'm sorry if I'm sounding vulgar, but name your price and we'll settle it right away.'

'But don't you want to see the Karachi Report fragment first?' asked Kenton, placing his palm on the folder.

Whitehead reached for the folder, his hands trembling in anticipation.

'I think, before any of you look at it,' said Kenton, making the collector pause, 'perhaps you should hear how I came – or think I came – to have this in my possession. And just as importantly, *what* it is that I claim to have.'

Whitehead reluctantly returned the folder to the table.

'The first thing I want to set straight,' said the schoolteacher, 'is that what I have in my possession – that is, what my family has had for generations in their keep – is only a *fragment* of what I think could be the Karachi Report, not the document in its entirety. It is in Burton's handwriting, though his signature is not present anywhere. And it's easy to see why: Burton didn't want to be officially associated with it. If you recall, he says – I think it was in the "Terminal Essay" – that he went undercover to complete this mission for Napier. The fragment I have with me looks like either the last two pages or the first two pages of a longer report. The two pages are on regiment stationery; the paper is watermarked "1846". Mr Whitehead, though this is not the complete report – its other pages were probably destroyed or lost – it is still going to interest you and, I imagine, every Burton collector.

'Now, the Karachi Report contains Burton's investigative findings about what went on in those underground brothels, solicited by British soldiers. As you all probably know, some scholars have speculated that Burton's "Terminal Essay" – that supplement to his translation of the *Arabian Nights* – might possibly contain traces of his findings from the lost or missing Karachi Report that would eventually get him into trouble. The details the "Terminal Essay" mentions are to be found in these two pages too. The difference is that this fragment which I have with me is the original source – the notes that were initially made. What I have are two pages from what could only be a part of the Karachi Report; the nature of the pages' contents indicates that these may have served either as a kind of preface to the report or as its appendix. The report, you remember, is meant to contain Burton's graphic description of what went on in these male brothels. These pages, however, are – I suppose somewhat disappointingly for some – devoid of the kind of detailed anthropological survey and description of sexual acts that Burton is famous for. They are, instead, itemized listings, gathered surreptitiously – possibly, even undercover – by Burton, of the various sexual services offered by the brothels and a list of the kind of clients that frequented them. What remains exciting and significant about the contents of this fragment is that it confirms the rumours Burton had heard: That boys were for hire and that some of the clients, shockingly – or, perhaps, not so shockingly – were actually high-ranking British officers. So while not exactly the full Karachi Report, the fragment tells us why Burton and Napier considered it scandalous enough to suppress or destroy.'

Here Kenton stopped, looked around at his audience and asked, 'How am I doing so far?'

'You have our attention,' Whitehead replied, 'but now to the main thing: How did you come to have it?'

'Hold on,' Kenton said. 'Let me first finish describing the fragment before you.'

Whitehead was about to interject again, but the schoolteacher held up his hand and said, 'There's another aspect to these meagre two pages that will make this an even more significant discovery... It may clear up something Burton scholars and collectors have speculated about for a long time.'

Had she actually caught the collector licking his lips, Kayal wondered, as she saw him lean forward to hear what was coming.

'In the margins of the second page, there is a scribble or a footnote, a kind of author's note to himself, and it says:

"*It now seems the only way I can confirm some details of what goes on here, things that are only whispered about on these premises, is to sample what is on offer myself. But should I, can I? Napier has already thrown a fit over his officers indulging in all sorts of homosexual porneia.*"'

Kenton paused and looked meaningfully at his audience. Kayal couldn't help noticing how different Whitehead and Neela's reactions were to this excerpt, the implications of which were clear to them all:

While the collector drew his breath in sharply, Neela was shaking her head, looking quite amused.

'Ah,' said Whitehead, 'you are referring to the tone of playful ambiguity Burton maintains throughout the "Terminal Essay", always making the reader wonder whether he had personally participated in any of the activities at the brothel.'

Noting Kayal's puzzlement, Neela explained, 'While Burton had no inhibitions about confessing that he had indulged in all kinds of sexual practices with women, he remained ambiguous and teasing in his references to his relationship with men. Scholars can only speculate as to whether he was bisexual. Several feel that he was not and his interest in sexuality was, in all likelihood, just ethnographic.'

'Yes,' agreed Kenton, 'but this note is also the first document that specifically and overtly indicates that Burton had actually considered it; had, perhaps, even gone so far as to sleep with one of them. What he's referring to here, I'm guessing, is the variety of tricks offered at these "boy brothels". Gay and queer, of course, have replaced "homosexual" today, but we have to remember that in Burton's day the term "homosexual" was considered acceptable.'

The schoolteacher paused for a moment, and then continued, his audience now leaning in to listen more intently. 'Right, then. Let me move on to how my family came upon this fragment. And I'll try to keep this short. I've always grown up with the notion in my head that our family – on my mother's side – are direct descendants of Sir Richard Francis Burton; a great-great-grandmother, some six generations removed, had been Burton's secret mistress during his brief furlough in Ooty. Her name was Parvathy Illankeeran and she was a nurse at the sanitorium where Burton was being cared for. He was recovering from fatigue that had set in following repeated bouts of fever in Karachi and was also being treated for an eye infection – which would develop into something called rheumatic ophthalmia. He had started showing the symptoms shortly after his arrival in Ooty. It is for the eye infection that he needed constant care and that's what Parvathy provided.

'Once he was on the mend, she found him restless and impatient with life at the club, yearning to mingle with some interesting locals, instead – preferably Indian women. Single British women at the club were both few and snobbish, taking a romantic interest in men only if they were officers. For his part, Burton had no interest in the married women who made themselves available, as the prospect of having affairs with them simply didn't tempt him.'

'Unless the woman happened to be Indian!' Whitehead retorted with a guffaw.

'Quite so. Parvathy was drawn to him and Burton took quick notice of it, asking to see more of her socially. It began innocently enough, with him wanting her to teach him Tamil, which he actually began learning in earnest. He was at this point already learning Telugu, but from a proper tutor. Burton was keen on knowing more about Parvathy's world – her circle of friends, her family. It was also his way of getting away from Ooty's club life, which he despised. Perhaps Burton got bored with it all, lost interest in Parvathy, discovered she was pregnant; whatever be the reason, he seemed to have left Ooty abruptly, cutting short his leave.

'Parvathy wasn't heartbroken; it was just that she hadn't been ready or prepared for this. She was with his child, but wouldn't tell him, fearing that he might read it as a ploy to entrap him and hold him back in Ooty. Or perhaps she couldn't tell him because she discovered she was pregnant only after he had left Ooty. After his departure, Burton would contact her only once, writing her the letter you now see in front of you. One gets the feeling that he did it for the sake of courtesy, because he expresses nothing of what he had once felt for her. And he never wrote to her again.

'She had the child – a daughter. She came from a traditional Tamil home and the birth, inevitably, was a scandal of sorts. Parvathy was disowned and she raised the child on her own. If there was one thing she refused to do, it was to run away from Ooty. She never married and threw herself into her job, devoting her life to her daughter whom she named Francesca Kalaiarasi. Her daughter settled in Ooty, like her mother, and cared for her until her death. Parvathy's story has loomed large in our family's history; every generation knows it and relates it to the next. My mother brought me up on it; she tells me she began whispering it to me when I was still in her womb.

'A key element in the story is the trunk; the few things that belonged to Parvathy, a little suitcase that contained some clothes – mostly nursing uniforms – a few photographs, some exercise notebooks and the valise that held these papers you see before you now. Because of the nature of its contents – a report regarding male brothels in Sindh, with reference to the British soldiers and officers who frequented it – my mother never showed it to me until I was twenty. I believe it has been the same for the children from previous generations. In fact, you only heard of its existence after you were old enough to understand, accept and come to terms with it. Nobody in my family had thought to make the papers public. I was the first one to entertain the idea. Times have changed, I feel, and my mother agrees. I am doing this with her blessings. Probably, nobody in the family had fully realized their financial and bibliographical value before my mother and I. We need the money and those devoted to Burton – scholars, collectors and a curious world – would be interested in knowing the truth: That the explorer had not fabricated such a report, that it had, indeed, been the reason for his disgrace in India.'

23

More Burtoniana

'Fantastic, absolutely fantastic!' murmured Whitehead, his fingers itching to touch the papers lying so casually now on the table. 'But,' he added, 'no one in your family knows why Burton left these papers with Parvathy, is that correct? None of you know how these papers came to be with her?'

'No, we don't. He trusted Parvathy, felt safe with her; she was so far removed from his world that he felt he could entrust them to her. At least, that's how I've explained it to myself.'

'A simpler explanation, according to me,' Neela interjected, 'is that Burton could, possibly, have forgotten his leather valise when he left?'

'That may well have been the case,' replied Whitehead, 'but it doesn't throw any more light on his actions.'

From his laptop bag, Kenton now removed another folder.

'This second folder contains the only documents related directly to Parvathy: Her birth certificate, some photographs of her, of Francesca Kalaiarasi, her daughter, and of her family and, perhaps, of more use as provenance – photocopies of records showing that she had worked as a nurse in the Ootacamund sanitorium during those Burton years.'

Kenton took the documents out of the second folder and passed the photographs around. Parvathy was more striking than beautiful, thought Kayal, and one could easily see why Burton would have been drawn to this woman. But it was their daughter, Francesca, with her high cheekbones, dark complexion and sparkling eyes, who had been the real beauty.

'Now, finally, let me pass around what I think could be the Karachi Fragment.' Kenton handed the folder to Kayal first. 'Since you came all the way to Ooty to see it and then couldn't,' he said and though he was smiling encouragingly at her, Kayal felt nervous and self-conscious.

'Listen, Ms Anbuchelvan,' chortled Whitehead, 'I've waited my whole life for this and I think I can afford to wait another few minutes – but no longer!'

It was just two pages, on ordinary stationery paper, listing names and addresses, the kinds of services offered at these male brothels and the prices charged for them. Apart from the list, which covered both pages, there were brief footnotes for a few entries, elaborating on the type of service offered. Kayal found it difficult to read Burton's hand; much of it looked hastily scribbled with a blue-ink pen. She turned the second page sideways to read the note to self Burton had jotted. Kayal felt a thrill within her as she ran her fingers over the handwritten words. Then, without delaying any further, she passed the folder on to the impatient collector.

'Nallathambi, I think we'll leave you alone with the papers now,' said Neela. 'I can go through them afterwards.' She gestured to the others to follow her out of her office room to give Whitehead the privacy he needed.

Once they were outside, the women asked Kenton if he would like a tour of the bookshop and he enthusiastically agreed. So they set off, leaving the collector to his rendezvous with this phantom-like piece of Burton ephemera, always whispered about, but never seen. That is, Kayal checked herself, if it was, indeed, the real thing. Well, she thought, we'll know in a short time.

'Nallathambi,' Neela had told her, 'would be the first to spot anything amiss in the papers, having spent years chasing Burton material. And then, of course, the usual step of authentication by Burton manuscript experts will follow.'

Fifteen minutes later, when they joined the collector in the office, they found him wearing an inscrutable expression on his face.

'I think, my dear Neelambari,' he said at last, 'we may have found that unholy grail after all.'

Neela laughed, pleased for him.

Kayal, delighted at what she was witnessing, glanced Kenton's way and noticed that he was just staring at the papers in Whitehead's hands. My God, she thought, it's hitting him fully now: That the manuscript Burton scholars and collectors had been pursuing in vain for more than a century was no longer just his family's private possession – it now belonged to the world.

'Well, come on! Is it as salacious and sensational as it is rumoured to be?' Kayal teased the collector.

'More so, my dear, much more so!' Whitehead exclaimed, looking chuffed.

'Let's not get carried away until it's fully authenticated,' Neela cautioned. 'More for Kenton's sake, than the collectors'.'

If, in the end, they turned out *not* to be the elusive Karachi Papers, the collector would sulk for a while and move on to the next conquest. Kenton, however, would be shattered; he seemed to have pinned all his hopes for a new future on staking a claim as Burton's unknown heir. Neela spent the next few minutes looking through the papers herself and Kayal could see that her boss was satisfied, even pleased, by what she saw. Neela put the papers away carefully back in the valise, and asked if anyone would like some tea.

'I think all of us would!' Whitehead said emphatically. 'And it would be nice to have it in the garden.'

'I'll make the tea and bring it out,' Neela said. As they shuffled out of the office and made their way out of the bookshop, Kayal lingered for a few moments in the office to tidy up and put the valise away in the safe while her boss saw to the tea.

In the garden, Whitehead addressed Kenton. 'I'm satisfied this is in Burton's hand and the voice in the text is vividly his own; the paper on which it is written too seems to be of that period. But I suppose any discussion of a price should come after the papers have been green-lighted by experts.'

'What does that involve?' asked Kenton.

'The standard procedure involves having it authenticated – an analysis of handwriting, paper and ink. The process is carried out by authorities we know in each of those areas,' Neela explained as she came out with the tea.

Whitehead continued, 'I'll have Nambeesan flown in from Thiruvananthapuram to authenticate Burton's handwriting and then we can move on to the rest – paper, ink and so on. I'll be very surprised if the inferences drawn are anything other than what we think we have here. But I am willing to wait. I've waited for forty years and a few more weeks won't matter now.' He paused. 'I'm feeling a little tired now, and I think I should be on my way.'

The collector slowly got up from the garden bench, steadied himself with his cane, and turned to head for the gate. 'Wait! Kenton,' he said suddenly, turning around, 'have you made any copies of it?'

'I made a PDF scan and it's on my laptop,' Kenton told him. 'But at this point, you'll appreciate my reservations about putting the scan on a flash drive and handing it over.'

'Fair enough,' said Whitehead. 'Of course, I can't wait to look at it again, but I won't deny myself the pleasure of sitting down with the manuscript, when it eventually becomes mine, to pore over in the privacy and comfort of my library.'

'So, Mr Selvaganesan, would you like to leave the Burton material with Biblio, then?' Neela asked. 'It will be very safe here. And I can begin the first steps towards authenticating it.'

'I'm afraid I can't do that,' Kenton replied, a new note of regret in his voice. 'I'm sorry, but as things stand, the authentication process may well be out of our hands.'

Whitehead froze in his tracks and then slowly turned around.

'What on earth makes you say that?' he asked. 'As the buyer, I have a right to examine all of it, before you put a price on it.'

There was a flicker of hesitation on Kenton's part and that was enough for Whitehead to sense a new development.

'What's happened?' he asked, his breathing a little short.

'I think what I would like – and what my mother, in particular, would want – is to put the K Fragment up for auction.'

'Why did you come to me in the first place, then?' the collector snarled.

'Our transaction, satisfying as it would have been financially, would have also remained private. But I want to be known for who I am, who my family is – to make it known to all those for whom Burton matters. That I am his descendant and the only solid proof of this is the Karachi Papers, notorious as they may be. It has become my legacy, my burden.'

'Ha! What would be the point of an auction? I will outbid them all!' thundered Whitehead, his breathing more a wheeze now.

'And if this material is, indeed, the Karachi Papers,' Kenton pressed on, 'the right thing to do would be to give every Burton collector a chance to bid on it.'

'Arcot Templar put you up to this, didn't he?' Whitehead spat out.

'Who's Arcot Templar?' Kenton asked, looking confused. When the collector continued to fume and refused to answer, the schoolteacher looked to Kayal and Neela.

'Templar's Heritage Auctions is the only auction house in India that deals solely with the auction and sale of books,' Neela volunteered. 'Sometimes, his grandiose ambitions get the better of him. But yes, once you make this public, he'll surely go after you to have your Burton material auctioned as a lot with Heritage. But I do need to say this, Mr Selvaganesan: it was unfair of you to have led us all into thinking you would deal solely with us as far as these papers were concerned. Apart from wasting our time, you've made use of our expertise and counsel for nothing.'

'Ms Adigal,' Kenton said, 'I am terribly sorry to drop this on you, believe me, but just before I left Ooty to come here, my mother felt strongly that this couldn't be just about the money or fulfilling the desires of collectors. It had to be about making the story of Burton and Parvathy known to the world. Why, then, you must be wondering, did I follow through with my appointment with all of you today? I felt I should begin by showing the Burton material to whom it would matter, bibliophiles such as you, who would have a deep appreciation and understanding of what the discovery of the K Fragment could mean to Burton collecting and scholarship. Besides, I will confess honestly, though rather sheepishly, that I was hoping to get your professional help on how I should proceed next.'

'I don't think Biblio should be involved any more,' Neela said firmly. 'However, if you are open to it, our suggestion is to bring this up at the next meeting of the Ziegenbalg Club and see what the others feel. The club, Mr Selvaganesan, is a bibliophile society of collectors from all over India, many of them authorities in the fields they collect in. As a seller, you would benefit from such exposure since these collectors would see to the best interests of the K Fragment. Arcot Templar will surely be there, pitching for Heritage. But it will still be up to you to decide whom you want to entrust it to.'

'I would like that very much. It will give me a chance to see what everyone else feels about this,' responded Kenton, making up his mind right away.

Neela touched Whitehead lightly on the shoulder, hoping to placate him. 'Perhaps the best thing to do is to share the exciting news with the club and see what our fellow collectors think ought to be done with the K Fragment,' she said.

Still bristling over Kenton's sudden reversal, Whitehead was in no mood to linger, but Neela urged him to sit down again, cajoling him.

'Nallathambi, aren't you forgetting how much you enjoy the thrill of a chase? Remember your audaciouness at auctions, bidding fearlessly? How long has it been since you really had that kind of fun, how long since you've really dared? You've been acquiring your Burtoniana easily, without the pleasure of the chase. Admit it, you've missed it. And now here is a chance again, after so many years!'

The collector looked sufficiently mollified and said, 'My dear, I've always deferred to you and will do so again – though now, the damn thing is going to cost me dearly; for all I know, I may be going up against the British Library, the Huntington and, for sure, Viscount Pilkington. But it will be mine. It *has* to be mine.'

'So it's best, perhaps, that I continue to keep the Burton material,' said Kenton, looking considerably relieved, 'until it is decided who will take custody of it and complete the authentication process. I think it makes sense to auction all of it – the books with Burton's signature and annotations, the letter to Parvathy and the K Fragment as one lot.'

'That's your choice entirely,' replied Neela.

Kenton rose from the chair. 'I best be going then,' he said, and before he could ask for the Burton valise, Kayal had already dashed back into the bookshop and fetched it for him. 'Thank you for your hospitality, and for your counsel,' he said, addressing the two bookwomen. Whitehead left soon after, still grumbling.

Heading back into the bookshop, Kayal said to Neela, 'I guess I'm not going to be jumping into those biographies, after all. I was rather looking forward to doing a study of Burton.'

'No reason why you still shouldn't, Kayal,' her boss said. 'In fact, I'd like you to. Who knows what Burton material may come on the market next? It's good to be prepared. Besides, Kenton taking this out of our hands doesn't change what an engaging figure Burton is and how much you'll still enjoy digging into his past.'

'The about-face he just did – whatever prompted that?'

'He may have realized that an auction would mean there would be no limit to what the K Fragment could fetch. On the other hand, who knows, we could just be the cynical ones, and that for mother and son it really *is* about finding a kind of vindication for the family through the K Fragment being made known to a Burton audience.'

It had grown quite late again at the bookshop and Kayal told herself she had to put a stop to her new work habit of lingering on at Biblio well after store hours. Paati, as usual, would be patiently waiting with dinner. Kayal decided to leave for the day and get started on the Burton biographies in the morning. She didn't have to be at the shop the next day – her visit to Cheran's garage to learn more about stocking private-press editions at the bookstore was scheduled for later in the afternoon, and she would have the entire morning to read. She would start afresh and make notes as she went along. It was high time she found out more about Burton's years in India.

24

In the 18th Bombay Native Infantry Regiment

The following morning, refreshed after a nourishing breakfast of slow-cooked quinoa sprinkled with organic flaxseed and walnuts, and a flask of strong black coffee, Kayal decided what she needed to do was focus on Burton's India years. The India section seemed the shortest in all the Burton biographies, consisting of some five chapters in each book. It wouldn't take very long for her to read through those parts, she realized, but then there were the two Burton monographs dealing with his time in India, *Goa, and the Blue Mountains* and the two pamphlets on Sindh that were just as crucial to finding out how he felt about his years in India. Another deep, comprehensive and up-to-date source online for primary material that she had discovered was Gavan Tredoux's Burtoniana.org. Her boss as well as Whitehead seemed to have missed out on this. Tredoux had published online, as recently as 2016, *The Book of Burtoniana*, a four-volume collection of Burton's correspondence, as well as recollections by those who knew him. Neela had also suggested she read up on the last few years of Burton's life – the years in Trieste as a consular officer, those spent in his London cottage working on *The Perfumed Garden* and, just as crucially, the years Isabel spent as a widow after her husband's death. In fact, for Isabel's side of the story, Neela had pointed out the Mary S. Lovell biography as being the best. Alongside Lovell's *A Rage to Live*, Kayal also kept open Fawn M. Brodie's *The Devil Drives* and Godsall's *The Tangled Web*.

She made notes as she read, moving from one biography to the other, correlating important events in Burton's life, as seen or interpreted by each of his excellent biographers. Brodie's book was swift and sympathetic; Lovell's was beautiful and intense; Godsall's was meticulous and balanced to the point of being critical of his subject. There were photos of Burton in all the books and Kayal looked at them with interest. Burton, she noted, was tall, with a swarthy complexion and piercing eyes. The eyes seemed to follow her everywhere, so penetrating was his gaze in every photo she looked at. After a morning of reading that threatened to swallow up the afternoon as well, Kayal paused to go over her notes, taking it all in slowly; and a sharper and clearer picture of the explorer began to emerge.

Richard Francis Burton was twenty-one when he reached the shores of Bombay. It was the evening of 27 October 1842. As was customary, he was stationed in a hotel until his posting came through and he could transfer to his regiment. Burton described the lodge as being filthy, reeking of 'tea and curry' all day. Lovell pointed out that Burton kept his remarks on the new country he found himself in deliberately low-key and off-colour, because he didn't want to sound like another breathless, uncritical Victorian travel writer. He deplored those aspects of colonial life among his people that most resembled life in England: The clubs, the snobbishness of its members and the tiresome tea parties.

However, emphasized Lovell, Burton was still the bigoted imperialist who thought God was an Englishman and the British were superior to the 'natives'. He himself would subsequently go on to record the number of times he had kicked a servant when he thought him to be 'lazy'. Kayal realized with a shock and a twinge of sadness that the Richard Burton she had imagined – as a man who always viewed Indians as equals – had been one more myth about this elusive figure.

What he seemed to possess, instead, was a ferocious curiosity, enhanced by a fondness for other languages and cultural, religious and sexual practices of different people that was not always shared by his countrymen. It was his gift for learning languages quickly that allowed him entry into new and alien cultures. A munshi he hired to teach him Hindustani had famously remarked, 'He was a man who could learn languages running.' Burton would always have a strong ethnological interest in anything he saw, touched and smelled here.

About six weeks later, Burton's posting finally came through; he was to join the 18th Regiment of the Bombay Native Infantry in Baroda. In Baroda, he quickly settled into a routine at the cantonment. While the other officers would go off to play billiards or hunt, Burton busied himself with his language lessons, studying for up to twelve hours in a day. Finally, he found the teacher he had been looking for, a Parsee munshi named Dosabhai Sohrabji and with him Burton's lessons were in the early hours of the morning, until 9 a.m. He knew the key to getting a staff appointment was through linguistic proficiency. He had been told, more than once, that 'sensible men who went out to India took one of two lines – they either shot, or they studied languages'.

Kayal had been curious to learn more about Burton's views on hunting; had he enjoyed it, had he disliked it? She discovered that he didn't hunt as often as the others, but had trained to hunt animals in the cruel way everyone trained then: By spearing pariah dogs while on horseback. It sickened him. Once, when he had shot a monkey, he felt severe remorse and wrote that it 'cried like a baby'.

Just four months later, in April, Burton took official leave and returned to Bombay to take his Hindustani exam, which entailed translating two books, reading a handwritten letter, carrying on a conversation with a munshi and writing a paper in the language. The exam was conducted by a reputed scholar named Vans Kennedy and Burton ranked first among the eleven candidates who appeared for it. He was keen now to tackle Gujarati and, on returning to Baroda, found a teacher, a Brahmin called Him Chand.

In June, the monsoon set in and it was relentless. Burton took to his books. The heat and humidity drove him to reading under a table, with a wet cloth spread over it to make him feel cooler. On 10 August 1843, regimental orders came, appointing him interpreter to his corps. A staff appointment! He had worked hard for it and was pleased at the outcome of his efforts. On 16 October in the same year, he travelled again to Bombay to sit for another interpreters' exam. But this time, he had a rival: The Company's best linguist, Lieutenant Palmer Rigby, who knew as many as six languages. Burton beat him, stunning everyone.

Burton, Kayal discovered, had been an unabashed bibliophile in India, spending a large portion of his salary of ₹180 on mess bills, language tutors and books. Soon, he would build a considerable library of his own.

Some biographers have speculated that he made an enemy out of Rigby by repeatedly performing better at these exams and that Rigby could well have plotted his downfall when it came. Perhaps, thought Kayal, he was the one who had sneaked on Burton to his superiors, exposing his role in the secret Karachi Report? But cross-referencing each biography, she noted that no one was able – or even desired – to substantiate this minor theory, because the rivalry seemed so much like another Burton embellishment. His biographers, particularly Godsall, pointed, in fact, to another possible early exaggeration of this nature: Burton had written that his tutor Him Chand was so impressed with him that he had allowed him to wear the janeu, the sacred thread that marked out a Brahmin. Godsall wondered how Burton could possibly have attained such a high status among the Nagar Brahmins; after all, an upanayana ceremony itself would have taken a week.

Perhaps the explorer wished it were so, she thought, and continued making notes.

Burton, Kayal discovered, had been an unabashed bibliophile in India, spending a large portion of his salary of ₹180 on mess bills, language tutors and books. Soon, he would build a considerable library of his own. Whenever he got the chance to visit Bombay, he would make it a point to haunt as many libraries as he could. In addition, he pursued the libraries of

British bibliophiles and collectors in India. One of his favourite libraries in Bombay was at the Court of Directors, which held a collection of Oriental manuscripts, several of which had never been translated. Later, when he visited Goa, he spent most of his time (when he was not pursuing pretty nuns in convents) in four libraries, copying out manuscripts. Whenever possible, he directly bought manuscripts (during his later years, spent away from India, his large personal library, acquired with such painstaking effort, would be burned down in a fire at a storage facility in Grindley's depository). Burton would also go on to form a friendship with Richard Monckton Milnes, one of the founders of the Philobiblon Society in London, a bibliophile club that had become more active than the Roxburghe, its members meeting over breakfast to talk about rare and curious books.

In September 1843, Burton was ready to sit for his Gujarati exams and made a trip to Bombay. Once again, he passed, as they say, with flying colours.

When he returned to Baroda in November, Richard discovered that he had been transferred to the newly conquered Sindh. And so, in January 1844, he set sail for Karachi. On board the Company's steamship, he would meet Captain Walter Scott, an engineer with the Company and the younger brother of the already famous novelist Sir Walter Scott. Burton and the younger Scott not only became fast friends, but also colleagues on the same project, a project that would culminate in the infamous Karachi Report and Burton's disgrace – if one were to believe his version and that of his wife.

All this while, the explorer's attention had also been keenly trained on women. There were two things he had noticed in the cantonment regarding relationships between the sexes: Soldiers sneaking off to have affairs with other officers' wives – a trend he didn't care much for himself – and the widely prevalent practice in these cantonments – of which he heartily approved – of British officers choosing to be morganatically married to an Indian woman. The custom entitled a British ensign or officer to keep an Indian mistress for as long as it was convenient for him to do so and discard her, after 'annulling' the 'marriage', as soon as he left the country or when his white wife or fiancée came down from England to join him at camp. It was assumed that the Indian women who agreed to such a temporary arrangement didn't mind moving on, moving out or moving in with someone else. It was the children of these marriages, the Anglo-Indians, who suffered.

In time, the practice would come in for severe criticism from some evangelical missionaries, who almost succeeded in putting a stop to it. Burton had been no exception, quickly embracing the tradition of taking a morganatic wife or *bubu*, as they were called.

He was of the view that this would help the British get to know the local people better and his Indian mistress was the first of many during his Indian years. It was here and now that his interest in sexual practices and techniques began to consume him. He made elaborate notes when making love, quizzing the women he slept with about what pleasured them.

When he reached Sindh, four days after setting sail, Burton was unimpressed by what he discovered, describing the place subsequently as 'an unhappy valley, a compound of sand, stone and silt...with visible as well as palpable heat playing over it'. The sight of Karachi dismayed him; its bazaar wasn't in the least colourful. Unable to recognize the potential of this port city as crucial to trade with far-flung places like Persia and Arabia, he concluded that it was a miserable place.

The cantonment was some forty miles away from the city and held five thousand British and Indian soldiers. Burton couldn't afford a bungalow and lived in a tent where it was hot and sweltering all the time, with temperatures rising steeply during the day. He wrote in his notebook, 'Nothing but sunshine seems to flourish here', and resumed his daytime practice of studying under a table, with a wet cloth spread over it to keep himself cool.

In October 1944, he travelled to Bombay to take the Marathi exam and topped once again. Returning to

Sindh in October, he hired, for the first time, a Persian teacher – Mirza Mohammed Hosayn of Shiraz – to learn the language. Walter Scott, the friend he had made on the voyage to Karachi, secured him a position as a survey assistant to the Canal Department of the Sindh Survey. Scott himself had been heavily involved with survey work. Their commanding officer here, Charles Napier, would play a crucial role in Burton's career. Napier couldn't speak a single Indian language himself and Burton found that he could easily make an impression. He enjoyed learning how to use survey instruments, something he had never done before.

Now he intensified his studies by engaging another Persian scholar – Mirza Dowd. It was around this time that he came up with the idea of disguising himself as a Persian merchant to get closer to the locals, particularly the old men in the mosques and the women in their harems. He probably considered this an effective way to test his Persian and took the help of his new munshi to dress up and pass off as Mirza Abdullah, the Bushiri. Burton stained his hair, now grown long, and his beard with henna. Eventually, he went so far as to set up a little shop in the Karachi market that sold dates.

It was at this juncture that the spectre of the Karachi Report began to cast a shadow on his life and it is from here on that Burton's biographers begin to question his version of events, primarily his account of Napier engaging him as a spy in the Great Game – a story to be picked up later by Isabel as well.

According to Burton, Napier seemed to have known all about him and his flair for languages, his recent experiments with disguises and even his ethnographic interest in various sexual practices. And so he was the general's natural choice for looking into the rumours of several male bordellos in the city entrapping his men. Burton agreed to the mission, provided that Napier kept it completely confidential.

Burton made several visits to all the brothels in the city and found three that catered exclusively to British soldiers. As soon as Napier received the report, he went about abolishing the brothels – and then misplaced the report, it seems, or sent it on elsewhere, when he should have destroyed it.

Kayal skimmed through the next few events and paused at the point, when a year later Napier was succeeded by a new man who was unsympathetic to Burton. Someone, Burton was unable to say who – perhaps, Rigby, his arch rival – informed the new commanding officer about the existence of the potentially scandalous Karachi Report. Napier's offices were searched, the report found and Burton disgraced. But why? The assignment, clandestine though it was, had been undertaken at Napier's request, after all. Had the report then contained some evidence of Burton's own involvement in the practices for which these brothels were notorious? Had he revealed how he had come to be acquainted with such intimate details of brothel practices? More trouble awaited him; he was ill, his infected eye had not healed and the new promotion he had been anticipating as Punjabi and Sindhi interpreter to the regiment was denied to him. It went, instead, to a mere novice, who knew just one language: Hindustani. Just one! Burton would brood incessantly over this humiliation and the injustice he had suffered, convinced that his career had been sabotaged by envious colleagues.

According to the notes Kayal had made so far, his trip to Ooty had taken place not long after the Karachi Report was written; so it was entirely possible that Burton had retrieved it from Napier and carried it along with him on this journey. And if that were so, could he have left it in Ooty, with Parvathy, his mistress in the hills? Why, then, would Burton confidently write that the Report had been found at the Bombay office? The only other explanation could be that what he had carried with him to Ooty were some notes or scraps of notes that he must have made while compiling the Report. And knowing what a stickler he was for taking notes and recording even the less sensational details of his life at this point, it made sense that he would want his own record of it, even if it were in the form of notes or fragments.

As she put away her notes for the day, Kayal's

thoughts wandered. She understood, for the first time, why Burton was so attractive to collectors – he resembled them in more ways than one: In his dogged, obsessive pursuit of the unknown, the elusive, the strange, the beautiful and the unattainable.

25

A Typographic Jewel

Kayal stood gazing at the Albion iron hand press standing handsomely in Cheran's garage, while she waited for him to finish up with another client. In the afternoon light, the Albion cast a shimmering, liquidy shadow on the floor. The wooden hand press and its iron version had always cast a spell on her as long as she could remember. In Biblio's book-arts section, she had stocked several books and some ephemera on printing on a hand press – from Lewis M. Allen's trade edition of *Printing with the Hand Press* to multiple copies of the Richard Gabriel Rummonds classic, *Printing on the Iron Hand Press*, with its array of splendid black-and-white plates of famous fine-press printers operating their choice of a hand press. Among the predominant presses for letterpress, the iron hand press had a special place in the private-press tradition, and among all the cast-iron presses, the Albion had its own mystique: William Morris had used an Albion to print his Kelmscott Press books. A typographic jewel in Kayal's collection, one she was thrilled and proud to possess, was *Three Essays*, printed by Frederic Goudy at his Village Press using the very same Albion hand press that Morris had used to print his Kelmscott Chaucer. After the Kelmscott Press had closed, Goudy had bought one of the Kelmscott Albions for the Village Press.

Kayal had found the book online by sheer chance. The bookseller had pointed out its condition – poor to acceptable, in addition to being an ex-libris copy – but was still expecting $40 for it because of what the colophon stated about this edition: 'One of three hundred copies, printed on handmade paper at the Village Press by Frederic and Bertha Goudy, utilizing William Morris's Albion hand press.' When the book arrived some three weeks later and she held it in her hands, Kayal felt a visceral thrill; she was holding a book printed on the same Albion as the Kelmscott Chaucer, the most famous (if not the most revered) private-press book in the world. She was drawn at once to the textured paper and the impression of metal type on the paper with rich black ink. She was often given to turning to the limitations page, just to read that breathtaking colophon again.

After Cheran saw his client off and joined her in the garage, she asked, 'So, did it come to you naturally, printing on the hand press?'

'Oh, no... Actually, my initial attempts had the opposite effect. For the longest time, I would just freeze, the way young writers do when steeped in other people's brilliant writing. I felt intimidated and was afraid to print a single page.'

'How...when did you get over that?'

'Well,' Cheran said after a brief pause, 'I think the process started when I began to learn about smaller presses, contemporary presses, pressmen who printed for pleasure, privately. There were – and are – so many one could read and learn about that looking at their work made me feel I could try something like that.'

'So your work, then – it's not mostly letterpress, is it?'

'God, no. If it were, I would not only have no work coming my way, I would be a physical wreck! Letterpress is fine enough when you can set type with a monotype caster or – as they do nowadays – compose digitally and print from polymer plates. But setting type by hand and printing a few pages at a time means you can't get very far, and you can't pull hundreds of proofs on a hand press. Of course, there have been some remarkable exceptions in the history of fine printing like Lewis and Dorothy Allen of the Allen Press, who produced large books by hand – they handset type for hundreds of pages, printed two pages at a time on a cast-iron press, hand-coloured the illustrations and hand-bound some two hundred odd copies. I print on the hand press for my own satisfaction and enjoyment. Small things – keepsakes, broadsides, the ephemeral things... I've not attempted a book yet.'

'May I ask why?'

'I guess, mostly because I'm waiting for the right material. The dilemma of every fine printer is subject: What kind of writing interests me enough to want to handset a whole book and print it by letterpress on dampened handmade paper on a hand press?'

'Surely, you have some favourite text you want to see printed that way?'

'Many, actually. I suppose I just haven't gathered enough courage to make a go of it. Also, I have to admit, some laziness speaks here.'

'*That* I understand.'

They laughed.

'I used to print a few things with my father and I just thought it was something absorbing to do, you know, with your hands. Like working on a craft. But it was different for my dad. I don't think he had any notion of fine printing, at least, not consciously; he was drawn to printing a page well and because he could draw, he began illustrating whatever text he picked up to run off the press. And then he had all this type from where he worked and some printer's flowers; so he began to use them in combination for titles and headers and vignettes, printing them in two colours – usually red and black. A handsome use of type and decoration.'

Kayal pointed to a striking-looking broadside still lying on the press. 'I see that you've just printed something nice-looking again... May I?' she asked. When he nodded, she went over and carefully picked it up. It was, once again, on beautiful paper, finely printed with blue metal arabesques, with the text in black in the most exquisite fount she had seen, called Cancellaresca Bastarda. The tiny colophon at the bottom attributed the text to Will Rueter of Aliquando Press:

> *The pleasures of the private press are many: The preservation of the art and mystery of printing; the discovery and development of a personal ideal and a sense of self-realization through craftsmanship and the use of materials; the choice and visual interpretation of a text which otherwise might not be printed; the exploration and maintenance of a distinct typographic individuality; the chance to experiment with letter form and ornament.*

'Well, I can't wait to turn Biblio, with Neela's blessings, into the first Indian bookshop specializing in out-of-print and in-print fine-press books!' Kayal said excitedly, placing the broadside back. 'I'm going to be turning away from modern firsts to focus more on press books, while Neela looks at antiquarian material. I shall leave signed books and modern firsts to Pokisha.'

'Good, I don't care much for modern firsts, however – '

'Let me stop you right there, mister, and ask why.'

'Well, they aren't very interesting bibliographically, are they?' said Cheran. 'It's mostly about "chronological priority", no? There are only three things to look out for – condition, pristine dust jackets and points – and once you've got that, it's settled. That can't compare to the number of tactile elements that go into the making of a fine book: The choice of paper and fine type, the satisfying three-dimensionality of a letterpress impression, rich ink in two to three colours, beautiful ornaments, pleasing typographic composition, immaculate presswork and decorative binding.'

'My comeback to that is this – something the English book dealer Claude Cox once said when talking about a first edition of Keats's first published book of poems: "Everyone likes fine copies, but the magic of first editions is not in the eye, but in the mind, in the heart."'

'That's *marvellous*, though only if we are still talking about antiquarian first editions, not modern firsts. It's not that I don't get the mystique of a beautifully preserved copy of a favourite book in its first impression, but there are such layers, in contrast, to a finely printed book. I recall another English dealer, Sophie Schneideman, remarking once, "Everything is so deeply felt in private-press books."'

'I'm beginning to see that,' Kayal responded. 'And here's my last shot: What about the dogged hunt one sets out on to ferret out the scarcer first editions? Doesn't that take quite a bit of collecting connoisseurship?'

'I'll grant that. *And* if there's anything really tricky and challenging in the realm of first-edition points, it has got to be the task you and Neela are carrying out – the hellish and thankless job of identifying modern Indian first editions.'

'Thanks!' Kayal said with just as much sarcasm.

'By the way, how familiar are you with fine-press books?'

'To be honest, not very. I can acknowledge that I have a few minor examples in my collection; but they've always beckoned very strongly and if I haven't drawn closer to them already it's because I know how much I'll start obsessing about them. I do everything obsessively.'

'Good. I can't think of anything else that's worth obsessing more about. I thought, rather than talk more about them, I'll show you a few examples of letterpress books. So let's go in.'

They went into the house, past his study, and into his bedroom. 'I've rightly set the scene of seduction here,' he said, grinning and pointing to his bed where he had laid out several handsome private-press books.

'I had them taken out of the shelves for you, just so we can get to all of them quicker; you'll have to sort of sit on the edge of the bed and look at them. I'm nervous about having them on a table – there could be stains on the surface that could get on the books. So now, to the books; rather than, I thought, me picking out what presses I think you should stock, I'll let you look at them at leisure – and then see which ones appeal to you the most. The fine-press or private-press production is an intensely personal one. Once you've seen what you want, I can give you more information about them.'

'And that's a promise?'

'Ha ha, yes!'

Cheran went off to work in his printing office with the offset suite, but returned almost immediately to offer Kayal some pongal ('I made it myself, and no, there's no ghee') and black coffee. Before he left her alone again with the books, he said, 'Oh, I forgot to mention that the collection is divided into four lots: This one, on the right, is books from all the classic presses from the past – Kelmscott, Ashendene, Doves, Essex and Eragny. I would think, rather than for the bookshop, you yourself ought to collect these presses. And the lot on the left consists of titles by private presses that are still in operation; and their work, though expensive in the deluxe edition, are still in print and often come up on the antiquarian market. The third set, in front of you, are typographic books, from type specimen books to the purely calligraphic or typographic book, beauties like Hermann Zapf's *Feder Und Stichel* and *Manuale Typographicum*. This last pile here, furthest from you, are journals – again, in print and out of print – on the printing arts. The Whittington Press has been bringing out a gorgeous yearly typographic annual called *Matrix* and you should try and find a complete run of them, the regular edition, at least, if not the deluxe, for the bookshop – or even for yourself!'

'All right, sir!' teased Kayal, at which he pretended to be embarrassed and scooted off.

Half-an-hour later, when he returned to look in on her, Kayal had a large pile sorted out and put aside for him to look over. It had proven difficult to pick out just a few, as Cheran had asked her to, but given how expensive most of them were, it had made sense to her to limit the selection and number of modern and contemporary fine presses to begin Biblio's collection. As much as it pained her, she would have to whittle her selection down to a smaller number still.

'Very nice,' he said, glancing over her choice of stock. 'Now let's go online and see which antiquarian bookshop specializing in fine-press books is selling what you want to stock up on. I have some favourite book-arts dealers – Entropy, Veatchs, Bromer, Woodbridge, Maggs, Claude Cox, Collinge and Clark, Michael Taylor, Rulon-Miller, Vamp and Tramp, so we could get started with them…'

26

The Z Club in Triplicane

The Ziegenbalg Club members, as many as were able to make it on a Friday evening, were gathering at the Book Arts Centre to decide, among other things on the agenda, the possibility of organizing and hosting the first antiquarian book fair in the country and – even though they did not know it as they walked in – the fate of a fragment of Richard Burton's Karachi Report.

When Neela called for a meeting, she had only hinted at some rare Burton material becoming available. Whitehead would be cross, she knew, and Templar would, when he was apprised of the details, feel, as the British put it, chuffed. The rest would be content to watch the two rivals prepare to outdo each other – or, wondered Neela briefly, would they too be drawn into the great game?

Kayal arrived early to get a moment with some of the collectors she had found things for, calling first on Roswitha Jose, who beamed brightly when the *Marg* issues were produced. She stopped to chat with several other collectors, bibliophiles and bibliographers, and noticed Clement Pandian standing in a quiet corner, wolfing down a sandwich. Kenton, who had arrived the day before, looked quite lost in this crowd. He seemed relieved and grateful when Kayal called out to him and, together, they went over to say hello to Pandian.

As she was introducing the two of them, Kayal noticed Arcot Templar step into the room. Templar's elegant appearance concealed his rapacious nature well. He was completely bald, very trim, always dressed with an eye to fashion, and with a ready, disarming smile that won people over swiftly. This was going to be tricky, Kayal realized, as he headed her way. There was no getting out of it now, she told herself, it had fallen on her to introduce Kenton around and... But Templar waved brightly at her and swept towards the conference room, probably eager not to miss Neela's announcement about the new Burton material that had come to light. Kayal seized the moment to remind Kenton and Pandian that they would be late for the meeting if they lingered outside, and the three hurried in, entering just in time to hear Neela say, 'We think the alleged Burton holograph could be genuine, undiscovered Burton material, along with the letter and the books with the explorer's manuscript marginalia providing provenance.' Neela paused, glancing quickly at Whitehead and Templar – one grunting glumly while the other cheered – before continuing. 'And there is reason to believe that it is, also, a fragment of the notorious Karachi Report, missing these many years.'

The room broke out at once in exclamations and murmurs; the members knew some Burton material was going on offer, but could hardly have guessed what it might be. And it was Templar, of course, who called out first, 'Auction! Auction!', making it clear to the room that Heritage would have some part in this fabled piece of Burtoniana.

Neela held up her hand, appealing for silence, and took another ten minutes to present a little background to the new Burton material that had surfaced, before introducing Kenton Selvaganesan, who shared his story. Whitehead, Kayal noticed, was looking quite distressed through it all, feeling, no doubt, that the Burtoniana he so coveted and that had come so tantalizingly close to belonging to him was slipping away from him as more and more collectors were let in on its existence.

When Kenton had finished speaking, Whitehead shuffled up to the front and said, 'Surely, no one else, not just in this room, but in the entire country, wants the Karachi Papers as much as I do. Can't the matter be settled reasonably between the owner and me? Now, Mr Selvaganesan has already expressed his wish that the K Fragment be auctioned, rather than sold privately, because his family wants to share their story with the world. I would like to reassure him, here and now, that I, with his cooperation and help, will do all I can, sparing no expense, to publicize it and make a fanfare of this Burton discovery.'

'Oh, I think not, sir!' Templar called out, his tone cutting. 'You've pocketed far too many highly auction-worthy items that way. This one *must* come up for auction.'

'What exactly are you referring to?' Whitehead retorted, looking outraged. 'Tell me...what?'

'Have you forgotten those Burton letters to Steinhauser? No sooner did we hear of a few being made available on the antiquarian market here than they vanished into your library before any of us could get a crack at it.'

'Collector's instinct, my dear fellow, knowing where to look – something you once admittedly possessed, but seem to have lost. If only you spent more time collecting books rather than auctioning them, you'd be snapping up finds too.'

'Gentlemen, a second please. Until the manuscript is authenticated, it's best to keep the discovery under wraps, you will agree,' Neela cautioned.

'I agree!' said Whitehead forcefully.

'Well,' drawled Templar, grinning ferociously at his rival who was now making his way back to his seat,'that would suit you nicely, wouldn't it? Keep it under wraps, while you quietly make a private deal with Adigal or the gentleman here and then announce to the world that you possess the great white whale of Burton's lost writing!'

'Now you're going too far, Arcot!' Neela snapped. 'It simply makes sense to keep this low-key until we're more certain of what we have here. Not that I mean to sound doubtful about its authenticity,' she added with an apologetic smile at Kenton, who waved her on, smiling back, 'but I'm sure even Kenton will agree that there is a good deal more to be explored concerning the provenance of the Karachi Report and the circumstances surrounding it.'

Roswitha raised her hand, indicating she had something to say, and Neela gratefully gave up the floor.

'It's evident,' Roswitha began, 'that these papers, though supposedly just a fragment of the elusive Karachi Report, are far too important a discovery to keep among us – just in terms of their potential to influence Burton scholarship, their impact will be enormous. I'm sure everyone in the world with some interest in the explorer – from collector to curator to bibliographer – will clamour for access to it. You'll have to let one of the big auction houses take a look at it. Sotheby's, probably, would be best, or even Swann Galleries. I don't think we have much choice in this – and I'm sure Neela has already tried to persuade you of this.'

'I won't have that!' said Templar emphatically, striding up to the front. 'I won't give up one more important artefact to the international auction houses when there is one right here. Why shouldn't the auction take place at Heritage? Let the curators and collectors and scholars and the media come here. Why should we go to them every time?'

Many in the room seemed to be in agreement, with some acknowledging their support with a nod, and Kayal, too, believed Templar had a point. Neela had anticipated this from the outset, having correctly read the reason for his interest in what Kenton had to offer; it would give him a chance to showcase his auction house to the world. She had known it wouldn't be settled so easily, and just as she was wondering why Whitehead hadn't raised an objection yet, he raised his cane for attention.

'How can I be sure,' he hissed, 'that Arcot won't have someone bidding against me? We all know he's done it before by having others anonymously bid for him on the phone – and when that became too obvious, his absentee bids were placed online.'

'Which is why collectors shouldn't own or run auction houses!' chided Jadwiga Hegde, a bibliophile-member from Mysore, who had never taken to Templar.

Unfazed, Templar just smiled and said dismissively, 'Rumours, all of them! It simply suits you – and many others as envious as you are – to believe them. When no one here thought to start up a book-auction house, I took the plunge and now it's the only one of its kind in India. The Karachi Papers must go up on sale at Heritage. It would be a shame to let them go out of the country.'

Neela looked in Whitehead's direction, waiting for a response. The others in the room also looked his way expectantly. The collector remained grimly silent, continuing to resist the idea, even as the collective pressure from a room full of his peers heightened. Then, sighing heavily, Whitehead nodded his agreement. Heritage would take the auction forward.

'So, it's decided then,' Templar announced. 'Heritage will sell the Burton material and, from here on, I will take possession of the books, the letter and the Karachi Fragment.' There was an unmistakable note of triumph in his voice. 'Following standard auction procedure, I will submit them to at least three document experts to authenticate and verify the material.'

The bibliophiles in the room had no argument with this, since any such material usually went to well-established experts in the rarefied field of authenticating British Raj documents.

'All through the process, the material will be in my – that is, Heritage's – safekeeping. If it is authenticated, we move quickly towards preparing a very special catalogue of the fragment: Description, provenance and other bibliographical notes. Since the provenance of this material is so unique – coming, possibly, from Burton's own living heir – there will be a biographical note from Mr Selvaganesan as well.' Templar turned to Kenton. 'That's something you should begin working on right away – telling your story. Prepare to be overwhelmed – the media interest in this is going to be intense. Besides, we at Heritage will be inundated with phone calls and emails, queries from every direction – Burton collectors, the media, rare-book institutions and specialist book dealers.'

Someone in the room yelled, 'What about the Antiquities and Art Treasures Act?' The reference was to the government stipulation that Indian antiques that had been in existence for ninety-nine years or more could not be taken out of the country or exported.

Templar snorted, 'You mean that sweeping hogwash you see at our airports?' Several in the room laughed because they knew how absurd it was of the government to consider anything that was old as automatically antiquarian or valuable.

'In any case,' continued the auctioneer, 'it won't apply to the K Fragment – our antiquities law requires manuscripts to have an illustration, illumination or painted miniature to be registered and evaluated. And since the K Fragment is bereft of any pictorial depiction, no one will bother with it.'

Once the question of the K Fragment had been settled, the meeting proceeded smoothly, focusing, chiefly, on the three-day antiquarian book fair that the club was hoping to organize and host the following year. If they could pull it off, it would be the first such book fair to be held in India, with an exclusive focus on antiquarian material. There was much lively debate and argument about what constituted an Indian antiquarian book fair, with several members speaking or raising questions at the same time.

After a point, Kayal lost track of who was saying what and sat back to enjoy the ruckus, cheering on a few and booing some others.

'The main thing that concerns me is keeping out the dealers from the regular second-hand market – we can't have them stock their booths with those container books. And then there are those who'll drag all their old, tattered books out.'

'Exactly! How can we make it clear to them that

the fair isn't just about a lot of old, crumbling, used books? They are so used to pitching a stall in book fairs around the country with towering piles of reading copies that they'll just turn up and then it's going to be difficult to turn them away.'

'Don't make it a public thing. Can't we just invite the few dealers we know who have a slightly specialist focus – fine bindings, limited editions and antiquarian books?'

'What fine bindings? What limited editions? What most of our dealers have is antiquarian Indian material, most of it in appalling condition. If it's not falling apart, it's because they've bound it in the most pedestrian way, taking away half the edition's value.'

'We shouldn't have a politician or a bureaucrat inaugurating it – let's plan towards getting somebody significant and famous in the world of bibliophily today.'

'Set the admission fee at ₹500 to discourage those who stroll into fairs during a weekend to idle away their time or look for cheap bargains. An antiquarian fair can't take such crowds. The items on display will have to be handled with care and if the whole world is allowed in, there could be pushing and shoving and possible theft. For this reason, there should be only one exit and all bags should be examined and purchases matched against receipts – standard practice in antiquarian fairs, annoying though it is.'

'Finally with a book fair like this, the few dealers in the country who stock anything even slightly specialized in the antiquarian sense and drag their stock from one standard book fair to another, hoping that in the chaos, there will be at least a few collectors interested enough to examine their choice stock and pay high prices – *they* will finally find the right milieu and takers for their material.'

'We have to make sure we get the browsers such material deserves – it doesn't matter how much they might end up selling, but to have an appreciative, knowledgeable browser look at such books will be a start.'

'But we need serious buyers too! It's not enough for the booksellers that people attending the fair have a sense of the value, importance and rarity of what is on display; they need customers who will pay antiquarian prices.'

'True, true! What's the point if books are not bought and sit there just for show? That would just be another posh exhibit and not a trade fair, where brisk business is done.'

For Neela, building an antiquarian book trade in the country, one with an established, vibrant market was of the utmost importance. And she cheerfully pitched in with the others, occasionally catching Kayal and Pandian's eye, chuckling along with them over such a virulent exchange of observations – learned, down-to-earth and business-centric on the one hand, but self-important and snobbish on the other – on bibliophilic matters.

Part Six

27

The Ghost of Reverend Thomas Frognall Dibdin

'Two of the most spectacular dates in the history of bibliophily,' said Neela, fixing her eye on the audience, 'are 17 June 1812 and 24 April 1911. These dates mark two of the most discussed auction sales in the annals of book-collecting history: The Roxburghe sale of 1812 and the Robert Hoe sale of 1911, leading to the founding of two distinguished bibliophile societies – the Roxburghe Club and the Grolier Club. Both periods have been referred to, at times, as the heroic or golden age of book collecting.'

She was addressing a packed college auditorium. Apart from students and faculty, the audience was made up of church dignitaries, bibliophiles and the merely curious. Filling the front row were a few members of the Anglican clergy from the Church of

South India, Reverend Satya and Robert Arulpragasam (who was beaming as though this gathering had been made possible by him alone). Also in the audience were several of the Ziegenbalg Club's stellar collectors. A little less than a month after its discovery, the Richard Heber collection had been duly catalogued and curated by Biblio, and on this Friday afternoon in March, the Heber exhibit had been formally opened to the public at Madras Christian College, prefaced by Neela's talk: 'Richard Heber and the Heroic Age of Book Collecting: The Extraordinary Library of a Legendary Bibliomane.'

'The Roxburghe sale of 1812,' continued Neela, 'for which England's famous bibliophiles – among them, Richard Heber and Thomas Frognall Dibdin – had gathered, led to the highest price ever paid for a printed book at the time. And assembled at the Hoe sale of 1911 was a galaxy of international collectors, librarians and book dealers, a virtual who's who of bibliophily, and there too the day ended with the highest price paid at that time for a printed book in auction history.

'To understand the bibliomania of Heber and Thomas Phillips and Dibdin,' Neela went on, 'we have to begin, not with the 1812 Roxburghe auction, but with the modern auction, the 1911 Robert Hoe sale at the Anderson Auction Company in New York. Several months before the auction, the buzz had already begun: The Hoe collection was full of rarities that everyone connected with the rare-book world wanted a piece of – and they would descend from all over the globe to the Anderson Gallery in New York to capture the top prize: A scarce vellum copy of the Gutenberg Bible

'Hoe had been a fastidious collector, always making sure he had the best copy of a rarity. His passion for a book's fine condition had ensured that he had remarkable copies of some of the high spots: For instance, the only perfect copy of Caxton's edition of *Le Morte d'Arthur*. Also present in the collection was a paper copy of the Gutenberg, a rich gathering of incunabula and fine bindings, including several Grolier bindings, Elseviers, Aldines, Caxtons, Wynkyn de Wordes, Pynsons, Bodonis and several first editions of English literature, many of which were inscribed or association copies. Further, Hoe had a quirk that purists had criticized him for, but that would, during the auction, earn him good points: His practice of replacing original bindings with contemporary designer bindings. The beauty of these rebound seventeenth- and eighteenth-century books attracted bidders to editions they would normally have ignored. What also excited collectors and dealers and librarians about the Hoe collection was realizing how unusual it was for such an impeccable collection to come on the market. Hoe explained why he wanted to do it: "If the great collections of the past had not been sold, where would I have found my books?"'

Neela paused as a murmur of approval swept through the hall, with some of the gathered book collectors even nodding and smiling.

'It was on an evening in January 1884 that several bibliophiles gathered at Hoe's house to talk about forming a club devoted to the art of printing and typography–and so was born the Grolier Club, named after the renowned French bibliophile Jean Grolier.

'Now let us return to the Hoe auction. Imagine the day: In the same room, perhaps for the first time in the history of bibliophily, had gathered the biggest names in book collecting. First, the book dealers. From Britain, the two most well-known names in rare-book selling, Quaritch and Maggs; from the Continent, Ludwig Baer from Frankfurt, Théophile Belin of Paris; from America, the legendary G.D. Smith, often referred to as the "Czar of the Auction Room", the beloved Gabriel Wells and, of course, Rosy or Dr A.S.W. Rosenbach, another "imposing monarch of the auction room". But what's interesting to note is that at that point in time, in that sale room at the Anderson Gallery, Rosenbach wasn't very well known. He was still in the shadows, especially in the shadow of G.D. Smith. Seated with Smith was a man few people recognized and probably wouldn't have bothered about if the gentleman hadn't been in the company of Smith. But, like Rosenbach, this bibliophile, too, was waiting in the wings, and his name was Henry E. Huntington. Just as Rosenbach would go on to become one of the most famous antiquarian booksellers in the world, Huntington would, in time, overshadow even his redoubtable peers J.P. Morgan and Henry Folger, to become one of the greatest among modern collectors. Morgan was the only famous collector not present in the room that day. He had, as usual, sent his excellent librarian Belle da Costa Greene – the mysterious, beautiful Belle, expert bibliographer, the most glamorous bookwoman of her day. On Morgan's behalf, she had already captured treasure upon treasure: Not one, but four Gutenbergs. Word was that the Hoe Gutenberg too would be hers that day.

'For that day, that was the prize – the Gutenberg in vellum. The sale catalogue – annotated by the gifted bibliographer Arthur Swann – described Hoe's copy as "the handsomest and most richly decorated Gutenberg Bible in existence... Except for two missing pages, which had been replaced by facsimile, its 641 unnumbered leaves could not have been fresher and crisper than the day they left the press at Mainz." An auction crier had been specially brought in from London. The high drama of the auction played out on the first day itself; as evening fell, the lot number everyone had been anticipating was called out and a hush fell over the room as the two-volume Gutenberg, bound in oak, was placed on the block. G.D. Smith called out the first bid of $10,000 in his trademark style – with a wink – and the auctioneer asked if anyone would raise it by a thousand. Several bids were made and from here on, the auction fairly galloped.

'When it stood at $21,000, an audible buzz started up in the room – an auction price for a printed Bible had just been broken. Everyone's attention was now focused on the remaining bidders seated ringside – Quaritch, Maggs, Widener, Belle (for Morgan) and, surprisingly, still in the race was Huntington as Smith ferociously outbid the others on his behalf. The Continental bidders pulled out first, throwing up their arms to signal that the bids had become forbiddingly high. At $30,000, even Quaritch dropped out and the race narrowed to Widener and Huntington. If Joseph Widener had been bidding for himself, he might have dropped out at this high a price. But he was bidding on behalf of his son Harry and was determined to secure the Gutenberg for him.

'Harry Widener, some of you may remember, was the Harvard scion who went down with the *Titanic* and, as a memorial to him, his mother had the Widener Library built for Harvard. In any case, now even Huntington began to grow nervous. Wesley Towner in his book *The Elegant Auctioneers* notes that "when the bid reached $40,000, Huntington apparently turned pale and said to Smith in a strained whisper that turned loud, 'Too much money. Nothing doing.' Smith, not taking his eyes off the prize, curtly said, 'Leave me alone. If you don't want it, I'll buy it myself...' And at $50,000, even Widener shook his head. The auctioneer let his hammer fall. It was now up to Huntington to accept the raised bid and Smith turned pointedly to him. Huntington nodded and Smith signalled the bid." The auctioneer announced loudly to the gallery that Henry Huntington had just become the owner of the most expensive book in the world. The audience cheered and Huntington acknowledged them by taking a simple bow. Fifty thousand dollars would seem little today to us, making you wonder what all the fuss was about. But we have to remember that this would be, in today's price, adjusting for inflation, nearly two million dollars. A bargain, really, even at that price because if such a perfect vellum copy of the Gutenberg Bible ever came up for sale today, it could fetch fifty million dollars, perhaps more!

'The chase continued at the Anderson Gallery in the ensuing days, with the same bidders hotly pursuing other rarities. Belle, once again, went up against Smith and Huntington, but determinedly outbid them this time for that near perfect Caxton folio *Le Morte d'Arthur* and secured it for Morgan at $42,800. She later said she had been prepared to go beyond the Gutenberg price, if it had to come to that. The Gutenberg paper copy went to Quaritch for $27,500. Smith also wrangled the *Book of Saint Albans* for $13,000 and the "tall copy" Shakespeare First Folio for $13,000. Smith's relentless bidding secured 5,500 of the 14,588 lots on sale at the Hoe auction. The Europeans – Belin and Baer – voiced their protest to the Anderson Gallery: "Your prices are as tall as your buildings!"

'I should,' Neela continued, 'mention in an aside here that a few years before the Hoe sale, Henry Folger had privately and secretly bought the Shakespeare First Folio for $50,000. Since he had kept it such a secret – not wanting anyone to know about the kind of stratospheric price he had paid – the world of bibliophily naturally assumed that the $50,000 for the Gutenberg Bible that Smith had bid on for Huntington was the highest price ever paid for a book. Apparently, Folger, looking at the newspaper headlines announcing this to the world, took much pleasure in knowing that it was he, not Huntington, who had been the first to break the record for the highest price paid for a printed book.

'This does not, of course, take away from the Hoe–Huntington Gutenberg copy the record hammer price achieved in an auction until that point. Also worth noting is that at the 1929 Kern sale, the dealer Gabriel Wells would make headlines when he bought Shelley's own copy of "Queen Mab" for $68,000. The price of rare books had become extravagant; Kern had bought this very copy for just $6,000 at the Buxton Forman sale not too long ago. The price of many items in the Kern sale had not only tripled and quadrupled, but shot out of all proportion. The twenties were indeed a heady time for rare books and those who collected them.

'To return to the Hoe sale, several other significant outcomes marked this watershed event: The entry of Huntington as the formidable new market force in the rare-book business, Smith sealing his reputation as the czar of antiquarian books and New York taking over London as the new centre for the antiquarian book market.'

As Neela paused for a sip of water and arranged her notes, Kayal took a quick look around the room. She noticed several members of the audience turning to each other to murmur, while others adjusted themselves better in their seats, some even leaning forward, indicating their growing interest in what Neela had to say next.

'The significance of the Hoe sale for our Richard Heber exhibit here today,' said Neela, pressing on, 'lies in the *provenance* of the books that were auctioned then. Where had Hoe bought his books? These were, largely, books belonging to the patrician book collectors of the eighteenth and nineteenth centuries and their renowned private libraries that had been passing through auction sales around the world, from one collector to the next, from Heber to Hoe to Huntington, and I would not be surprised if a part of those great collections is now in the private libraries of at least a few Indian collectors present here with us today! Thus, these books are not just rare, valuable and beautiful; they also have a certain pedigree. It is not uncommon to hear dealers or collectors referring to something as "the Hoe copy" or even as "the Heber–Hoe–Huntington copy", tracing the marks of ownership. The ownership bookplates of all three collectors remain in the book, raising the value of such a copy, not only in the market but also in terms of its heightened desirability in the eyes of a collector.

'Now, we will rewind to the beginning of the golden age of book collecting and locate another landmark moment in the history of bibliophily – the Roxburghe sale of 17 June 1812, which inspired many young collectors, ushering in a new era of British book collecting. Just as the Hoe sale, a century later, would draw the most pre-eminent collectors and dealers of the day, the Roxburghe sale was attended by England's famous bibliophiles, most of whom were wealthy, distinguished noblemen and noblewomen, with the finest libraries in the country. Also present at the sale were the two persons who concern us the most: Richard Heber and Thomas Frognall Dibdin. They were not as wealthy as the rest of those present in the room. Nor did they enjoy the privileges of peerage. But they would, in the years to come, prove to be the greater champions of bibliomania.

'For the patrician collectors gathered at the Roxburghe sale, book collecting had become an exciting game, a favourite sport. And every sport throws up its own poet and chronicler to both record and serenade the game; just as cricket had Cardus, bibliomania had Dibdin. The writings of Thomas Frognall Dibdin, bibliomane and bibliographer, whipped the sport of book collecting into a frenzy. John Carter described this famous sale as "a battle of Homeric quality and Dibdin was its rhapsodist".

'On that day in June, if there was an air of expectancy and excitement in the auction hall, it was because of the influence of Dibdin's *Bibliomania*, a work that had done much to stir the passion of bibliophiles and collectors in England and on the Continent. It was the first major work on bibliomania, impassionedly evoking the world of rare books, book hunters, fine bindings and paper, printers and bibliographers. The effect was electric, making bibliophily something to be both desired and regarded with awe.

'Like the Gutenberg at the Anderson Gallery, Roxburghe too had a star item on the block: The Valdarfer Boccaccio, that would go on to fetch £2,260 – which would be more than £150,000 today. And two bibliophiles, both aristocrat collectors, would clash for it: The Marquis of Blandford and Lord Spencer. What *was* the Valdarfer Boccaccio that was so highly coveted? The Venetian Christoph Valdarfer had printed in 1471 a beautiful copy of Boccaccio's *Decameron*, but because of its risqué contents, most copies had been burnt or otherwise destroyed and only a few survived in good condition. The Valdarfer Boccaccio that turned up at the Roxburghe sale was, though blemished, still the best-known copy in existence. It is to Dibdin that we must turn to get a first-hand account of the Roxburghe sale.

'I'd like to read an excerpt from his entries, made in his overwrought, but affecting style:

> "*At length the hour of battle arrived... For two-and-forty successive days – with the exception only of Sundays – was the voice and hammer of Mr Evans heard... At last it was the turn of the Valdarfer. I have a perfect recollection of this notorious volume... It had a faded yellow morocco binding, and was a sound rather than a fine copy... On his right hand, leaning against the wall, stood Earl Spencer: A little lower down, and standing at right angles with his lordship, appeared the Marquis of Blandford... The honour of firing the first shot was due to a gentleman of Shropshire, unused to this species of warfare, and who seemed to recoil from the reverberation of the report himself had made!— 'One hundred guineas,' he exclaimed. Again a pause ensued: But anon the biddings rose rapidly to 500 guineas...*

'A thousand guineas' were bid by Earl Spencer – to which the marquis added 'ten'. You might have heard a pin drop. All eyes were turned – all breathing well-nigh stopped – every sword was put home within its scabbard – and not a piece of steel was seen to move or to glitter, except that which each of these champions brandished in his valorous hand… 'Two thousand two hundred and fifty pounds,' said Lord Spencer. The spectators were now absolutely electrified. The marquis quietly adds his usual 'ten,'… and there is an end of the contest.

"Mr Evans, ere his hammer fell, made a due pause – and indeed, as if by something preternatural, the ebony instrument itself seemed to be charmed or suspended 'in the mid air'. However, at length, down dropped the hammer. The spectators stood aghast!... The price electrified the bystanders, and astounded the public! The Marquis's triumph was marked by a plaudit of hands, and presently after he offered his hand to Lord Spencer, saying. 'We are good friends still!' His lordship replied, 'Perfectly, indeed I am obliged to you.' 'So am I to you,' said the Marquis, 'so the obligation is mutual.' He declared that it was his intention to have gone as far as £5,000. The noble marquis had previously possessed a copy of the same edition, wanting five leaves: 'for which five leaves,' Lord S. remarked, 'he might be said to have given £2,600'… The battle languished towards its termination (rather, we suspect, from a failure of ammunition than of valour or spirit on the part of the combatants): But

not-withstanding, there was oftentimes a disposition manifested to resume the glories of the earlier part of the day, and to show that the spirit of bibliomania was not made of poor and perishable stuff."'

Neela paused to take in a deep breath. When she resumed, she emphasized, 'But of more significance than the sale is what took place *after* the auction; Dibdin proposed that the bibliophiles gathered, heroes all, should repair to a pub and dine together to celebrate and commemorate the Roxburghe sale. On 17 June 1812, the Reverend Thomas Frognall Dibdin and a coterie of fellow collectors and bibliophiles dined together at St Alban Tavern and the Roxburghe Club, the first bibliophile society, was born. That evening, they drank a toast to all the distinguished printers in the world, and this would become a tradition at every annual Roxburghe gathering, with a growing line of fine printers added on to the toast. Nicolas Barker in his bicentenary history of the Roxburghe Club gives us an idea of how these toasts are usually recited: "The toasts, with occasional textual variants then and since, were and are, in canonical sequence: 'The immortal memory of John Duke of Roxburghe, of Christopher Valdarfer, printer of the Boccaccio of 1471, of Gutenberg, Fust and Schoeffer, the inventors of the art of printing, of William Caxton, father of the British Press, of Dame Juliana Barnes and the St Albans Press, of Wynkyn de Worde and

Richard Pynson, the illustrious successors of Caxton, of the Aldine family at Venice, of the Giunta family at Florence, of the Society of Bibliophiles Francais at Paris, the prosperity of the Roxburghe Club, and the Cause of Bibliomania all over the world.'" Barker later adds that when St John Hornby of the Ashendene Press died, his name became part of the canon in the Roxburghe toast. There were gathered that evening at least eighteen "enthusiastic and resolute bibliomaniacs", and one among them was Richard Heber, then a young collector. Dibdin and Heber grew very close in the years that followed, but even Dibdin was a little mystified by his fellow bibliomaniac. Heber was a very private person and, unlike many collectors, who liked to write or speak about their book-hunting exploits and treasures, he was quiet and modest. And yet, though shy, nearly everyone who knew him spoke of his cheerful, helpful nature – he readily gave his books to friends and young scholars. He was a witty, entertaining conversationalist.

'Dibdin spoke of Heber's book collecting as an "ungovernable passion" and a remark like that, coming from a fellow bibliomaniac, reveals the magnitude and depth of Heber's bibliomania. He was, in fact, that rarest of collectors – a child bibliomaniac; he began collecting when he was six years old and was buying books right up to the morning of the day he died. What we know of Heber and his collection today is mainly from a small handful of sources. A biography of him, long overdue, is yet to be written. Scholar-collectors such as Dibdin, Fletcher, Di Ricci, Munby and Hunt have written about Heber's library and his circle of collectors and it is their writings and research that have now given us a more complex and complete picture of the man.

'Born on 5 January 1773, Heber went to Brasenose College, Oxford. By this time his bibliomania was already in full bloom. His father discovered from booksellers how much over his allowance – £100 – he had been spending on rare books and wrote several letters to him, urging him and pleading with him to put an end to his bibliomania and, when that had no effect, even threatening to cut off his allowance. Luckily for Heber, he had a sympathetic aunt in London, who indulged his bibliomania and allowed him to hide at her house the books he was acquiring at a dizzy speed. She kept Heber informed of auctions taking place and mailed him book catalogues. When he visited London, she entertained his large circle of bibliophile friends and even allowed booksellers to call at her house.

'When his father died in 1804, Heber's allowance not only went up from £100 to £10,000 a year, but he also inherited much of his family's vast estates across the country. Now he could collect with a serious focus and he chose early printed books on poetry and drama. His standards were exacting – the moment he found a better copy of an edition he already owned, he would acquire it at once, attending every auction sale in the country and in Europe. As for the lengths he would go to to acquire just one book, we have the testimony of a friend, who recalled: "On hearing of a curious book, he has been known to put himself into the mail coach, and travel three, four or five hundred miles to obtain it."

'Like the best book collectors, he was also an expert bibliographer with a phenomenal memory for his books. Once again, we have the recollections of a friend who was given the following instruction by Heber to retrieve a book from his library: "If you will take the trouble to go to my lodgings, you will find them bound in five volumes, small quarto, rather thick, in vellum covers, standing, to the best of my recollection, on a lower, right-hand shelf of the white painted bookcase, opposite the windows, in the room at the head of the back staircase."

'Heber book-hunted everywhere, beginning with the London auctions, which often procured the best books, and then on to Europe and the various auctions houses there and, finally, homed in on the vast collections of books – treasures, really – that were being dispersed by monastic libraries in the process of being dismantled. After a while, he was buying entire rooms of books. Instead of bringing them back to his house in Pimlico or Hodnet, he began storing them in houses in Europe that he had rented or bought simply for the purpose of housing the books somewhere.

'At the house where he finally came to live when he turned recluse, he made certain that his favourite books – first editions of English literature and rare bibliographical reference books – were at hand. At last count, after a thirty-year period of fierce collecting, his books were spread over several cities – Paris, Antwerp, Ghent, Brussels, Frankfurt – and the areas where his country houses were located. Such huge and, what seems indiscriminate, buying might suggest that Heber didn't look after his books, but his anxiety, each time, over purchases he had made – such as the occasion on which he booked an entire carriage on the train for his books and rode along personally with them – proves his concern for their condition. Dibdin recalls once seeing Heber collating his books from 6 a.m. until 10 p.m. without taking a break. At auctions, says Dibdin, Heber would bid very unobtrusively; he would take a seat in the front row, just below the auctioneer, and signal bids with just the slightest raising of a finger. Sometimes, he would have dealers bid for him, even though he was present in the room. He was secretive about his book buying and even bid against himself at an auction so that friends wouldn't suspect how many bids he had going in the room.

'There was some vague talk of marriage, for Heber was still single. It was thought by all that Heber would marry – or had contemplated marrying – Frances Mary Richardson Currer, a book collector of some reputation, whose library was said to have contained some fifteen thousand to twenty thousand rare volumes. Frances Currer was a serious collector, with a formidable library of her own. A lady who was also a bookwoman in the rare-book game was an unusual thing at the time, dominated as it was by the circle of gentlemen-bibliophiles, and she seemed the perfect match for Richard. But theirs remained a book friendship. And Heber remained a bachelor until the end, though for a brief period, controversy surrounded his friendship with a young collector, an antiquary named Charles Hartshorne. Increasingly, Heber began spending more time at home with his books; he suffered terribly from gout and every outing to an auction or bookshop was not without discomfort and pain, but his bibliomania helped him withstand it all. The last thing he did on the morning of his death was to send his coachman to a bookseller with a list of books he wanted. When Heber died on 4 October 1833 at his home in Pimlico and was buried at Hodnet, Shropshire, his library was the largest private book collection in the world.

'The Heber sale, listed in sixteen volumes of sale catalogues, happened in many parts. It took as many as sixteen auction sales, between 1834 and 1837, to disperse his library fully. Henry "Measure" Miller bought heavily. So did the great manuscript collector Thomas Phillips, who bid on large lots. The Bodleian and British Libraries also benefitted from the low prices at the Heber sale. In turn, these books and manuscripts would, as we have already seen, eventually find their way to the Hoe sale and, from there on, to the collectors of today.'

Neela looked around the room, taking in her audience, row by row. 'And now, here they are,' she said, gesturing to the curated exhibit, 'a part of that Heber library, right before you, to view and examine and take in the bibliomania of the ages. Except that what we have here, ladies and gentleman, is something entirely unique: A portion of Richard Heber's library that didn't come from an auction, but directly to us from his library. Such a provenance for Heber's books has been unknown for a century-and-a-half – nearly everything institutions and collectors around the world possess of books and manuscripts that once belonged to Heber is from an auction lot. We have the honour and privilege and, I'd like to add, the bibliographical thrill, of seeing and touching books that have come to us directly from the home of Heber, from his house, his very bookshelves.

'How these came to be in the possession of his half-brother Reginald Heber, Bishop of Calcutta, is something we can only surmise. There are several possibilities. We think of Reginald Heber as the clergyman, but forget he was a poet, an accomplished hymn writer and a church historian. As a student at Brasenose College, Oxford, he was regarded as a thinker and critic. As a bishop in India, he felt compelled to travel widely in the north and, on one such trip, extended his travels to the south, pushing towards Trichy even though he was clearly exhausted and near collapse. That first Sunday in a church he even managed to give a short blessing in Tamil. And it was just a little later in the day that he died, overcome by the heat and illness.

'As with his brother Richard, books obviously played an important part in Reginald's life – who's to say he wasn't a modest collector himself? So, perhaps, when he left Hodnet for his bishopric in Calcutta, he took with him a portion of Richard's books, given to him, perhaps, by Richard himself as a farewell gift? Another possibility is that Reginald's wife Amelia and his children, who would join him in Calcutta just months later, could have brought these books along – sent, perhaps, by Richard himself to his brother. Or, maybe, these books weren't with Reginald at all or even with Amelia, but after Richard's death, his sister-in-law could have, while settling the affairs of the estate and sorting through the books, bequeathed them to St John's church in Trichy in memory of her husband.

The books may have stayed there, later becoming a part of the Heber College library, and when the Trichy College merged with Madras, the books were transported and finally housed at Heber Chapel, Tambaram. Today, while there are two biographies of Reginald Heber, there isn't a single full-length one of his brother Richard.

'The exhibit features many remarkable editions, stunning examples of the art of the early printed book and original editions of Keats, Coleridge, Wordsworth and Shelley. It includes a remarkable copy – Keats's very own – of his *Poems 1817*, with his ownership signature, and – this is the kicker – inscribed and signed to his betrothed, Fanny Brawne. I also want to point out one other item in the exhibit: A most interesting association copy, an extremely rare sale catalogue from 1662, that of Lazarus Seaman, significant for being one of the earliest surviving printed book catalogues in the world, inscribed by Dibdin to Heber! How come, you may well ask...

'In June 1817, Thomas Frognall Dibdin was forced, as heart-wrenching as this must have been for him, to auction a portion of his books to settle debts; the bibliographer frequently went through spells of having sufficient funds and not having enough, compelling him to sell his best books. The 1817 Dibdin sale contained some of his most cherished rare works, particularly some high spots in bibliography. And it was Heber who bought most of the lots at the Dibdin auction. The Lazarus Seaman catalogue even has a special signed binding, executed by none other than Charles Lewis, Dibdin's favourite binder. So you see, we have editions here that Keats and Dibdin had actually once held in their hands. There are other books here that Dibdin might have handled, for they carry his beautiful bookplate, a heraldic device, engraved and printed for him by the printer Bulmer.

'My dear fellow bibliophiles, before I finish and let you explore and savour the Heber collection on your own, to experience privately its myriad bibliophilic delights, I feel impelled to point out that book collecting isn't only about bibliomania; it's also a form of scholarship and an art in itself. Heber and Phillips and Hoe were scholars and artists in their own right. The scholar-collector Thomas Tanselle wrote, "Collectors create a view of the past through their collections – by the scope they set themselves and by the arrangement they impose on the artefacts. They have the pleasure of taking objects from disparate sources and fitting them together into a coherent entity. They are creating order in the same way that historical scholars do... The fun of collecting increases, paradoxically, in proportion to the seriousness with which one takes it." Imagine the fun Heber must have had! The awe that we feel today in the presence of his books was felt all those years ago by that celebrated book dealer John Carter himself, when he said, "No bibliophile can look unmoved on the small black oblong stamp of *Bibliotheca Heberiana*, however warmly he may deplore library stamps… "

'Since Heber's library was so vast – bibliophilic treasures hunted for everywhere and bought from countless auction sales, private collections and monastic libraries – we take in, through these books exhibited here today, the heroic bibliophilism of not just Heber, but of all the collectors before him, reaching back to the very beginnings of book collecting. And it continues to be the same, even *after* Heber! Though the books, catalogues and manuscripts exhibited here were not a part of the Heber sales after his death, we are still thrilled at simply knowing the extent to which Heber's books fuelled the bibliomania of the great modern collectors and the collections of the great rare-book institutions. Through Heber, we can draw a straight line from the first stirrings of bibliomania in the Middle Ages through the golden age of book collecting in the nineteenth and twentieth centuries and, finally, to the scholarly bibliophilism of our own modern bookmen and bookwomen – from Robert Hoe to Mary Hyde Eccles, the first bookwoman elected to the Roxburghe Club. Today, for those of us – collectors, dealers, librarians – involved in India's antiquarian and rare-book world, especially here in Chennai, having a portion of Heber's collection at hand is akin to having a talismanic presence, a bibliophile charm, a magnificent example to inflame our own bibliomania, our own quest and love for antiquarian books and manuscripts.'

28

Lot K

The following week, early on Thursday morning, just minutes after Kayal had opened the bookshop and let herself in, the phone began to ring insistently. It was Neela, calling to say that the Burton material had been authenticated. Heritage had received written responses from each of the documenting authorities and Templar had phoned her the previous evening, asking her to come by and view the letters.

'I'm calling you from Heritage,' Neela explained. 'I've just seen the letters confirming the material as being Burton's. The handwriting and style have been verified in all three items – the books, the letter *and* the K Fragment – as his own. The stationery paper is of the kind commonly supplied to Company staff in those days. On the issue of the ink alone, particularly in the K Fragment, there are two opinions: One claims he has no doubt it was the ink used then, while another feels the ink was the kind used a few years later.'

'Does that still mean the K Fragment will be counted as the real thing?' Kayal asked.

'Well, it's not unusual to have a small difference of opinion or slightly varying views in the verification of manuscripts and since, in this case, there's one strong opinion in favour of the ink, there will be no problem.'

'God, Neela! So the great game begins.'

Neela laughed and Kayal caught the excitement in her voice too.

'Hey, what about the Bannerman first edition?' exclaimed Kayal, referring to the scarce *Sambo* copy she had uncovered in Ooty.

Neela knew exactly what her associate had in mind because she had wondered briefly about the same thing with the big Heritage auction now looming close.

'I know... A good time to put it up for sale, right? With all those big bidders present.'

'Exactly, Neela,' Kayal responded. 'Where will we see another powerhouse crowd like this again at an auction?'

'But something is keeping me from letting it go, Kayal. Somehow I feel when it comes to this little book it can't, or shouldn't be, about who can bid highest for it but who wants it – who deserves it – the most.'

Both of them knew that this needn't always be the collector who can pay whatever it takes to knock it down; there were other bibliophilic considerations at play here, such as the fitness and rightness of ownership. Eventually, after further discussion, they decided on keeping it out of the upcoming auction.

'I've been trying to call Whitehead,' Neela said, 'but can't reach him on either of his phones. If he calls the bookshop, you can give him the fantastic news yourself. Or have him call me – I was hoping he could join me at Heritage to view the letters. Though, knowing him, he's probably rushing over to Heritage even as we speak.'

'I know! Will you be coming over to the shop later?'

'Yes, but I may have to attend a few meetings before I do that. I'll probably be there much later in the evening.'

A little later in the day, Whitehead himself turned up at Biblio, waving his cane, looking highly charged.

'Have you heard yet? Have you?' he asked breathlessly.

'Just a little while ago,' Kayal replied. 'Mr Whitehead, Neela has been trying to get hold of you.'

'Oh, I've been on the phone all morning – Kenton rang to tell me as soon as he heard from Heritage, and then Templar called to confirm it. And, soon afterwards, there was a flurry of calls from collectors and curators, not to mention our own club members. And then I was off to Heritage, looking over those authentication reports – they are all shipshape, by the way.'

'Shipshape?'

'All in order, all to our satisfaction.'

'Great. That's one of the things Neela was eager to convey to you.'

'Paper, ink, handwriting and style stand verified; its provenance – as coming from a lost, hitherto-unknown Burton heir – is, in the opinion of these experts, more than just highly plausible; it is, rather, most likely.'

'Terrific. So, will it be up for auction in the coming Heritage sale?'

'Yes, a few weeks from now, the first Sunday in April.'

'That's really soon!'

'It can't be soon enough for me,' Whitehead snapped back. 'Some of us have waited long enough for this – a whole lifetime. And when the day comes – presumptuous as this may sound on my part – I will carry it away too.'

'Anyway, here's to the auction. And I'm not going to wish you luck, Mr Whitehead, because I know you won't need it. To see the Karachi Fragment with you will be just as thrilling for Neela and me.'

She walked the collector to his car and hurried back inside to finish up with Burton. With the news of the Karachi Fragment being declared genuine and an impending auction around the corner that promised to be make auction history, there seemed more substance now, if not the same urgency, in her need to return to Burton's life in India.

———

The first news of some sensational Burton material coming on the market came in the form of a tweet that appeared just a few hours after Heritage had made a formal announcement of an important auction coming up on their calendar, which would feature, as its central piece, nothing less than a fragment of the fabled Karachi Report by Sir Richard Francis Burton. It was re-tweeted almost immediately and, by the end of the day, the BBC had begun to show an interest in pursuing the story. They wanted to interview Kenton and the angle they were keen to explore was the even more sensational discovery of a still-living descendant of the explorer.

While the schoolteacher basked in all this new-found attention ('I've become a local celebrity in Ooty,' he told Kayal when she called him, 'and rather notorious at the school!'), Whitehead, as the preeminent Indian collector of Burton, and Templar, as the owner of Heritage Auctions, were being courted by the media, who wanted them to comment on what such a discovery would mean to Burton collecting and scholarship. As expected, it sparked immediate interest in libraries with a large Burton holding, from the Royal Geographical Society and the Huntington to the British Library. While bibliographers speculated on how that knight of Burtoniana, Quentin Keynes – who had pursued the Karachi Papers all his life – might have reacted to such explosive news, the media focused on Viscount Pilkington's blustery announcement that he would attend the auction in person and bid on it until the 'holy grail' was knocked down to him.

Some newspapers and magazines wanted to publish the K Fragment, along with the Burton–Parvathy letter, but they were politely but firmly turned down by Heritage. Auction houses were not obligated to disclose details and in terms of sheer publicity, the K Fragment would be of more interest if some of its mystery was retained. Lord Das issued a press statement that the special catalogue in preparation would offer just a hint of the fragment's contents, meant purely as a teaser, but it would be enough to establish that it was, indeed, in Burton's own manuscript hand.

Across a platform of reactions, the dominant tone was one of scepticism. Burton scholars and fans weighed in on blogs, shot off letters to newspapers, appeared on panel discussions on television, saying that while there probably was, somewhere in the world, an unrecognized Burton heir, maybe even two, that missing heir couldn't possibly be Kenton Francis Selvaganesan. The Indian media, too, now got into the act, enthusiastically celebrating him as Burton's long-lost Indian heir.

A week after Heritage's notice, the auction house followed it with a catalogue showcasing the K Fragment. The catalogue, though slim, was lavishly produced in full colour, printed on fine paper and contained an account of Kenton's discovery, in his own words, an introduction by Arcot Templar on the importance and significance of the K Fragment for Burtoniana, a two-paragraph text excerpt from the report and two photographic reproductions of the K Fragment. The first image, also found on the catalogue cover, was of the handsome folder that Cheran Perumal had designed to hold the K Fragment. The cover of the folder was made from colourful Nepalese Lokta handmade paper with the title, 'The K Fragment', beautifully etched into a recessed rectangle decorated with typographic fluerons. The second was a close-up image of a portion of the fragment, offering an impression of Burton's manuscript hand. The most interesting aspect of the fragment – Burton's little note on having no choice but to sample the wares of the brothel himself – was, of course, not displayed in the catalogue. This was reserved for the eyes (and pleasure) of whoever would carry away the prize of the auction. A PDF of the catalogue was made available for viewing on the Heritage website.

The Heritage auction had been slotted for a Sunday morning in the first week of April. The standard practice, even when the heart of an auction was some rare, extraordinary item, was to have a series of lots precede it, before rolling out the evening's centrepiece. Heritage, rather unusually, had chosen Lot K – the K Fragment – as the first one to come up for bidding, feeling it would have too disruptive an effect on the auction if brought out in the middle, and wouldn't get the importance it deserved if kept for the end. Among those expected to bid with every intention to win were the Huntington Library, the British Library and the Royal Geographical Society. Curators and rare-book librarians from these institutions would not, however, be putting in a personal appearance, but would bid over the telephone or online via Invaluable, a global live-auctions marketplace that offered online bidding services to several prestigious auction houses.

Rummaging around in her Alwarpet apartment, Kayal gathered her notes on the Burton biographies once again, this time sharpening the focus of her research on two critical points: Burton's trip to Ooty and what his biographers had to say about the Karachi Report. So far, she had read only Burton's version, which had been a straightforward account of events that were now highly disputed. What she needed to know was how most Burton scholars viewed the existence, or non-existence, of the Karachi Report. She sat still for a few minutes, thinking to herself how odd it now felt to dip back into Burton's life at precisely that point where the Karachi Report had become a source of controversy in his career.

But first, Burton's journey to Ooty. All accounts of his life were unanimous about the details. In July 1846, Burton, along with several soldiers, came down with cholera. By September, he had to be hospitalized in Bombay, and the disease had such a debilitating effect on him that he was granted two years' sick leave. Burton was miserable about this – he didn't want to be on leave – but he would have to follow the Company's orders and spend that time in a sanitorium in Ootacamund, a genteel hill station in peninsular India, healing.

In January 1847, Burton left in a *pattymar*, spending a month in Goa, before continuing his journey to Ooty by road. Here, he stayed in a hotel run by an

Englishman. When he first arrived amidst the hills, he was delighted, embracing everything that was different about an Indian hill station and appreciating how the very air was so different from that of the plains. Then the cold got to him, as did the air of lethargy that hung over the place.

Burton would later remark in his first published work, *Goa, and the Blue Mountains*, that during the periods that Ooty was not in season, it turned into a dull provincial town. The *Bombay Almanac and Directory* of 1843 described the Nilgiris or Blue Mountains as 'exceedingly beautiful and of the grandest and most romantic description in the world', but Burton complained, 'Nothing could be duller or more disagreeable.' He was sick of the cold and dampness that pervaded the hills.

He wrote:

> *You have ventured into one of those uncomfortable localities – a cold place in a hot country...life on the Nielgherries – a perfect anomaly. You dress like an Englishman, and lead a quiet, gentlemanly life — doing nothing... At the same time, your monthly bills for pale ale and hot curries, heavy tiffins, and numerous cheroots tell you, as plainly as such mute inanimate things can, that you have not quite cast the slough of Anglo-Indian life.*
>
> *During your first fortnight, all was excitement, joy, delight. You luxuriated in the cool air. Your appetite*

improved... You praised the vegetables, and fell into ecstasy at the sight of peaches, apples, strawberries and raspberries, after years of plantains, guavas and sweet limes.

The end of the month found you in a state of mind bordering upon the critical. You began to opine that the scenery has its deficiencies... And now, sated with the joys of the eye and mouth, you turn round upon Ootacamund and inquire blatantly what amusement it has to offer you.

Is there a hunt? No, of course not!

A race-course? Ditto, ditto!

Is there a cricket-club? Yes. If you wish to become a member, you will be admitted readily enough; you will pay four shillings per mensem for the honour, but you will not play at cricket.

A library? There are two: one in the Club, the other kept by a Mr Warren: the former deals in the modern, the latter in the antiquated style of light – extremely light – literature... By some peculiar fatality, the book you want is always missing. And the absence of a catalogue instead of exciting your industry, seems rather to depress it than otherwise... Is there a theatre, a concert-room, a tennis, a racket, or a fives-court? No, and again no!

Then pray what is there?

We will presently inform you.

Ooty was really more a holiday place for officers of the Madras Presidency and Burton unexpectedly found himself feeling like an alien among his own people. The English had turned the hill station, surrounded by Toda tribes, into an English village. The snobbish, unattached Englishwomen here would have little to do with anyone below the rank of field officer (a good reason, Kayal thought, for him to pursue an attractive local woman like Parvathy). With little to do, Burton set about making his first attempt at translation: The Pilpay fables, written by the 'Indian Aesop'. He also made attempts to learn Telugu and Toda, though not with the enthusiasm he had displayed earlier for other regional languages. Towards the end of his stay, he had managed to make a start with writing a travelogue, making this his earliest foray into writing. Wow, Kayal thought, Ooty became the place where Burton not only tried his hand at translation for the first time, but made his debut as a writer as well!

When there came the mention of Burton coming down with something called rheumatic ophthalmia, an infection of the eye which affected his vision, Kayal sat up, her heart racing just a little bit. But she couldn't locate any mention of a nurse who had attended to him. After just four months in Ooty, he was described as having persuaded the doctors that he was ready for active duty and left for Bombay in September 1847 – this time, stopping in Calicut on his way back. In the short time that Burton had been in the Blue Mountains, Sir Charles Napier had resigned and returned to England. Sindh was under Bombay's rule now. But Burton was happy that he could return to the Sindh survey office. So that was that, Kayal noted. No official mention of Parvathy anywhere, or of the Karachi Report while in Ooty.

Back in Sindh, he mastered Persian and began learning Arabic. He took an exam in Persian and did splendidly. His interest in Islam grew as he immersed himself deeper and deeper into Sufism. He would pray and fast and wait for experiences of ecstasy. It's quite probable that it was at this point that the idea of going on a pilgrimage to Mecca, disguised as an Iranian merchant, began taking shape in his mind, if it hadn't even earlier. He passed his Sindhi and Punjabi exams and even had a working knowledge of Multani now.

The big blow came in April 1848, when the Second Sikh War broke out. Confident that he would be made official translator, since he was the only one in the regiment who could speak both Punjabi and Sindhi, Burton applied for the post. But, to his shock, the job went to a young officer who only knew Hindi. From here on, Burton would attribute his failures to his role in preparing the Karachi Report, convinced that he had been ostracized for this alone, and punished by having all further possibilities of career advancement blocked.

Dejected that his seven years in India had been what he looked upon as one more failure, he applied for more sick leave and noted later how 'sick, sorry and almost in tears of rage' he was as he said goodbye. He left for England in March 1849. He remained an officer on the payroll of the British East India Company for a further thirteen years (foregoing nineteen years of pension from the Indian Army), though he would never see action in the subcontinent again.

Kayal read on, her interest intensifying when she discovered that Burton had returned to India in 1876, this time, with his wife Isabel, and visited Ooty again. It was clear that he attached no sentimental value to this visit, describing the place as he saw it now as *'a rotten hole full of middle class, respectably pious and water swilling paratts! A race that disagrees with me.'* Why such a virulent reaction, Kayal wondered. Had there been a scandal all those years ago, making him flee just four months after his arrival? A scandal that had pitted all of Ooty's proper, stuffy colonialists against him? If that had, indeed, been the case, Burton wasn't telling.

Kayal reviewed her notes on Burton's last years. The pilgrimage to Mecca and Harrar had been done, the search for the headwaters of the Nile and the sighting of Lake Tanganyika over, the translation of the *Kama Sutra* and the *Arabian Nights* completed. After some years of consular service in Trieste, Burton and Isabel were now back in London. His last year was spent working on a translation of the most sexually explicit text in existence then – *The Perfumed Garden*. Isabel, he wrote, was nervous about its publication.

In October 1890, while working on the last page of *The Perfumed Garden*, Burton became seriously ill and died shortly afterwards. Three days or so after his demise, Isabel locked herself in her husband's study and, with the help of a maid, sorted through his papers in order to decide what she preferred to keep and what she wanted to discard. Having completed that task, she destroyed several of his letters and manuscripts, along with the unfinished translation, by setting the lot on fire. Her act was widely criticized and even labelled 'a crime'. Outraged, Burton's friends turned their backs on her. There was a public outcry in the papers. Mary S. Lovell, in her biography of Burton, *A Rage to Live*, seemed to offer a reasonable defence of Isabel's actions. For now, the question remained: Was the Karachi Report one of the manuscripts that Isabel had thrown into the flames? If she had, no mention had been made of it, either by her or any of the people who delved into Burton's life and wrote about it.

Sitting back once she was satisfied with her reading, Kayal realized she now had two sets of notes: One was a broad outline of Burton's years in India; the other was a clutch of details on the Karachi Report –

what Burton and Isabel had said about them and the different conclusions their biographers had come to. Napier's records showed that he had closed down some brothels, but there was no mention of Burton's report – or even a reference to any report that might have led to Napier's actions. But if such a report existed and Burton had asked him to keep it confidential, why would Napier have mentioned it?

Arguing against its existence, Burton scholars were asking why, if the Karachi Report had caused such a disruption in his career, there was no mention in the Company's records of Burton being in trouble. His records were clean, with not a single mention of disrepute or disgrace. However, Kayal found two letters in *The Book of Burtoniana* that touched up on Burton being under a cloud, and Napier unwilling to assign him a posting. Something about Burton having disobeyed Napier, and the men finding him too 'bumptious'. She didn't know how this fit in with the rest of the narrative.

Kayal turned again to the other questions his biographers were raising: Burton had been just one more staff appointment among hundreds; why would he have been singled out by a senior officer for such a clandestine mission? Burton's disappointment at being denied the interpreter's post and blaming it on his role in the Karachi male-bordello scandal seemed totally uncalled for when one thought about it logically. Since he already had two staff appointments as interpreter, it was perfectly in keeping with the regulations governing appointments within the regiment that a new man, even one with fewer linguistic skills than Burton, would be preferred over him. It would seem it had been too ambitious and unrealistic on Burton's part to expect a third such appointment.

As a famous explorer and translator, looking back at his life, had Burton despaired at not having distinguished himself or established a reputation to reckon with in his early years? Had he invented the scandal of a notorious, sexually oriented report that had supposedly kept him from all further advancement in the Company to explain away his reasons for leaving India, feeling defeated and a failure? Besides, as his biographers reminded readers, Burton loved a good scandal; he hated to be thought of as one more conventional, prudish Victorian.

And what of Burton and the Great Game? In her biography of her husband, Isabel Burton explored this idea further, claiming that Kipling had, in fact, based the character of his fictional secret agent Strickland (described as 'the unconvincing Sherlock Holmes of all disguises') on Burton. She also recorded that Napier had used her husband more than once as an intelligence officer, disguised as a local, to infiltrate the ranks of rebellious tribes in the hills. There didn't seem to be any evidence for this, nor for the other claims that the Sindh Survey was only a front for spying on any advances Tsarist Russia might have been making in Central Asia and towards India. There was some evidence, however, that a few British officers were using trained Indian natives as spies, called Pundits; their mission was to travel, disguised as Buddhist pilgrims, to Afghanistan, Turkistan and Tibet to collect information on any brewing rebellion. But if Napier and Burton and the Sindh Survey had, indeed, been a part of this, there was no record of it.

This led to the inevitable question: Even allowing for Burton's mischievous embellishments, why would he make up a thing like the Karachi Report if there had been no basis to it? Kayal took a while to think this through. It was probably safe to speculate that given how Burton was inclined in those later years, he would be curious enough to visit female and male bordellos, and interested enough in the goings-on there to make notes. Had he availed of the services offered by those brothels, slept with the prostitutes? With the women, very possibly, but unlikely where the men were concerned. He had, possibly, simply an insatiable ethnological fascination for sex.

Burton's biographers felt that the notes he had made while visiting the brothels may have eventually become the notorious 'Terminal Essay' at the end of his translation of the *Arabian Nights*. The ten-volume *Arabian Nights*, published in 1886, had a 'Section D' at the end for notes on 'pederasty'. Burton's notes and an 18,000-word essay in the tenth volume was one of the earliest published discussions in English of same-sex practices. But Burton's knowledge of such practices in male brothels could just as well have come later.

Somewhere on her shelves, Kayal knew she had an abridged version of the Burton translation. There! On the bottom row. She sat down on the floor, pulling out the heavy, one-volume *The Book of Thousand Nights and a Night*, and hurriedly turned the pages to the end. Luckily, this edition contained the 'Terminal Essay', and Kayal pored over the notes introducing the essay. This was the one section, the notes said, the one part of the *Arabian Nights* that was not from the *Tales*, but in Burton's own writing – his own little supplement to the *Arabian Nights*. Most readers generally knew that Burton's *Arabian Nights* was a translation, but not everyone realized that in the Burton translation there were supplementary chapters such as the 'Terminal Essay' that were the translator's own original writings. She glanced quickly over the first few paragraphs that read:

> *In 1845, when Sir Charles Napier had conquered and annexed Sind, despite a fraction (mostly venal) which sought favour with the now defunct 'Court of Directors to the Honourable East India Company', the veteran*

began to consider his conquest with a curious eye. It was reported to him that Karachi, a townlet of some two thousand souls and distant not more than a mile from camp, supported no less than three lupanars or bordels, in which not women but boys and eunuchs, the former demanding nearly a double price, lay for hire.

Being then the only British officer who could speak Sindi, I was asked indirectly to make enquiries and to report upon the subject, and I undertook the task on express condition that my report should not be forwarded to the Bombay Government, from whom supporters of the Conqueror's policy could expect scant favour, mercy or justice. Accompanied by a Munshi, Mirza Mohammed Hosyn of Shiraz, and habited as a merchant, Mirza Abdullah the Bushiri passed many an evening in the townlet, visited all the porneia and obtained the fullest details which were duly despatched to Government House.

But the 'Devil's Brother' presently quitted Sind, leaving in his office my unfortunate official: this found its way with sundry other reports to Bombay and produced the expected result. A friend in the Secretariat informed me that my summary dismissal from the service had been formally proposed by one of Sir Charles Napier's successors, whose decease compels me parcere sepulto. *But this excess of outraged modesty was not allowed.*

Although several biographers and collectors had looked extensively for the report Burton mentioned, they had failed to turn it up. Why? Kayal made a note in the margin: *Kenton Francis Selva's copy part of the missing report?* But as she read deeper into the 'Terminal Essay', her notes began to reveal new aspects to the issue and difficult questions now began to persist, questions that most of Burton's biographers had repeatedly asked. She made a note of them and rang Neela.

'I've been going over my notes on Burton – from all the recent reading – and some things don't add up... Like, who was it that tipped off Napier about the bordellos? Who in the Bombay Government House cared enough to haul up Burton for it and summarily dismiss him from service? It's strange, isn't it, that Burton doesn't name them? By the time he began publishing his books and articles, most of these officials were very old or dead – so what compunctions did he have in not naming them?'

'Kayal, you're not telling me anything new,' Neela remarked. 'These gaps in Burton's account are well known. Most Burton collectors like Whitehead are well aware of them. And the way they've usually explained them is by pointing out that the records of Burton's years in India have always been scant; so no absolute conclusions can be drawn. You were right, though, to bring it up. These questions would remain valid if Burton hadn't been telling the truth about the Karachi

Report. But now that we may have to acknowledge that he *wasn't* dissembling and that there could well have been such a report all along, it would be interesting to view these lacunae in Burton's story again, but from *his* perspective; in other words, assume that there must have been, after all, a conspiracy against him, as he claimed. So far everyone has used the lingering problems in his Karachi story *against* Burton; it would be interesting, even if only in some academic fashion, to see how they might be used to bolster his theory instead. But you can do that later, perhaps, once the auction is behind us and we return to our routine here.'

Of course! What was I thinking, Kayal admonished herself as she hung up. She ought to have known that Whitehead and Neela and scores of other Burton scholars would have arrived at the same puzzling dead ends where the Karachi Report was concerned. Kayal put away her notes. Time, then, to get over to the bookshop. The Burton of the books would have to wait; out there, very possibly, was his own flesh and blood, on the verge of announcing his presence to the world. It's going to be an interesting but hectic week, thought Kayal, as she rushed out of the flat, dodging her grandmother's question about lunch.

29

Under the Hammer

By 9.45 a.m. on that first Sunday in April the auction house was thrumming with activity. The serious bidders had filled the front rows that had been reserved for them; several auction regulars at Heritage took their customary seats, while the rest were occupied with the largest gathering of bibliophiles, bibliographers and collectors Kayal had ever seen. The usual suspects were there, of course: the Ziegenbalg bibliophiles, local dealers and collectors and some auction addicts. But also present – in the hope of snagging the K Fragment for their rare-manuscript collection – were the curators and special-collection librarians from the Nehru Memorial Museum and Library, the Sarasvathi Mahal Library, Kolkata's National Library, the Connemara

Public Library, the Salar Jung Museum and the Asiatic Society of Mumbai.

A row of young house clerks with laptops and phones occupied both sides of the aisle, ready to take online bids; these would, primarily, be the bids

At an auction, a rarity can go either way; it may realize a price that falls well below what it should have gone for or — as is frequently the case — considerably more than anyone had estimated.

from the famous institutional collectors abroad, such as the Huntington, the British Library and the Royal Geographical Society. They would be the serious game players, Kayal knew, whom Nallathambi Whitehead and Viscount Pilkington, the two most formidable private collectors of Burton, would have to go up against. The two, she anticipated, would either be outbidding each other or slashing down the offers of other institutional bidders in the room, who wished to take the prize away from India. The auction catalogue that Heritage had mailed out had put down an estimated sale price of anything between ₹25 lakh to ₹35 lakh for the Karachi Fragment. It was an inconsequential amount for the rare-book institutional libraries in the West, but significant for Indian collectors and librarians.

Two days ahead of the auction, the K Fragment had, as was the custom, gone on display at Heritage, allowing bidders to preview it. Bidders – as well as what collectors often cheekily referred to as the 'non-bibliographic public' – had streamed through Heritage to get a second look at the item, or register themselves and collect their bidding paddles. The K Fragment was now housed in a blue clamshell box, made by the binder Pandian. The papers inside were laid loosely in a chemise which was encased in a decorated, calligraphed buff folder that Cheran had made. Commissioning Pandian and Cheran to make a special binding for the papers had been Arcot's initiative to give these loose, slightly soiled stationery sheets some decorative and typographic flourish.

As he took the rostrum, Lord Das became keenly aware that, among all the book artefacts he had auctioned here, nothing more unique had ever graced the Heritage auction before.

Kayal looked around the room for her posse, hoping to also catch sight of the notorious Viscount Pilkington, the only big auction player from the West to have actually made the trip from London to bid in person. Whitehead, she noted, had taken his favourite place, the aisle seat in the second row on the left. Kenton seemed content to stay at the back, probably wanting a fuller view of the proceedings. Neela was in a row mostly occupied by the Ziegenbalg Club collectors. Arcot Templar was all over the room, greeting people and ensuring that the more promising collectors had a copy of the catalogue. Finally, she spotted the Englishman, furiously typing on an iPad. It surprised her to see that he was wearing jeans and had long hair. Ah, so the Viscount is a cool dude after all, thought Kayal. If only he hadn't been such a rabid Raj worshipper... Seeing the auction was going to start, she quickly took the seat her boss had saved for her.

'Ladies and gentleman,' Lord Das called out, appearing suddenly on the podium and tapping his gavel lightly. 'We now come straightaway to the main item of the morning, the centrepiece of today's auction at Heritage, a fragment from Sir Richard Francis Burton's Karachi Papers.'

A hush fell over the room.

In his plummiest voice, Lord Das announced, 'Heritage Auctions is proud to offer this legendary piece of Burtoniana for sale.'

On cue, two porters rolled in a small filigreed cart with a velvet cushion, on top of which lay Pandian's magnificent custom-made clamshell box containing the star item.

How dramatic, thought Kayal, greatly amused at the sight of the cart.

The porters stepped back as Lord Das nimbly danced around the cart. Lifting the box gently off the cushion, he slowly opened the lid, smacking his lips as though he were about to unveil a gourmet dish, before announcing, 'May I present, ladies and gentlemen, fragments from the long-lost – and presumed missing – infamous Karachi Papers.'

Many in the audience immediately stood up or craned their necks to catch a glimpse of the item, but all that was visible was the handsome folder inside which the papers lay.

'Laid in with the fragment,' added Lord Das, 'is a letter by Burton in his manuscript hand and two books, with the ownership signatures of Burton *and*

Johann Ludwig Burckhardt. These two titles, books by Burckhardt, are of extraordinary significance for being such remarkable association copies. The three items, then, comprise Lot K, which is now open for bidding.'

To get things going, Lord Das himself opened the auction with a bid of ₹50,000. 'Bids in increments of fifty and upwards, please,' he announced. It was a considerable bid to kick off with and the auctioneer's purpose was to indicate to the more serious players in the room what the reserve price for this item might be. The reserve had been set at ₹10 lakh, a sum that, of course, remained undisclosed to the players. No one except Lord Das, Kenton Selvaganesan and Arcot Templar knew what the reserve was, though the more seasoned auctioneers would, perhaps, have been able to make a good guess. From the start, Lord Das had known it was going to be difficult for Heritage to put a price on this lot. It wasn't, after all, just another piece of writing in Burton's bibliography; it was a piece of Burton mythology. Since the property belonged to Kenton, it had been left to him to set the reserve price, but the schoolteacher had deferred to Templar in this matter and the director of Heritage had settled on this price. A veteran auctioneer, it had fallen to Lord Das to throw a bid out there that would speed things up and quickly take them past the reserve price, allowing the real contest to begin.

'One,' offered Antara, raising her paddle, just to get things rolling. She didn't want the prize – unless she could actually get it for her bid, which was unlikely.

'I have a lakh,' Lord Das stated, pleased with the swift bid which, more importantly for him, was the correct bid. People calling out wrong bids were a trial at auctions.

'One-and-a-half,' someone called out from the back.

Kayal recognized a local antiquarian dealer, bidding for a private Japanese collector who probably wished to remain anonymous.

'One-and-a-half lakhs. I am looking for two.' Das looked around the room. 'Let's not dawdle, ladies and gentleman.'

The two players the crowd had their eyes on, Viscount Pilkington and Nallathambi Whitehead, had not yet made a move.

A clerk tracking online bids raised her paddle.

'Two lakhs, online!' Das called out quickly.

From here on, paddles were raised in quick succession, with online bids continuing to raise the bid higher and bids from within the room coming mainly from the Indian librarians and curators. Still there was nothing from Whitehead or Pilkington, or even the famous American and British rare-book institutions.

When the call reached nine and a half lakhs, the bidding paused. The crowd, which had been quiet so far, began to murmur, people turning their heads this way and that to see where the next bid would come from. Lord Das looked at the online bid callers. They shook their heads.

'Nothing from the room?' he prompted.

Finally, after a tense twenty seconds, Whitehead raised his cane and gently brought it down, tapping once.

'Ten with Mr Whitehead!' Lord Das cried out in relief. The reserve had been met and now the bid increments could be upped. By how much would the K Fragment exceed its reserve price, Das wondered momentarily and then quickly brought his attention back to the room, announcing that the bidding could now begin in higher increments, making the crowd stir in anticipation.

Viscount Pilkington placed his first bid by a slight wave of his catalogue. Kayal recalled Neela telling her that he seldom called out or used his paddle. From him there always came a tiny gesture with his catalogue to let the room know he was still in the bidding.

Das, with his practised eye for recognizing the bidding gestures of collectors, caught it quickly and called out, 'Eleven lakhs with Viscount Pilkington.'

Many in the room whirled around or rose halfway in their seats to take a peek at the Viscount.

Without wasting another moment, Whitehead tapped his cane hard. Twice.

'Thank you, Mr Whitehead,' Lord Das called out. 'The bid stands at thirteen lakhs.'

Since neither of the two principal players was articulating his bids, those in the audience found themselves swivelling their heads from one man to the other, as if following a tennis match, to catch the all-important gesture or nod.

Pilkington raised his catalogue and once he was certain Lord Das had seen it, raised it higher. And just as Lord Das was about to call out a doubled bid again, the British collector raised his catalogue even higher.

Lord Das swallowed. The gesture meant that the Viscount had tripled the bid.

'Sixteen lakhs. The bid is against you, Mr Whitehead.'

Whitehead tapped his cane four times, but the sounds were so faint, Lord Das had strain to catch each one.

'Twenty lakhs, ladies and gentleman!' Lord Das exclaimed, looking very pleased. The reserve price had just been doubled!

Suddenly, a clerk raised a paddle. A new player, online.

'Twenty-one lakhs,' purred Lord Das.

'One of the big three?' Kayal asked Neela in a whisper.

'Has to be.'

They were both thinking of the Huntington, the British Library and the Royal Geographical Society.

Before Pilkington or Whitehead could make a move, another clerk had his paddle up.

'Twenty-two,' Lord Das announced, his surprise evident in his tone.

'It *is* them!' Kayal exclaimed. 'They've woken up.'

Abandoning his cane, Whitehead called out, 'Twenty-five!'

Lord Das didn't have time to state the bid, as it was raised almost immediately by someone calling out very loudly and commandingly, 'I make that thirty!'

Lord Das and the auction veterans in the room looked around, startled. It was Pilkington. The silent bidder had chucked his catalogue and had, perhaps for the first time, actually called out his bid!

Whitehead, chasing Pilkington, raised it to thirty-five.

'Thirty-six!'

'Thirty-seven!'

'Thirty-eight!'

Not to be left behind, the online bidders pursued with equal gusto.

Until Pilkington snorted and called out, 'Fifty!'

Lord Das's voice trembled just a tiny bit as he acknowledged the bid. 'Ladies and gentleman, we have fifty lakhs for the elusive K Fragment!'

Kayal looked expectantly at Whitehead. Would he drop out now? He had mentioned in confidence earlier that ₹50 lakhs was as high as he would take it. 'Seventy!' trumpeted Whitehead, not the least bit perturbed.

It looked like this lot would set a new auction record for Burtoniana! Turning around, Kayal noticed Kenton looking quite overwhelmed by what was unfolding.

Pilkington wasn't expecting it and swore aloud, his surprise and annoyance apparent to all.

'That was terribly foolish of Whitehead. He's overplaying his hand,' Neela whispered to Kayal, looking concerned.

'Ladies and gentleman, we now have seventy lakhs for the K Fragment!'

Both collectors waited to see if any of the online players would step in.

No paddles went up. Kayal and Neela realized at once what must have happened: The three great rare-book institutions had probably decided not to pursue the Karachi Papers any further. From where the bid stood, it could easily climb higher and they did not consider the lot worth that much. All of Lord Das's attention was now focused on the two remaining bidders in the room.

'Seventy-five.' Finally, from Pilkington.

'Eighty,' right back from Whitehead.

Oh God, thought Kayal, he's lost his head.

Neela said, 'I was afraid of this – I should never have let him bid. I should have done the bidding for him. This will tie up his finances for *years*! Let's hope he's outbid.'

'Eighty-five,' Pilkington called out easily; he had every intention of clinching it at one crore and the crowd began to sense this too.

'Thank God!' said Neela, breathing more easily. 'There's nothing wrong in being the underbidder in a contest like this. Nallathambi can still hold his head high.'

Lord Das waited.

Nothing from Whitehead.

'The bid is against you, sir,' Lord Das reminded him.

Pilkington relaxed, looking around the room, even smiling and nodding at a few people.

Lord Das was happy to knock it down at where the bid stood; the K Fragment had reached dizzying heights this evening, commanding a stratospheric price that even Heritage hadn't dreamt of. Thanks to the bibliomania of the rival Burton collectors, the value of this slender piece of Burtoniana had skyrocketed.

Whitehead picked up his cane, which had slid to the ground, straightened himself up and said calmly to Lord Das, 'Ninety.'

'Enough,' Pilkington murmured. 'I bid one hundred.'

More gasps around the room. It was the might of the pound sterling speaking. This was one of the toughest odds Indian collectors faced in the international antiquarian market, the way the Indian rupee stacked up against the dollar and the pound.

'One crore,' the auction crier repeated, slowly and softly, uncharacteristically for him.

'That's it, Neela!' Kayal exclaimed. 'Whitehead's strung him up as far as he can. Now he'll quit.'

Neela's comment about how the collector was playing with fire was drowned out by a sudden uproar in the room. The crowd was practically up on its feet.

'What? What is it?' Kayal asked Antara, tapping her on the shoulder.

'Whitehead just placed a counter-bid.'

Lord Das was asking the room to quieten down. 'One-and-half crores now with Mr Whitehead. The bid stands at one-and-a-half crores against Viscount Pilkington.'

A stillness now descended on the room. All eyes turned to the English collector.

For a few seconds, Pilkington looked hesitant, undecided, and then, meeting Lord Das's eyes, firmly shook his head.

'Sold to Nallathambi Whitehead!' Lord Das called out and, forgetting himself, added rather shrilly, 'Beautifully done, sir!'

The room burst into applause, cheers and hoots, followed by clamorous, heated conversation. People were boisterously congratulating Whitehead. Kenton bounded across the room, manoeuvring his way through the crowd, and shook the collector's hand. From the other side of the room, Arcot Templar mimed the gesture of doffing an imaginary hat to acknowledge his old rival's moment of triumph.

In all this, where was Pilkington, wondered Kayal, scanning the room, and grinned when she saw him pushing past the crowd to the exit in great haste. He's not going to come around here for a long time, she thought to herself.

Neela didn't bother going up to Whitehead. Her brows knotted, she watched the scene unfolding before her. Kayal leaned across to her. 'Are you worried for him?' she asked.

'He may have won,' Neela told Kayal, trying to speak above the noise in the room, 'but he doesn't realize how this is going to put a dent in his collecting. It is going to cramp his collecting style for a long time to come. What is he going to do in the future, when other things he badly desires come on the market and he lacks the funds to buy them?' She knew how a collector's mind worked; once the chase was over, the eye turned automatically to a new prize. 'Arcot though,' she added, 'is going to do very well out of this after the fat 23 per cent buyer's premium he'll be slapping on to this sale.'

There were still eleven lots to get through, but Lord Das was unable to get the room to settle down in order to continue. He decided, under the circumstances, that the best thing would be to announce a five-minute break and then resume.

Several in the audience, including Kayal and Neela, made their way out, leaving behind only those who were keen on bidding for the coming lots.

'Neela, what time is the Ziegenbalg Club party?' asked Kayal, as they pushed their way through the crowd and out of the auction premises.

'Seven, I think.'

The Ziegenbalg bibliophiles had arranged a lavish reception with drinks and dinner for its members and their guests in honour of the evening's winner.

'I'd like to go home and check on Paati for a bit,' Kayal told her. 'Shall I join you later for the reception?'

'Of course. I wish I could slip away too!' said Neela, 'But there are too many people I've promised to spend time with this evening. You take off.'

30

Dark Bibliophily

The Ziegenbalg Club reception in honour of the winner of the auction was being held at the handsome exhibit hall of the Book Arts Centre. Since the champion had turned out to be one of their very own, Neela, joining the party at around 7.30 p.m., sensed real jubilation in the air. Arcot was buttonholing important bibliophiles in the room, booming, 'A spectacular success, wouldn't you say?'. Indeed, Nallathambi Whitehead, the new owner of the K Fragment, was not the only one being fêted in the room. Nearly everyone present – collectors, librarians and dealers alike – had realized that the pay-off trickled down to two supporting players in the room. After today's high-profile auction, Templar and Heritage had inched a little closer to realizing the dream of joining the league of such international auction houses as Swann or Sotheby's. And then there was the other star of the evening – Kenton Selva, a real Burton heir in their midst! That wasn't something you saw every day.

It was at this point that Neela noticed her associate dashing into the room, slightly out of breath.

'Hey, didn't I say there was no rush to get here?' she said, walking up to Kayal.

'I know,' said Kayal, trying to catch her breath. 'I hurried back for a reason.'

'Everything okay at home?' Neela asked, concerned.

'Nothing wrong at home. It's actually something else – '

A pair of rare-book librarians from Shimla passing by them stopped to say hello. Kayal waited impatiently, but as soon as they moved on someone else came and borrowed Neela. Her boss stepped away, signalling at Kayal to give her a few minutes. Kayal headed for the bar, asked for a cocktail, drank it quickly and asked for one more. I may as well find Kenton, she thought, and wandered around the room, finally catching sight of him on the balcony. She stepped out on to the wide balcony, where it was cooler. The night sky was black, with a crescent moon piercing it. Kenton was standing there by himself, puffing on a cigarette. Kayal walked up to the schoolteacher, her heart pounding.

Moving up silently behind him, she asked, keeping her voice even and steady, 'It's your handiwork, isn't it?'

'What?' Kenton replied distractedly, turning her way. 'Oh, it's you. Handiwork? What handiwork?'

'The Burton fragment. Rather, should I say, the *Selvaganesan* fragment?'

There was silence, and then a flicker of... something...on his face, and then he straightened his shoulders. When he spoke again, his voice was even. 'How did you catch on?'

Kayal had expected feigned indignation or firm denial, but not direct admission. Was he trying to hide a grin, she thought, alarmed and offended.

'How do you think?' she shot back.

'If I knew, Clever Girl, I wouldn't be asking,' he said patronizingly. 'I thought I had it neatly tied up.'

'Well, not neatly enough. You—you're not denying it.'

'What would be the point? I think you've got me. And, anyway, the auction's over and I've got what I wanted.'

'If Whitehead's already paid the sale price, you do realize, don't you, that you'll have to give it back?'

The schoolteacher remained silent, sipping at his drink. He didn't seem troubled at all, and Kayal grew more perplexed. 'Isn't that what the hoax was about? It had to be about the money...'

The mention of money seemed to set him off. He

burst into a fit of laughter. 'Oh, yes, of course the money,' he said finally, 'and a few other trivial things. So what now? Are you and Neela going to bring the roof down?'

'Neela doesn't know yet, but I'm heading her way now to tell her what I know. After that, it's up to her – and, I suppose, Whitehead and Templar and, maybe, even the Ziegenbalg Club – to decide how this will be dealt with. Not kindly, I imagine.'

'Look, before you and Neela begin trumpeting this around – '

'Trumpeting!' Kayal said angrily, cutting him short 'You've dragged us and the bookshop into this...this despicable form of deception.'

'Listen, this is no time for exposure or explanations. There's a celebration on... And don't worry, I'm not running away anywhere with the money. I can explain it all, but let's take this elsewhere. Just make sure Neela and you show up at my suite here in the Book Arts Centre building – Suite 402 – at 9 p.m. And be on time.'

Giving Kayal no time to respond – shocked as she was with the sudden transformation of the quiet, unassuming schoolteacher she had known thus far – Kenton strode out of the balcony, crossed the reception room quickly, and headed straight for the bar.

At 9 p.m., the bookwomen of Biblio knocked on the door of Suite 402. Neela had turned ashen when she had heard Kayal's suspicions about the fragment and when Kayal told her that Kenton hadn't bothered to deny his role in the deception, she'd became alarmed.

'Hello! Hello!' said the schoolteacher brightly, as he let them in.

Neela ignored him.

'Good, you people are on time,' he carried on, 'but don't take a seat here in the living room just yet. Please step into the bedroom and wait there.'

'What for?' Neela asked curtly.

'You'll have to wait and see,' Kenton replied archly. 'Just a few minutes or so, but you must be quiet in there.'

The women exchanged puzzled glances, but did as they were told, perching themselves on the bed once inside.

Kenton, placing a finger on his lips, said 'Just listen.'

Leaving them in the bedroom, he went out and pulled the door behind him, keeping it slightly ajar so that Kayal and Neela could hear anything transpiring in the other room.

They waited in silence. A short while later, they heard someone knocking on the door of the suite.

And then they heard Kenton opening it and saying, 'Come in quickly, gentlemen.'

'Have you lost your mind? Why are we meeting here?'

Templar? Was that Arcot Templar's voice? Kayal mouthed the name in a silent query. Neela nodded gravely.

'Yes, bloody foolish!' said another voice. 'I thought we were meeting at my place.'

Whitehead! Kayal restrained herself from getting to her feet.

The voices came in clearly through the gap in the door.

Kenton was saying, 'I didn't feel safe meeting there. I'm more comfortable here. Let's bring this to a conclusion and I can be on my way quickly. You have the rest of my money?'

Templar's voice replied. 'Of course, as agreed. Here – half from me and half from Thambi,'

'Thank you, gentlemen. This will come in handy. And now, my precious K Fragment, if you please.'

'I have it right here,' said Whitehead.

The sound of a briefcase clasp unsnapping, a faint rustle of paper and the briefcase snapping shut again.

Kenton spoke again, 'It was worth all the risk just to see Pilkington go down.'

'You should have seen his face when Das knocked it down to me.' Whitehead's voice squeaked in excitement.

The women heard the three men chortle and congratulate each other.

'Well, it's all right for the two of you,' Templar was saying, 'but if this ever comes out, I'd be ruined and it would mean the end of Heritage. The two of you will get away practically unscathed. Except for your reputation, the both of you have nothing to lose –'

'Perhaps Kenton doesn't,' Whitehead countered, 'but reputation is everything to a respected collector. Something, my dear Arcot, you've long forgotten, having turned tradesman. The Ziegenbalg Club will throw me out, the bibliophile community will take me to task and Neela – my God, poor Neela – will be unforgiving.'

Kenton chimed in almost at once, his voice barely masking his snarkiness. 'Oh, that reminds me, Nallathambi. You can ask her yourself. She's here. And Kayalveli is with her too.'

'*What!*' Whitehead and Templar exclaimed together.

'There was nothing I could do, gentlemen. They seemed to know everything already.' Then Kenton called out, 'Do please join us, ladies!'

'You better be joking, Selva,' Templar growled threateningly.

'I wish he were,' said Neela, stepping into the room with Kayal.

The Katpadi rivals averted their gaze and stared at the ground, as if willing it to open up and swallow them.

'This is why I called you here tonight,' Kenton said, addressing Kayal. 'To see for yourselves that the hoax was not just my handiwork, as you had concluded. Why don't the two of you sit down? We obviously have much to discuss.'

Neela glared at him, and Kayal knew she was wishing they could refuse his sarcastic invitation. But they had to get to the bottom of things. There were two sofa sets in the living room, and a chair that Templar was sitting on. Neela strode towards one of the sofas and took a seat next to Whitehead, who sheepishly made place for her, moving his bulk to the corner. Kayal sat down next to Kenton.

'Well?' Neela snapped, addressing Whitehead and Templar, ignoring Kenton completely now.

But her colleagues remained tongue-tied, their eyes not meeting hers, and it was Kenton who spoke again.

'It was all done in the spirit of the Great Game. Book collecting is a great game too, isn't it? And we played it well; most of what we put out there is genuine. Two out of the three Burton documents are the real thing. The Burton books *are* Burton's books, with his ownership name and annotations in his hand. The letter from Burton to Parvathy, his nurse, *is* genuine. Were they lovers? There's no evidence of that, except Parvathy's own word; that was her story to her family and we had no reason to disbelieve her. From there, it was a small leap to finding Burton's papers among her belongings, one of which could easily be a fragment of the Karachi Report. After all, the history of the game of book-collecting has been studded with forgeries and – pardon the pun – biblio hoaxes, has it not? Monsieur Chalon, Ireland, Wise…'

'You're hardly in their league,' cut in Neela.

'Well…perhaps not. But the three of us had our little reasons. Templar will now get collectors to pay a little more attention to his auction sales. Whitehead has become what he wished most for: The greatest collector of Burton. And I – well, I did it for…I know you're thinking money, but no, not just for the money. I also did it for my family. I've never been able to take the Burton–Parvathy story seriously myself, but it was different for my family, particularly my mother, who had made a fetish out of it and invited the scorn and ridicule of relatives, friends, colleagues and, well, our whole community. This was a way to show those mockers, those sceptics, that it was high time they took my mother seriously. That our family does, after all, descend from Sir Richard Francis Burton.'

Arcot cleared his throat and tentatively asked Neela, 'However did you find out?'

'It was Kayal who found out, not me. Looks like none of you did your homework properly. And, regrettably, neither did I. But Kayal sensed something was amiss.' Neela turned to her associate.

'On my way home on the bus after the auction this evening,' Kayal began, 'I was looking through the pictures on my phone that I had taken today and remembered that I had a few of the K Fragment from the Saturday morning when Kenton first came to Biblio with the Burton material. Just before we broke for tea, Neela asked me to put away all the material in the safe and that's when I quickly peeked at the fragment again and took a few photos. I know it was sneaky of me and I don't know what made me do it – Neela would certainly have disapproved – but I was so taken with the material I couldn't really stop myself. Later, I glanced at them quickly, but the text didn't make much sense then and I decided to return to the fragment after I had finished reading up on Burton. On the bus this evening, I finally read the fragment. And something I saw there made me freeze. I had seen it before, of course, but without sensing anything odd about it.'

'What was it?' asked Kenton, leaning forward.

'It was your use of the word "homosexual".'

'What of it?'

'You had Burton use the word interchangeably with "pederasty". You know what I'm referring to – that footnote or note to self Burton is meant to have hastily scribbled in the K Fragment that you drew our attention to when you first brought over the manuscript to show us.' She quickly drew up the fragment on her phone and read, '"*It now seems the only way I can confirm some details of what goes on here, things that are only whispered about on these premises, is to sample what is on offer myself. But should I, can I? Napier has already thrown a fit over his officers indulging in all sorts of homosexual porneia.*"'

'I'm all ears, but I have no clue what you're talking about.'

'Something about that triggered questions I had had about Burton earlier, which I had dismissed or put off. I looked over my notes. There was nothing there but the thought kept needling me until I realized that what had bothered me was the memory of some things I had read, not in the Burton biographies or bibliographies, but in fairly contemporary ethnographic texts; things I happened to be reading in connection with Burton's work on sexuality. And it all fell into place. Scholars had noted, quite casually, that Burton had never used the words "homosexual" or "homosexuality", because he could *not* have. The words didn't come into use in the English lexicon until 1892 – that's two years after Burton's death in 1890. Also, in Burton's timeline, the writing of the Karachi Report – as he claimed –

takes place in either 1845 or 1846. A year later, in 1847, he came to Ooty. "Pederasty" was the word he used constantly. However, in *your* version of the Karachi Report, Burton uses the word "homosexual" while refering to his observations of what goes on in the lupanars or brothels. Even in the one substantial piece of writing about same-sex practices in different cultures that Burton attempted—his notes on pederasty in the 1880 "Terminal Essay" at the end of the *Arabian Nights* – the word "homosexual" does not appear. Here, too, Burton uses "pederasty" or "sodomy". I then looked up the word's origins to find out when it had first been used. I discovered references to its first ever use in German even earlier than in English: First in a private letter, written in 1868, and then in 1869, in an anonymously published pamphlet. But even that was twenty years after the so-called Karachi Report was supposed to have been written. I had to conclude then that the fragment could only be a fabricated document.'

Struck, Kenton swore. Then, taking a deep breath, he said, 'You know what? I think I couldn't stand to repeat or reiterate Burton's offensive references to gay sex – especially oppressive biblical rhetoric like "pederasty" and "sodomy", and I must have made a subconscious, instinctive substitution. I knew enough to know the word was acceptable then but unacceptable today without realizing it would be at least a decade before it would be in circulation. Still, how the hell could I have missed something like this?'

'The question is, how did the others miss it?' Kayal asked pointedly. 'You were simply lucky there. The experts who verified it missed it because they were not Burton scholars or bibliographers, but overpaid experts whose expertise was limited to analysing the material, not Burton's work. And none of the collectors, bibliographers or scholars bidding at the auction spotted it because the full text of the K Fragment had never been published or shown to them. If it had, more than a few people showing interest in it would have figured it out.'

'I'm not interested in learning more about Kenton's part in this,' Neela said. 'What shocks me, makes me so very angry, is the part you two seem to have played in this. When Kayal told me all of this just a few hours ago, I felt terrible that the two of you had been duped by Kenton – only to come here and discover that the deception ran far deeper. Why did you do it? Why would you deceive me – *us* – betray the bookshop? It looks like it's Kayal and I who have been deceived all along.'

Whitehead looked up now, and his face indicated his current state of mind. He seemed devastated, at his own betrayal, at the prospect of being exposed and the unthinkable aftermath that would surely follow, damaging all of them.

'I would be grateful if Biblio doesn't go further with this,' he said, looking pleadingly at Neela and Kayal, 'and I will come clean and tell you about my part in this, as much as I know.'

Templar looked at Whitehead in exasperation and asked him to simmer down. Kenton still had a supercilious grin on his face, as if watching a scenario he had scripted play out to his satisfaction.

31

Richard and Parvathy

'Well, at least for a time, I was a victim of this hoax myself,' began Whitehead. He sighed. 'Let me begin at the end. No one bidding at the auction would have gone away with a forgery; no one would have thrown away their money on it, least of all, Pilkington. The plan was – and all of you saw it happen just so – that no matter how high the bid, I would bid higher, until everyone dropped out. The K Fragment would never have been discovered as a forgery, because no one else in that room would have won it. That's how we designed it. Because even the highest bidder, be it the British Library, the Huntington or an unstoppable Burton collector like Pilkington, wasn't ever meant to have it. No, this piece of Burton forgery *had* to come to me, so it would stay undetected and continue to be thought of as the holy grail it was proclaimed to be: Part of the long-lost, fabled Karachi Report, now unveiled at last. Bid for and won by the greatest Burton collector in the world. After this coup, how could I *not* become *the* greatest Burton collector of all time?'

No one said anything for a while. The only sound in the room was the rattle of the old air conditioner.

Whitehead fiddled with his cane, took a deep breath, and continued. 'The fact that it was a forgery and my part in the deception were revealed to me by Arcot and Kenton only a week before the auction. From the time I heard about such a fabulous possibility, when Kenton called to say he had a unique piece of Burton holograph, through the moment I first laid eyes on it in the bookshop and on to the day it was authenticated a few weeks ago, I was blissfully unaware that it was not the real thing. And ever since Ms Anbuchelvan first brought news from Ooty that it could be the elusive Karachi Papers, I had been dreaming about them, living in the hope that they would be mine. All that was shattered when Arcot and Kenton revealed to me that though the K Fragment had been verified, it was something Kenton had fabricated. When they first hinted at the origin and provenance of this 'K Fragment' – well after the Ziegenbalg Club meeting where it was decided Heritage would auction it – I wasn't easily persuaded. But, soon enough, I found myself going along with their fabrication, because as an old Burton man, I have, as every Burton collector has, quite given up on ever finding the Karachi Report. It is probably a fiction, the last enduring myth about Burton, and I *had* to be a part of it. Why did I go along with them after such knowledge? I'll come to that later. First, I think we'll need to know what happened before all this, before any of us had heard of such a Burton "treasure", and only Arcot and Kenton can tell us that.'

Whitehead leaned back into the sofa and closed his eyes, as if in relief, perhaps at having confessed his part in the affair.

'I'm sure Neela and Kayal have already guessed what was in it for me,' said Templar, his voice quiet but matter-of-fact. 'I, too, wanted a part of that Burton myth, wanted my auction house to be known as the one that had landed the coup of selling the rarest, most-sought-after Burtoniana in auction history. And that chance fell into my lap one morning, when a schoolteacher from Ooty unexpectedly presented me with a near-perfect forgery of what we now know as the K Fragment… But I am getting ahead of events.

'About six months ago, Kenton contacted me, introduced himself and asked me if I would like to come up to Ooty to take a look at some very interesting Burton material for sale. I went, of course, silently thanking my bibliophile goddess that he had not offered it to anyone else. Once I arrived at his home, he filled me in on his family history, their connection with Burton and the details of Parvathy's life. He then handed me the material, the books, the letter and the fragment from the Karachi Report. It was not for me to believe or disbelieve him. The Burton material he was handing me would speak for itself, because I was going to have it carefully examined right away. Kenton said that was fine with him; he was confident all would turn out well. And it very nearly did, except for the ink used in the fragment. The books and the letter stood out as authentic, but there was a shadow on the fragment. That was enough for me. I confronted Kenton and after some half-hearted evasion he admitted the fragment alone was his creation; the books and the letter were genuine. That, of course, had already been established. And as forgeries go, it was pretty good. Even I had to admit that. He had done his homework.'

Kenton jumped in. 'The ink I used was carefully chosen for its antiquity, an old ink called Blackburns, which I expected to pass off as an ink that was in circulation at the time Burton claimed to have written the Karachi Papers. I didn't know, until much later, that Blackburns in Birmingham, famous for manufacturing nibs for fountain pens, didn't make this ink and market it until 1859, after which, it was so widely used in the Bombay Presidency that it became commonplace. But that was *after* 1859, not before. But it was the closest thing I could find to the kind of ink Burton must have used and so I went with it.'

'So, you see, Neelambari,' Arcot continued, 'I had the material checked out several months ago. When I sent it out again last month, this time to another trio of document experts, I was confident of the findings. The little doubt about the ink had me worried, but since it wasn't far off the mark, it didn't come in the way. I offered Kenton a handsome price for the Burton books and the Parvathy–Burton letter, which he accepted. And then it occurred to me that his fragment was of some curiosity value too, being as well-made as it was, and asked if he would part with it. For a price, of course. Kenton was happy to let it go.

'It was when I asked Kenton why he had made such elaborate arrangements to concoct such a thing, the reasons he put forward – to vindicate his family, and lure Pilkington and crush him – made me sit up and start thinking. What if we did, indeed, put it up on the market? Not just anywhere, but at Heritage. This time, I thought of using Kenton's fragment in an entirely different way: Auction it, but control and manipulate the sale so that it goes to the bidder we want it to go to. My own reasons for wanting to do this grew. Heritage had been suffering; we were not getting enough consignments from private collectors and rare-book institutions abroad. Most of them go to the more established auction houses. It wasn't enough to have Indian or even Asian collectors and institutions consigning their lots to us – there just aren't enough of them to sustain an auction house of our scale. I figured that after a headline-grabbing auction sale featuring something like the K Fragment, Heritage would no longer be that obscure little book-auction house in far-off India. From here on, everyone who mattered in the book world – private and institutional collectors, scholars, librarians and bibliographers – would be curious to see what Heritage was going to be up to next. Would there be another fabulous bibliographical treasure like the K Fragment in one of our upcoming lots, waiting to be plucked?

'So this was my play, dirty as it was, to be in the big league. I felt confident enough to unleash it on the world. I felt I had made sure of the most important thing – it would never leave our hands and no else would ever get a chance to examine it, because the highest bidder would be Thambi. If other players at the auction, in some momentary frenzy or loss of their senses, bid absurdly high, Thambi would, at every turn, bid higher, until every contender, every rival – even that arrogant, obnoxious, unstoppable Pilkington – would feel it was beyond him or her and bow out. And that's more or less exactly how it went down this evening.'

Templar stopped here and gestured towards the schoolteacher. 'But you have to ask Kenton his reasons, because he had the best ones.'

When the schoolteacher did not speak up, Whitehead prompted him. 'Kenton, it's your turn to say why you created the fragment, what you hoped for. I think they should really know how you feel. They need to know – all of us owe it to Neelambari and Kayalveli.'

'The two of you think you know why I created this,' Kenton said sardonically, addressing the women, 'but you don't have a clue. That whole thing about wanting to demonstrate to the world that I was Burton's lost heir and prove that Burton was not lying about the Karachi Report was just a sham, a mask. I couldn't care less. You see, as I said just a little while ago, I've never really believed completely in the Burton mythology embraced by my family. I'm the sceptic at home. But taking him seriously for my mother's sake revealed something else to me: The way Anglo-Indians had been treated while the British were here. I mean, most of us know what it was like for them in India *after* the British left, but there's hardly any information at all about the plight of Anglo-Indian children in India while the British Raj still flourished.

'When I began to find out more about Parvathy and her illegitimate child, things changed for me. I saw how Anglo-Indians were scorned by Indians and disowned by the British. They were disparagingly called half-castes. I was conflicted and angry, but now, for the first time, my rage was directed at the real culprits: The British soldiers and officials who had no compunctions about fathering children and then abandoning them. It didn't matter to me if it was Burton or another British soldier who had abandoned Parvathy. My family had been insisting for generations that it had, indeed, been Burton and had been proud of the fact. So the villain in my family had a name: Sir Richard Francis Burton.'

Here, Kenton paused, smiling ruefully at everyone; he seemed more despairing than triumphant now. 'My family was already in possession of some Burton material,' he continued slowly, 'and it was when I got to thinking that I could sell it to bring some much-needed money into the family that the idea struck me: I could cook up some sensational Burton material to sell. But this piece of fake Burtoniana would not be done for the money. No, I had another target in mind: Those people who worshipped Burton, the Burton collectors, and one, in particular, whom I wanted to take down – Pilkington. He was the one I wanted – this scholar-collector, whose shameless veneration of the British Raj had assumed megalomaniac proportions. I wanted to see him humbled in public, to watch his habitual smugness replaced with the shaken, defeated expression that I saw today as he lost the K Fragment to Whitehead. I wanted to crush him – and I did.'

'You're really saying this wasn't done for the money?' asked Neela, her voice sharp and full of doubt.

'For the money too, but also to bring the spotlight back – however much these lost Burton papers could help me to accomplish that – to Parvathy and her child. You'll probably be glad to hear that my mother has now stopped speaking to me; she feels I've stained our Burton legacy. But I did it so the bastard family of Sir Richard Francis Burton wouldn't have to be pariahs any more. I saw this as a way to make the world of fawning Burton admirers discover his other side. Over the years, my family has squandered all the things that could have proved we were Burton's heirs, leaving me with the unenviable task of inventing a connection between Parvathy and the explorer. Could there have been a better thing, a more sensational, controversial thing than the Karachi Report to show as our legacy, our inheritance, the crumb that Burton had left us? For my family, their connection to Burton remains something real and true. My mother, especially, will always believe in it, even if the rest of the world scoffs at it. Growing up with the idea of Sir Richard and Parvathy in my head, as all the children in our family have for generations, their coming together is more family history than fable.

'My own obsession with Burton, unlike my family's,

was intellectual. For the others in our family, claiming blood ties with him was, you could say, a caste thing; we felt a cut above both Anglo-Indians and Tamils, because we were descended from Burton. He was the means that justified our claim to pedigree and we have, over each generation, found ways to hold it over others, particularly in our own mixed community of Anglo-Indian Tamils.

'I, however, became steeped in Burton and felt convinced that this would take me places, get me out of my stifling provincial milieu to something finer, larger, with a wider horizon. One day, following through with my efforts to observe Burton minutely, I made a study of his handwriting as a lark. This was an idea that occurred to me because I have always had a gift for calligraphy. At school, over weekends, I give students basic lessons in calligraphy – entirely gratis. Immersed in Burton, I had long known about the futile search for the Karachi Report that scholars and bibliographers had undertaken over the years. I began wondering about the Report; what did it actually contain? It fired my imagination in a way that nothing so far about Burton had done. So I invented, for the pure pleasure of seeing something being born on paper, a whole page of the K Report – or, at least, what I imagined it would read like. It was, again, as easy as play for me; it was stimulating to probe the culture and practices of Indian and Persian brothels. I felt a bit like Sir Richard himself, foraging in the forbidden, stomping around on similar anthropological grounds.

'I must have made dozens of versions, each of varying length. I already had the paper, the stationery, Burton had left behind, which I had discovered among Parvathy's belongings. The ink alone was a challenge, but one I solved to some degree, if not very satisfactorily. It was clearly foolish to try and cook up the entire report; so a safe bet was a fragment from it, like an index or a footnote.

'When I had it ready, I started considering the names of possible collectors I could approach. I wanted to foist it on Pilkington, but if he didn't fall for it, it would mean an even more bitter defeat for me. I looked at possible Indian collectors and when Heritage popped up as an auction house based in India that dealt with books, especially Burton material, because its owner apparently had a keen interest in the explorer, I realized I had a good shot at putting it up on the market. Templar has told you the rest. And when he offered to buy it privately, I said yes.

'A few weeks after our deal was firmed up, Templar called again to say something more could be done with my fragment. But he wanted to see me first, before he said anything more. He said that he would come to Ooty as soon as he could manage it. When we met, he told me he had something in mind, something that would also involve an important Burton collector called Whitehead – and that I was not to breathe a word of this to anyone. Our little hoax, he said, would bring each one of us the thing we desired the most. I was about to turn him down, to say that I wasn't going to make anything more of my creation, when the implications of what Templar was saying hit me: If I agreed to whatever plan he had in mind, every Burton collector was going to want my concocted Karachi Report, was going to come after it. In one masterstroke, I could fell the tribe of Burton collectors and, possibly, bait in the one I wanted the most – Pilkington. I was in.'

'For my plan to work,' said Templar, picking up the thread now, 'I had to rope in Thambi – however disagreeable the prospect seemed to me.' Kayal heard Whitehead grunt from his corner at this, but Templar carried on. 'I knew I had to do some grovelling before he would come to see it my way, but it had to be done. If I was to rig the auction in such a way that only one bidder, my chosen bidder, would be the winner, it couldn't be just anybody for hire to play the role; it had to be a famous, respected Burton collector. And no one has wanted the Karachi Report more than Nallathambi Whitehead; the esoteric world of Burton collectors know this. Thambi was the key to staging this plan successfully; I could easily have paid someone to do my bidding online by proxy or on the phone –

a common enough practice that keeps the bidder's identity a secret – but crucial to the sale was the auction drama of two devoted Burton collectors, Whitehead and Pilkington, going head to head. But what I had to gamble on was Thambi's desire to be *known* as the Burton collector who now owned the Karachi Papers. Would it mean more to him, I wondered, than actually having the report in his possession?'

'Just days before the auction,' Whitehead cut in, 'Arcot and Kenton asked to see me in private. There was a way, they said, that I could be the owner of the Karachi Report. But before they said anything further, I would have to swear myself to secrecy – in writing. I was to give my word that if I didn't like what they were proposing, didn't agree with it, I would walk away and keep mum about what I had been told. And when I heard that the Burton material was an invention, I was heartbroken. I did suspect some minor fraud would be involved, like breaking an auction rule or two, but never imagined the magnitude of the deception. I was shattered to learn that it was a forgery that all of us had been losing our hearts to. I was so bitter, initially, that I wanted to have nothing to do with it. But as I sat there, with the minutes ticking away, the temptation grew and grew – to have the collecting world witness me grabbing the great Burton prize, this great white whale of Burtoniana. I confess to losing sleep over it; if it all went according to plan, I told myself, I would be, at the end of it, the collector who had carried away one of the most coveted trophies in the world of antiquarian collecting – the most tantalizing piece of Burton rarity that had come into the market in many decades.

'I finally acquiesced, just as I suspect Arcot always sensed I would. Not just because he knew I wanted it badly, but also because he knew it would set me back financially to go up against all those great institutional collectors at the auction and deal the winning bid. It's true that I am wealthy, but I am not some software tycoon who can spend that kind of money and not take a hit. I was prepared to outbid everyone, but it would have meant selling half my collection to meet the hammer price. So a couple of days later, I said yes.' He paused, then turned to Neela. 'I can't tell you how sorry I am, my dear Neelambari.'

Neela stared at the collector for a long time, as if she were looking at a stranger and asking herself if she had ever really known him at all. Kayal thought she saw her eyes glistening. She had never seen Neela look or sound so angry and wounded. 'It's unacceptable to have dragged us and the bookshop into this,' she said finally, her voice steady and cold.

'I can see how you were a victim in this too,' Neela continued addressing Whitehead without directly looking at him. 'These two preyed on your desire to own a rare Burton document. Still, Nallathambi, you could have walked away. You had a choice.'

Templar said hastily, 'Neela, I didn't know Whitehead would drag you and the bookshop so deeply into this. But once he did, it's true that I let you roll with it. It was good for the plan; your unwitting involvement in it added legitimacy to such an astonishing discovery – both the K Fragment and the existence of a living Burton heir. The hypothetical outcome was to be this: Kenton would get a decent monetary pay-off for his troubles from both Whitehead and me – though not the fabulous sum the auction was expected to wangle out of the highest bidder, of course! He would also get his fifteen minutes of fame as Burton's living heir and – perhaps, most important of all for Kenton – the chance to thwart Pilkington and put him squarely in his place. Which he did today and quite admirably, too. For Whitehead, the glory of bidding and snapping up that holy grail of Burtoniana and for Heritage and me, a higher profile in the international auction business.'

'How sorry you must now be, gentlemen,' said Neela with a grim smile, 'that you involved us. You might have got away with it, if you hadn't made such shabby use of us. And what a pity too. Just when I thought our small, intimate world of book collectors and collecting in this country, with its burgeoning antiquarian and rare-book market, was coming into its own and looking for ways to be deepened and nourished, bookmen like you come along and very nearly destroy it.'

Neela looked around the room, then announced that she needed a word alone with Kayal. Kenton nodded and asked them to use the bedroom. After a short conference there, the women returned, but remained standing.

'I'm going to ask that you hand over the fragment,' Neela said firmly, looking at each man in turn. 'That's the deal if the three of you do not want this entire episode going further than this room. Kayal agrees with me. Let me tell you what we intend to do with the papers. They will remain in Biblio's custody, under lock and key – to be brought out and held over your heads in the future if we sense or smell some dark bibliophily is afoot.'

Whitehead and Templar exchanged swift glances, relief flooding their faces, and urged Kenton to hand over the material. The schoolteacher hesitated for a moment. Then, with a shrug, he asked Kayal to help herself to the folder. Kayal snatched it up before he could change his mind, and passed it over to her boss.

'As I was listening to all of you,' said Neela, tucking the folder into her bag, 'I got to wondering why I hadn't been more sceptical of the fragment from the start. And I realized it was because I very much wanted the fragment to be the real thing, not for the money or a share in the glory – because Biblio's role has always been behind the scenes – but to be part of a significant discovery in the antiquarian manuscript and book world. I guess I'm just as vulnerable as the next bibliophile. But I believe it was also because I had such implicit faith and trust in our bibliophile community, especially in the two of you, Nallathambi and Arcot, whom I regarded as old colleagues and friends, that I left the matter entirely in your hands. If it hadn't been for Kayal's sustained interest in digging deeper into Burton, the hoax may have never come to light and we'd still be the foolish bookwomen of Biblio. Still, I suppose Biblio will have to pay in some small measure for our part in this and I dread to imagine what form that might take. And now, if you gentlemen will excuse us, Kayal and I have a bookshop to run.'

Epilogue

A Romance of Bibliophily

Several months later, on a brisk December morning, soon after Kayal and Neela had got the bookshop open for business, the priest's familiar face appeared at the door; he was impeccably dressed as always in his firmly pressed cassock and starched collar. He greeted them warmly, and said he was on his way to Mount Road to finish an errand but had stopped briefly on the way to give them something.

'A little gift from a very grateful college,' said Reverend Satya, reaching into his bag and taking out a couple of books individually wrapped in plain white transparent paper that revealed the shadowy contours of two antiquarian volumes, one large and heavy, the other small and light. 'And what better offering, we thought, than something from the Heber collection itself?'

'Oh, there was no need at all...' protested Neela weakly, while Kayal looked wide-eyed and delighted.

'This is for you, Neelambari, and this one's for you, dear Kayal – I hope I've got it right. Anyway, I suppose you can switch if you like the other better!'

Neelambari unwrapped the book to find she was holding one of the three volumes of Dibdin's *The Bibliographical Decameron*, which she recognized at once with a frisson of pleasure – it was the copy inscribed and signed by Dibdin to Richard Heber. She could only manage a soft, shaky 'thank you'. This was the one exquisite association copy, apart from the inscribed 1662 Lazarus Seaman catalogue, that she had coveted the most from this long-buried collection.

'Oh my God, look!' Kayal shouted, thrusting her gift towards her boss. 'Fanny Brawne's copy of Keats's *Poems 1817* with the poet's personalized inscription to her on the flyleaf!'

The priest seemed to have sensed exactly what each desired, perhaps from having looked into people's souls professionally for so long. 'My heartfelt thanks again,' he said and hurried out, a figure in black disappearing out the door.

The women spent the next fifteen minutes poring over each other's treasures, and then sat chattering, unable to believe their luck. In their possession now, suddenly, was a tangible and glowing token of that golden time of book-collecting.

'Kayal!' Neela exclaimed suddenly. 'There's something I wanted to show you first thing this morning, but Reverend Satya's visit made me forget – let's step into my office for a minute.' Kayal followed her into the office, where Neela bent down to the safe and retrieved *The Story of Little Black Sambo*, the Helen Bannerman first edition. Neela opened the book carefully to its preliminary pages. 'Look: A prelim page that must have got stuck to the title page, making us miss it.' And there, to a corner, was an inscription: *For Alice Bond who made it happen, fondly, Helen.* Kayal could only look on in astonishment, still trying to fully grasp what she was seeing.

'How about that for an association copy, huh?' Neela asked, and they both burst out laughing, unable to believe their luck.

'This must be what kept you from auctioning it off!' Kayal cried out.

Neela smiled, 'I just couldn't bring myself to put it on the market.'

'Think of it, Neela, if you hadn't held it back, we'd never have discovered the inscription. What a close call!'

A first edition, first printing of an already scarce children's classic had just turned into a unique copy: Not only had there been no known copy in the market bearing any association value, there had been no copy anywhere with Bannerman's manuscript signature in it. A $12,000 copy had just turned into a $50,000 edition.

Finally, after quietly gloating over their find, Neela and Kayal put the book away carefully and lovingly in order to get on with the day – there was much to do.

Things at Biblio had heated up since the Burton auction. Their first catalogue of modern Indian first editions had been out for a while now and enquiries and orders were pouring in. Kayal had managed to gather a nice stock of private-press books and was busy getting the information out to a new line of young but committed collectors that Biblio had acquired over the summer. The bookshop was also gearing up to participate in the first ever antiquarian book fair in India, set to open in January 2018, which was just around the corner now, and the bookshop was focused on acquiring interesting and new stock to display at this very first Indian rare-book fair.

It must have been a week or so later that, quite out of the blue, Neela heard from the firm of Yashudo, one of Japan's most distinguished antiquarian bookshops, that a private collector in Kyoto had bought what was, without much doubt, the Karachi Report. The firm of Yashudo added that this information had to be kept in the strictest confidence. They themselves hadn't had a chance to see it; nor were they likely to be shown the item even if they called on the collector. But one of their board members was a dear friend of the collector in Kyoto and he had viewed it; what's more, their man had even seen the paperwork and documents from the most trusted firms, all swearing to its authenticity. But this was all they could tell her; they knew nothing further of its provenance. Oh yes, there was just one more detail they could add: It had been acquired at a very dear price.

Neela tried to dig further using her wide connections in the antiquarian trade, but drew a blank. The Kyoto collector had kept his mania for Burton a secret, always purchasing his Burton items anonymously, and without a name or even a hint of one, it was impossible to track him down in a country which abounded in secretive collectors. Neela shared what she had heard with Kayal alone, and the two bookwomen briefly speculated if Kenton somehow figured in this, though they were more certain that Templar and Whitehead could not possibly be involved. They would not be so foolish.

However, when Kayal tried reaching Kenton in Lovedale, she was told he had quit his job in August and immigrated with his mother to Australia. He had not left behind a forwarding address. The trail had grown cold, and a little suspicious. Whoever was behind it, the women concluded, it looked as if this troubling piece of Burtoniana would always have a way of surfacing – there if not here and here if not there – keeping Burton collectors salivating. For now, the bookwomen had no interest in the affair – besides, they had no desire to go on another wild goose chase, and turned their minds to the upcoming antiquarian book fair.

'So, what are we offering at the fair that no other dealer will have?' Neela wondered aloud as they began handpicking the choicest stock for display.

'Oh, that would easily be our recently acquired stock of private-press books,' replied her associate.

'Then let's go take another look at them.'

Kayal had already shelved them in bookcases, and they now began singling out the books from the fine presses they felt would draw an audience at the fair, displaying each of them attractively on a wide table. The first thing Neela and Kayal had noticed about these books was that they didn't use dust jackets; instead, the covers, whether hardbound or paperbound, were of lovely marbled paper. The title, instead of being printed on the spine or the front cover, was printed elegantly on a label and pasted on. The ink was usually in two colours, red and black. The paper had a creamy, laid texture, and the letterpress impression of hot metal type on it was satisfyingly deep. And, unlike trade editions, the page margins were wide, the illustrations were wood-engraved, the presswork immaculate and handsome, the whole of it warmed by ornaments.

'Perfect!' exclaimed Neela, as she caressed them, taking in, with her hands and her eyes, the physical and typographic sensation of a finely printed book. 'Okay, so here I am, a keen but undecided customer stepping into Biblio's stall at the fair. Now you tell me, Ms Kayalveli Anbuchelvan, why I should bother with these beautiful, expensive books.'

Kayal began to tell her customer exactly that, and found that she could not stop.

Kayal's favourite section in the bookshop comprised the shelves dedicated to the book arts, the art and history of manuscripts and the printed book.

Acknowledgements

My deepest thanks and gratitude to Poulomi Chatterjee, my editor at Hachette India, for enthusiastically jumping into the bibliophilic spirit of the book. She closely shaped not just the novel but also how it should look and feel in the hands of a reader, making this in every way a better book than the one I started out with. Also at Hachette, thanks to Thomas Abraham for his keen support and to all those who read and worked on the manuscript at various stages. Grateful thanks and appreciation to Sonali Zohra for her deftly bookish illustrations, Bhavi Mehta for the lovely cover art, lettering and design, and the valuable inputs offered by Ranjitha Ashok, Ajoy Alexander and Chandra Siddan after reading an early version of the manuscript. I owe a debt of gratitude to colleagues, friends and family for their steadfast support and warmth.